MAKING MIDLIFE MARVELS

Forty Is Fabulous 4

HELOISE HULL

Henwin Press LTD

Copyright © 2021 by Heloise Hull

All rights reserved.

No part of this book may be reproduced in any form or by any electronic or mechanical means, including information storage and retrieval systems, without written permission from the author, except for the use of brief quotations in a book review.

Any appearance to real people is purely a coincidence and should not be inferred.

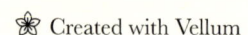

❦ Created with Vellum

Making Midlife
Marvels
———————————

The final book in the Forty Is Fabulous series is here! Drink the wine, eat the food, and finish the adventure.

Mistakes? I've made many. My ex- can attest to that, but none bigger than accidentally giving life to the dying god.

Now, he's coming, full of vengeance and wrath, determined to destroy me and everything I hold dear.

But it's how you end, not how you begin that matters.

I'm determined to fix my mistakes. The only problem? Who can I trust if I can't even trust myself?

Turns out, even my body is a lie, and sometimes, it's hard to remember whose side I'm on.

All I know for sure is that a final showdown is coming, whether I'm ready or not.

Time is ticking, and while I may be immortal, this world I love is not.

I am the fiery Eye of Ra
>   Who went forth as the terrible one,
>   Lady of slaughtering, great of respect,
>   Who came into being as the flame of the sunshine.
>   —Coffin Texts, Spell 316

Before You Begin

If you missed the announcements in the previous books, there's still time to download and read *Making Midlife Memories*, book 1.5 of the *Forty Is Fabulous* series. It's a short story about Ava's vision the first time she astral projects with Manu on her way to see the Council. The events in the short story directly precede the second book in the series. However, it is not necessary to have read it to understand what follows. Think of it as a bonus scene!

If you'd like to read *Making Midlife Memories*, simply sign up for my newsletter, and I'll send you a free copy. You're under NO obligation to stay on my list, but if you do, I promise I only send out new release notices and sales/giveaways every few months. You can also follow me on Amazon for new release updates.

NOTE: If you do choose to read *Making Midlife Memories*, please know the novella is grittier than Ava's story thus far. Be prepared for blood, sex, glory, and even an ancient

Roman recipe for honey fritters. If you're cool with that, then sign up and I'll send you a copy!

FORTY IS FABULOUS SERIES
MAKING MIDLIFE MEMORIES

HELOISE HULL

Prologue

EGYPT BEFORE MAN

The flames of flickering reed torches barely touched the blackness of the temple. My bejeweled sandals echoed loudly on the mosaic floors of cerulean lapis and blood-red marble. Deep, lacquered and fragrant wood from the cedar forests of the east lined the coffered ceilings, and Thoth's own wedge of sacred ibis stood at attention down the hypostyle hall. Their long, sharp beaks terminated in a wicked curve that made my stomach curl unpleasantly, but they only watched, carbon copies of his own aloofness.

Thoth himself strode in front of me. As the official advisor to our lord, Ra, nothing happened in the land—or any other land for that matter—without Thoth knowing. The same, however, could not be said for me. I honestly had no idea what was about to happen. It was true that I had begun to shun my husband Shu, but of what consequence was that to Ra? Shu had failed him. We were outcasts in the court's eyes. And I would not forgive Shu for his crimes, either.

"Are you nervous, Tefnut?" Thoth murmured softly. He was hard to read. At times, he seemed enamored by me, shyly asking if he could

accompany me on a walk through rainy fields of newly-sprouted green barley. During those times, he seemed like a child, a boy I needed to hold and reassure. It was the other times, the times when I saw the calculations speeding through his mind faster than an abacus, that I wondered if the shyness was also an act.

"Yes. I freely admit I am. What is going on? Is Ra displeased?"

Thoth grimaced. "He is unhappy about the Demon Days business, but what's done is done."

"Thank you for that," I murmured. "I know you had no small part in helping my daughter give birth."

"It was nothing."

"It was a gamble with Khonsu," I said darkly, picturing the sadistic god with moonlight for armor. "Nothing is assured where he is concerned."

Thoth expertly maneuvered around the praise. "How is Nut?"

I trilled happily for a moment, thinking of my daughter. She was the sky, and my son Geb, her husband, was the earth. It was because of their nature that they had to stay apart. When they embraced, there was nowhere for anyone else to be. The sky met the earth in divine love and shoved out the rest of us. That was before Ra's maker of prophecies revealed their children would overthrow him, so it was decreed that Shu would keep them apart forever. And he did, his loyalty to Ra absolute over his loyalty to me and our children.

Until Thoth gambled for those five extra days, and Nut gave birth to five more gods. I stayed with her, dotting her head with cool dew drops and breathing soothing, rainstorm air on her heat-slicked body. Five beautiful little gods, one born on every extra day.

But Ra could hardly count that as betrayal. If anyone should be punished, it should be Thoth. I wondered how he had escaped divine justice, and I wondered why I never wondered that until now.

Carefully, I answered, "Nut wishes she could be with her children and frets over them. She misses Geb, but I am allowed to visit, for which I am eternally grateful."

Thoth nodded once, taking my small thanks in stride. We were *nearing the inner sanctuary. Suddenly, he paused. When I glanced at him, his eyes were alight with fire.*

"Thoth?"

"What do you wish to be?" he asked.

I shifted uncomfortably. "Be? Whatever do you mean?"

"A mother, surely."

"Yes," I allowed. "I enjoy my children."

"For whom?" he asked more urgently.

"These are not questions I'm comfortable answering to you, Thoth."

His face was hurt. "Why?"

"Leave it be."

Thoth met my gaze for a moment longer. I thought I heard a deep sigh as he pushed through the ivory and bone doors, and we marched into Ra's inner sanctum. Cavernous braziers roared at the edges of the known world. The sun god was difficult to look at, even for me, his daughter. His lambent skin, his bronzed hair, the light came from within and beamed to all corners of the earth.

Ra sat on a dais of obsidian, surrounded by none. Only two lions flanked his throne. Thoth took his customary place at the foot. How did he bear the forge-like temperatures?

Ra rapped his scepter of myrrh wood and stood. He had already set for the day and was nearing his nightly death. His face drooped, its shine less bright. I found I could blink away the blind spots fairly easily.

But that didn't explain what I was doing here.

Gently, with Thoth's help, Ra dismounted the smooth dais and took three steps to me. We had no audience. Only the crackling flames kept time.

Ra didn't utter a word. When I opened my mouth to explain something, anything, I found I could not speak. Fearfully, I tossed my head, begging Thoth to tell me what to do. He always knew what to do.

When Ra placed his wizened hands on my shoulders, I flinched.

With the strength of the sun, he squeezed and turned me around. Moving quickly, he shifted down to press his palms on my shoulder blades. Where he touched, hot pain seared against my skin. I gritted my teeth, refusing to cry out in agony.

Oh, but I was burning.

Once, I'd watched the Greek Titans punish their father, Ouranos, for imprisoning them. After they castrated him with a sickle, they whipped him, and I remembered wincing at the expert way the whip struck his arms, his back, his legs. His golden blood poured from wounds that healed an instant later, the whip singing through the air just in time to strike the pink flesh. Not once did Ouranos cry out.

The Titans invited gods from afar to watch their spectacle. Ra said they were trying to send a message and cement political ties for their fragile, new-found power. He sniffed his disapproval, and we left the merrymaking halls of Mount Othrys before the feast. Now, I almost wished for an audience. See how my own father tries to degenerate me? See how he fails?

I felt Ra's thumb press against my back and the heat tapered off. There was no coolness to balm my wounds, and I dared not summon any rain in the temple of Ra, but at least I wasn't on fire anymore. He stepped away, and they brought me a polished mirror. I didn't want to look, but his face brooked no disagreement. There. Black tattoos winged around my shoulder blades, the rivulets still smoking from where Ra had bestowed them on me.

His Left Eye. His Right Eye.

Chaos and Order. The moon and the sun.

Everything inside of me demanded to scream. To rip my hair and clothes and cry that it couldn't be. So this was my punishment? It was not my fault! My heirs were destined to overthrow Ra. That was the prophecy. As much as Thoth whispered to Ra, no one escaped destiny. All Ra had left was his fury at losing, and he passed that fury to me.

Ra's voice was wispy and faint as if the ritual had taken more than energy. As if it had taken parts of his very soul. "We welcome a new Eye," *he announced.* "Rage across the arid lands, my daughter."

My body burned, bristling with unrestrained chaos as I looked to Thoth. Even from this distance across the hall, I could see his grim smile of approval. If everyone else saw the smart, quiet advisor, the problem-solver, the lord of wisdom, I saw deeper. I saw the cunning crocodile teeth hidden beneath the surface of the water.

Of course I saw them. I was the water, after all.

The question remained. Why did Thoth want me to become the Eye of Ra? What did he gain? For Thoth never did a thing without a gain in return.

I took one look at the hall, the acanthus columns, the braziers sparking with cassia incense, and I let the chaos consume me.

What I mean to say is, I ran. And I didn't look back.

Chapter One

MY ANAMNESIS REVEALED itself in fits and starts. The memories of my life with my father Ra, with my husband Shu, and with Thoth were all coming back. It was like watching a hidden message emerge under the heat of a flame, the ink blooming to life to reveal the truth. The men in my life had all ill-used me. And now? Now I remembered.

Now I was pissed.

There were beautiful moments, like the birth of my children and my grandchildren, but Ra's court was like any MILF court. Conniving and dangerous. Even for the gods, a long, happy life was never guaranteed.

It was bizarre to think I married my twin, Shu, and that I birthed twins, Geb and Nut, who then also got married. Before regaining my magic, incestual mythology was an abstract thing. Now... It was a little too close to home. Or maybe that was me as Ava talking. It was hard to separate the two.

Honestly, I didn't even know if she really existed or if she was a figment of my imagination—someone my brain created for this new reincarnation? Honestly, these were questions I doubted I'd ever answer.

I hoped that each woman I became embodied one aspect, one part of me. Even the scary ones. They were all bundled in the messiness of my being. Of my soul. They were all little slivers of me. At least—

"Hey, remember when you weren't lost in existential dread and could help navigate? Let's go back to that."

I scowled at my blue-haired companion. I loved Thessaly for coming to rescue me in Nibiru, but she sure was cocky now that we were back in her homeland.

"Hey," I shot back. "Remember when you didn't talk more than a word at a time? Let's go back to that."

Thessaly flipped through the air, landing like a cat on the balls of her feet and fingertips. She eyed me with piercing purple eyes and an unsympathetic face. "Now is not the time for wallowing. The Council was arresting everyone on sight when I left, and if what you say is true, that's the least of our worries."

Thoth's face wavered in my mind. I replayed his gruesome death by chaos and the way he smiled as I rent the flesh from his body. My gut twisted when I thought about his consequent rebirth on Aradia and the mirror of that smile on his immortal mouth in the crypt. Not only had I gotten myself stuck here, I'd played right into his hands. I was constantly playing into his hands. He'd advised Ra to make me his Eye. I knew that now. I just didn't know for what purpose. He'd also wanted me to look in the Emerald Tablets so many millennia ago. The reason there was obvious—to curse me. But the why was still a mystery.

With all of this intrigue and realm hopping, I suddenly felt as ancient as I was. They say you're only as old as you feel, except I felt like I'd been exhumed from a coffin in ancient Egypt, given a shot of espresso, and told to go save the world. I guess it was better than my actual age, which was measured in time before the dawn of humans.

Something hard hit my calf. "Hey!"

Thessaly took aim with another rock. "Stop wallowing."

"I should get some time to wallow."

"Deal."

"A one word answer. I like that."

"I wasn't done. When you get some free time, you can wallow, but I don't predict that for at least a few years."

"A few years?"

Thessaly aimed another rock at my face with no mercy. "Owww!" I yelped as she scored a hit to my temple.

"Correct. Besides finding a way out of Nibiru, a safe way at least, we have to convince the Council we are not the danger, keep an archon imprisoned, and neutralize a god. The Archon Wars lasted two centuries, so a few years would be your best case scenario."

"Yeah, but there's only one god on the loose."

Thessaly gave me a once-over that made my skin goosebump.

"Fine," I amended. "Two, if you include me. Which I don't."

Thessaly picked up another rock and tested its weight in her hands. "Like I said, there's no time for wallowing."

I didn't argue. Instead, I swung the subject back around to her. "Why don't you tell me where we're going? You came stampeding into Nibiru like a woman with a plan. You've got a plan, right?"

Thessaly's face, while always grim, went Grim Reaper. "My birthplace."

I stopped inching my way down a deadly slope. When Thessaly had appeared, my fear and shame overwhelmed me, and I'd clung to her, crying my eyes out. I kept blubbering about mistakes before she snapped, "We all make mistakes. It's called being alive."

Now, she was looking at me intently. "You're about to see my greatest mistake."

"Your birthplace? With a bunch of other sirens?"

Her nod was curt. "None of whom are well-inclined towards me."

"Are you going to give me a little background before we get there?"

"No."

"Back to one word answers, I see."

"Yes."

"Why? I need all the help I can get. Are they going to try to maim us on sight? Will I need my powers? Tell me now, because I'm exhausted and they aren't as strong here. I don't want you to rely on something that might spit and sprinkle instead of blowing stuff up."

"I'm not sure. Whether they try to kill me again remains to be seen, however, there will be plenty in my family who will be delighted to recall my many mistakes. But whatever you do, keep your powers hidden."

I was snagged on one part. "Did you say 'again'? As in you've been maimed here before?"

"Yes."

"I can't believe I'm saying this, but I miss the Thessaly who was all talky-talky. Does this have to do with your curse?"

Thessaly's face turned to stone. "Yes."

I let it go. Clearly, I wasn't getting anymore out of this stubborn siren.

All around us, Nibiru's landscape was changing again. I'd seen Hypnos's Cave, the spring pillar held aloft by Krios, and some deep circle of hell where I'd stashed

Thoth's consciousness. Thessaly had led me up, away from all of that.

I knew from our previous conversations that she had grown up in a fishing village. The thing was, I didn't smell fish or the ocean.

I smelled burnt desert winds and salt. And an undercurrent of something noxious. Something savage.

The light from the travertine stone and salt made my eyes water. It was the only thing wet in this desiccated land.

Then, a woman with a voice as hard as the terrain hobbled into view. Ignoring me completely, she appraised Thessaly, probing with her eyes and weighing her worth alone. The old woman looked as ancient as the landscape, her face a mask of wrinkles. Except for her hair. She had the same shade of hair as Thessaly.

After a moment of her hard gaze, she turned around and began hobbling back the way she came.

As she went, she called, "Welcome home, cursed one."

Chapter Two

CERULEAN BLUE SALT beds crackled under our feet as we entered the village. Huts of white logs dotted the parched expanse. The air felt staid, as if breezes couldn't summon the strength to blow.

How could anyone live here?

We passed a hut and I realized my mistake. They weren't made of white logs. They were made of bleached bones.

As we walked, I stole glances at the woman. Her mouth was set in a firm line, and her face had such a stern, familiar quality that I knew she and Thessaly were related, even without the hair. "I suppose you're hungry, eh?"

When it was clear Thessaly wasn't going to respond, I cleared my throat. "Thank you, but we really have to get out of this realm. It's a matter of life or death—"

The old woman cut me off with a cackle as my stomach betrayed me in a big way, grumbling from here to Earth, probably.

"You can't go saving the realms without a proper meal.

Although we haven't had a proper meal in ages, we at least have some sustenance. Isn't that right, Tess?"

Thessaly winced as if the old woman's words struck her in the gut. While I didn't understand the price the siren paid by coming home, clearly it was high.

We neared a thick cluster of huts surrounding a smoldering fire, and Thessaly slowed to a crawl. "I'll stand guard outside of the village. I don't want—"

"Nonsense. You'll come in and say hello to your mother," the woman interrupted.

Thessaly crossed her arms and blew hot air from her cheeks like a petulant teenager, but she didn't argue. "Yes, Grandmother," she said dutifully.

When I looked at Thessaly, her head was bowed, and my heart broke a thousand times. All of my friends had sacrificed so much to help me and what had I done? Let Thoth escape. Failed.

I let my fingers find Thessaly's and squeezed. She finally glanced up, her purple eyes unnaturally bright.

More dark figures emerged from the huts, and I saw colors I'd never imagined before in their eyes and hair. There was one woman, however, that reflected Thessaly perfectly. One woman who had the same blue hair and purple eye combination I had grown to admire. One woman who shared the same scowl and angry tilt to her jaw. It was the same woman who looked like she wanted to kill us.

"Say hello to your mother," Grandmother chided. The three were like carbon copies of each other at three stages of life.

Thessaly's mouth moved, but only the faintest of whispers emerged.

The middle-aged woman crossed her arms. "She is not welcome here."

Grandmother harrumphed. "You don't get a say, Acantha. In fact, gather the remaining water. I'm dry as a dancing bone in summer."

Thessaly's mother—her actual mother—gave Thessaly the most sour look I'd ever seen. The type of look I'd reserve for Jim at his most nitpicky, passive-aggressive worst. Thessaly's face stayed stoic, but I knew my siren better than to take her at face value. My fingertips found her palm and squeezed again, just to remind her that I was still here.

Grandmother snorted. "Acantha means thorny. She was the most disagreeable baby, squalling at all hours of the day and night. Nobody slept for a year. If the gods had spent more time in Nibiru, I would have sworn that Athena herself was punishing us for that attempt to drown Odysseus." Grandma looked critically at Thessaly. "At any rate, it's a small mercy that sirens can only bear one child every thousand years. Well, come get settled. We'll find some water, I suppose. Perhaps there is a strip of dried fish we overlooked."

Some food sounded more divine than any intervention the gods could cook up, and I was looking forward to seeing how ancient beings from another realm lived. Although, the salt-rimmed huts and barren land didn't exactly match the vision in my mind. I was expecting oceans and sea shanties and, I'll admit it, mermaid-like creatures braiding each other's hair. Or at least, a fountain. Something watery. There wasn't anything even water-adjacent here. Not one shell or a stray piece of seaweed.

Thessaly still wouldn't meet my eyes. I followed her, ducking under the doorway of femurs, and entered the dark hut. The homes must have been the only place of respite from the blinding landscape. Despite that, there was no fire and no cooking utensils. No pantry or warm atmosphere or anything to suggest this was more than a place to merely survive.

I was having a hard time reconciling the reality in front of me with Thessaly's story of her pearl necklace and fishing with her father. In fact, I hadn't seen one man here at all. The questions piled up faster than I could form them, with more lining up right around the corner.

From up close, I could see how invasive the salt truly was, as if the seas had dried up, leaving a thin, crackling layer on everything and everyone. They'd given up on keeping it at bay long ago. Salt coated Acantha's eyelashes and the tips of her hair. It sparkled in a macabre way over cracked lips and blistering skin. Nothing was untouched.

Acantha bustled in the corner where a shelf of bones held rounded bowls. Carefully, she took two and gave them to Grandmother and me, completely ignoring her daughter. Her face was hard, creases wrapping her eyes and mouth in tight lines. I got the feeling they weren't laugh lines.

I looked down at my hands and fought the urge to gag. The bowl was, in fact, a split skull, bone-white and smoothed out. Human, from the size of it. Inside, a thin layer of water sparkled at the bottom. Grandmother nodded for me to drink. "Water's scarce until the next deluge, but this should help. Go on, now. Drink up."

Slowly, I raised the skull to my mouth and drank the tepid mouthful. Like everything else, it tasted salty, like demon tears. I didn't know what exactly had happened to Thessaly's home, but it was something horrible.

After a few minutes of awkward silence, Grandmother said, "Tell us about your quest." She sat in a rocking chair constructed from various bones with a skinned hide covering the seat like a cushion. I did not want to know what sort of animal it came from.

"It's not a quest," Thessaly spoke for the first time. She looked to me as if in some silent plea. *Don't say a word. Let me handle my family.*

"Oh really?"

"Quests died with the gods," Thessaly said.

Acantha's voice was sharp, a perfect match for this inhospitable habitat. I wondered if the land had made her this way, as a glacier carved out a gorge. "The gods are not dead, girl," she snarled. "They will return. They always do."

"No, they won't. Stop wishing for it."

I jerked my head to Thessaly. The sirens wished for the gods to return? Well this was a plot twist.

The bone chair creaked as Grandmother rocked, her fingers twisted together calmly as she watched me. I had a feeling she understood more than she let on.

"If it's no quest, what is this life and death business?" she asked.

"Ava is mortal. She will die if she stays here," Thessaly said simply. "We have to get back to Earth."

I approved. A lie was better when it stuck to half-truths. I had no doubt I would absolutely die here if I couldn't find a way out. At least, Ava would.

Inwardly I cringed. Having to talk about myself like that in the third person was just… weird. This body felt more real than anything else in the world. But of course I would think that.

"You'll stay, though," Grandmother said. Creak, rock. Creak, rock.

Acantha snorted in derision. "Of course she won't. And good riddance. Nobody wants her here. Simply sheltering you in my home is almost more than I can manage. My shame will follow me for a century for this."

Obviously, her mother was an expert at wrapping her daughter in humiliation, as if she were merely wrapping yarn around a loom. It must have been centuries since mother and daughter had seen each other, but time had healed nothing. If anything, whatever happened between the two of them had sunk deeper, festering and infected.

"Acantha," Grandmother rebuked.

Acantha whirled on Grandmother next. "How can you welcome her back? Look what she has done to us! What sort of evil has she wrought to even be here? Well, Daughter? How do you come to be?"

"Enough. Get the bowls ready, Acantha." Grandmother turned her age-wise eyes to us. "Would you help us catch the rains?"

I started to say if she wanted rain, I could make her some, but Thessaly gave me a slight shake of her head. Instead, I nodded with my mouth half open. I'm sure I looked a little slow.

"Good. Grab as many bowls as you can and set them out. But only take as many as you can keep an eye on or they'll wash away with the floods." She gave me a dead serious look. "Making these bowls is a messy business."

I nodded, sure of the truth of that statement.

Grandmother rose from her chair as creakily as the bones that formed it. She battened the chair with a piece of rope that looked as if it had been made from twisted strands of siren hair while Acantha arranged their two siren hair beds as high on the shelf as possible. There was nothing else inside. Nothing to suggest hundreds of years of occupancy. No pictures, no mementos. Nothing soft or comfortable to relax on. The inside of the hut was as harsh as the outside vistas.

"What's going on?" I asked.

"The deluge. Don't do anything, Ava. Just hang on."

"I—"

"The waters are coming."

"But I could—"

"No!" Thessaly hissed.

Clumps of sirens whipped their heads around and hissed back at us. Their teeth sharpened as they snarled, and their hisses followed us to the dry sea bed. Nobody said an actual word or threw anything, but their blows landed just the same. Thessaly was not welcome here.

I didn't want to push her, so I said, "Is there anything I need to know?"

"Misery loves company." She wedged three bowls between her legs as she sat and held onto two others in her hands. "I did this to my village. We have no water and no food, no seas and no fresh meat, because of me. Be thankful they limit themselves to hisses only. For now."

Chapter Three

A DULL BUZZ began in the distance. "The waters are coming," Thessaly warned as the sound grew to a roar. "They flood the whole land and recede just as quickly. Don't let your feet leave the ground," she ended with a shout.

"Or what?" I called nervously. The heat and humidity were rising exponentially, and the sweat made my clothes stick to my skin.

"You'll be swept away, and I don't know where the waters empty, so I won't know where to search for you."

And then the world was drowned.

The gush turned into a torrent, and yet Thessaly had the gall to add, "Whatever you do, don't use your powers."

"Why?" I screamed back, feeling the force of the currents tugging at my thighs.

"At best, it will give them hope to think a goddess walks among them. You do not want to give sirens hope."

"And worst?"

"They will want to feed on them."

The water surged higher, and it was all I could do not

to part the waves. Around us, sirens were jumping to collect water in their skullcap bowls while others snapped up iridescent rainbow trout and slipped them inside their chitons. Where I came from, we used to call that the redneck purse, but it was usually lipstick and credit cards we'd slip inside our bras.

I tried to keep myself steady as the water rose. A slick fish smacked me in the face, leaving a sticky substance on my skin. A siren dove after it, her sharp teeth snapping inches from my cheek. I yelped as she gulped the morsel down.

In my fascination, I forgot about my own skulls. They began to drift away, and I lunged desperately after them. As soon as my feet left the ground, I churned and swirled in the raging waters, while the sirens dove and swam and came up sparkling in the air. They filled and collected, but I couldn't keep my nose above the waves. Some goddess of water, I made. Another wave washed over me, taking me with it.

My feet tumbled over each other and my voice became bubbles. What was worse? Getting swept away or revealing my powers? Because Thessaly seemed to think it was the latter.

A cold hand gripped my ankle and yanked—Grandmother. Wiry and strong, she pulled me back down just as the roaring quieted.

It ended as quickly as it came, the waters swirling in blues and greens until suddenly, they receded. I saw now why the salt line was at a certain height along the bone huts and why it clung to the sirens' eyelashes and hair tips. I thought I could almost understand why they chose not to crumble it off of their bodies anymore. They had given up and given in to the land.

"The waters come every twenty-one days. I don't see a

rhyme or reason, but it's the only water available to us until the next cycle. We need very little food and rarely need to drink, but our skin needs to soak every day," Grandmother explained. "Most of what we manage to collect is doled out day-by-day, drop-by-drop, to adorn our parched and drying skin. We've found over the years that applying it like a tincture directly under our navel seems to be the most effective at keeping us alive."

I wanted to say something so badly, give them some stores to see them through in case the deluge ever stopped coming, but Thessaly's look strangled any of those ideas. So, I simply said, "Thank you for sharing some of your precious water with us."

Grandmother accepted the thanks with a noble nod of her head. I wondered if she was the matriarch for the entire siren village. I was getting matriarch vibes, at least. It was probably the only reason we were still alive.

"How long will you stay?" Grandmother asked.

"We leave tomorrow, if that is agreeable to you."

Grandmother gave her prodigal granddaughter a long look. "No. It's too dangerous for Ava to stay the night here. You'll leave tonight. But come, let's sit and hear what you have to tell us."

Thessaly brooked no argument, and since I'd caught no water, I tried to make myself useful by helping Acantha with her bowls. I got a fierce snarl for my efforts. Backing away with my hands up, I went to sit cross-legged on the ground as they laid out the hides and rearranged the shelves and chairs again. It only took a few minutes. There was no fire to stir back to life or pots and pans to bang. No sounds of hearth and home. This place was the complete opposite of Nonna's kitchen. I couldn't shake the desolate feeling creeping up my neck and bristling along my arms. Nor could I forget the fact that these were demons.

"Can you go up to the other realms, like Earth?" I asked. "To fish or collect food and water there?"

"We could, but ever since the curse, sirens have mostly stayed here in Nibiru."

I looked to Thessaly who kept silent. Was it possible the entire village was cursed, too? What exactly were the constraints of her curse?

"Thessaly," Grandmother scolded. "Have you not told your companion anything? Child, I think it's time you explained how you are here and not bound to that rock."

Thessaly bowed her head. "Yes, Grandmother," she whispered.

"She brings disgrace to our village merely by being here," Acantha objected. "Do you wish to further curse us with her presence? I, for one, wish I had kept my legs closed to the gods, although it was the only good thing in my life. Perhaps, I should have strangled her at birth."

"Acantha, do as I asked and gut the fish."

"But Thessaly is the youngest in our house now," she objected immediately. "It should be her job."

"And yet, only she seems to have figured out how to end a curse of the gods. Go and do not question me again."

Acantha gathered the still-flopping fish, grabbed a sharpened jawbone, and went outside, muttering under her breath. In her absence, a few sirens entered and dropped off a fish or two, as if they were a tithe to Grandmother. Their conversations had the harshness of some guttural language I didn't understand. They looked with suspicion around the hut before leaving.

Grandmother turned her eyes back to us. "Well?"

With a deep exhalation that seemed at once apprehensive and cathartic, Thessaly began her tale. And it was the wildest fish tale I'd ever heard.

Chapter Four

"SIRENS DO NOT BEAR MEN, in any sense of the meaning. We do not enjoy their company, and we do not physically birth males. Every thousand years, a siren is allowed to mate with a god to produce a new siren. My mother was the last siren to be chosen for this honor."

There were no sounds in the hut save for Grandmother's creaking bone chair. I clung as tightly to Thessaly's story as I did to the skulls. A portal to Aradia could have opened wide, and I might have missed it.

"My father was different. Glaucos was a simple fisherman before he found the dog's-tooth herb and consumed it. He noticed when he rubbed it on the fish he was about to cook, that they would leap out of the frying pan and swim back into the sea. He deduced the magical herb granted longevity or health or something of the sort. But it was immortality that the herb bestowed. Afterwards, he became a god of fish and was taken into the bosom of the Greek sea gods."

"Your father was as much of a scoundrel as the rest,

child. Do not look to the past through a rosy-fingered sunset."

Thessaly stood at that, her hair becoming an electric crackling sheet behind her. This seemed like a fight they had nursed for many years, a scab that never healed.

"He was different. He loved me," she insisted.

"No, Thessaly. He did not," Grandmother said, her voice more gentle. "Sit down. You're going to break something, carrying on like that. Your father would have used you like every other god. I'm only thankful that he vanished in the Archon Wars before he could break your heart."

Risking a demon's wrath, I broke in between their argument. "Acantha seems to miss the gods. But not you?"

Grandmother snorted. "I'm too old to be anything but a realist. Now go on, Thessaly. Sit."

Thessaly slumped to the floor, all the fight extinguished from her body, but she added petulantly. "He did love me."

"Get on with the story."

Thessaly continued, muted slightly. "Usually, the gods pursue a siren for a day, consummate the union, and are never heard from again. Glaucos, however—"

"Loved *me*," snapped Acantha. Her shadow filled the door frame, arms crossed, and she wore a familiar blank look on her face. "If Glaucos ever came here to dote on you, it was because of me. And look where it got us!" She spread her arms. "Powerless. Even our voices are gone. He was too soft on you. He let you dream too much."

Thessaly winced with every syllable, her dog star hidden behind the storm clouds of her mother.

Grandmother gave them both a reproachful look. Clearly, she nursed some hurt for whatever Thessaly did, even if she still loved her, too. Siren lives were as complicated as mortal ones, it seemed.

Acantha stalked closer, fish guts still glistening on her hands. "Didn't she tell you? We have no siren song. The only thing that happens if we venture to the mortal realm now is death. We are captured like beasts. All because of her. Our entire kind was cursed and punished. We only get enough water to survive. But what is survival without our songs? If the gods returned, surely Glaucos could convince Poseidon to lift this curse."

Thessaly suddenly stood. She took one look at Acantha and fled.

And that's when I realized how big of a problem we really had.

I gave her mother a glare of my own before I raced after my friend.

Forever, Thessaly ran and I chased her, long sharp cracks sounding from where our feet hit the brittle-dry salt beds. "Thessaly! Wait!" I cried over and over. The only answer I received was the flutter of her long hair streaming in neon against the aggressive white of the landscape.

After a half hour, she finally slowed. Cautiously, I came up behind her, as if she were a wild animal. There were strange wracking sounds coming from her, and by the time I got close enough, I knew what they were.

She was crying. Thessaly was actually crying.

My chest heaved, and all the aches on my body complained even louder as I sat down next to her. We remained silent for a bit, my arm in her lap and another around her shoulder, before I noticed the landscape had changed.

"Where are we?" I asked in wonder. It was cooler and the salt had given way to bare dirt. A broken set of wooden pillars lay in pieces like a long bridge.

Thessaly shook herself slightly. She blinked a few times, as if to refocus on the present. "It used to be the dock where my father and I would go through the nets from our catches in the world above. This is where I wanted to take you. This is where we can go home."

"But Thessaly——"

"Yes," she said bitterly. "If I help Aradia defeat the gods again, my village and family will be cursed to live like this forever. And my own curse will continue to reassert itself, no matter what you do."

"I can never lift the curse?" I asked, incredulous. "Not even with chaos magic or mother magic or anything?"

"Only the god who set it can do that. I'd hoped, since they were gone, that maybe their powers were broken—or at least a little ragged. Ragged enough that whatever powers you seemed to have would be enough to end the curse forever."

"Poseidon did this to you? Why?" A sob ripped loose from Thessaly again, shaking me to my core. "I'm sorry. You don't have to tell the story. And I'm sorry I'm not strong enough on my own."

"It's not about strength," she said, her purple eyes clearing of tears and turning to steel. "It's about wrath. Because of Poseidon's wrath, my entire village suffers. He wanted to send a message. Demons are nothing more than backs to be broken. So, he took our most precious possession. He took everyone's songs but mine and bound me to that rock near Aradia. Technically, the sirens can still travel between Earth and Nibiru, but without the power of our siren song, we're vulnerable to mankind. I've glimpsed cousins and family over the centuries who dared seek food or a better life above. Some managed to hunt and nourish themselves, but usually, it is them who were caught. I've seen cousins tangled in nets, friends mistaken for fish and fileted, and even an aunt stuffed and mounted as a decoration for the prow of a trireme."

I swallowed hard, remembering something Grandmother said. "Was this because of Odysseus?"

"No. That was before I was born. And Poseidon would have deeply enjoyed Odysseus's death. It was Athena who favorited that mortal hero."

"Oh. Right," I said, not knowing that at all.

Thessaly stared at the dilapidated dock as if mired in memories. "You already know I once loved a mortal man. That was only a half-truth, as he was only half of a man." My brow furrowed and Thessaly added, "The other half of him was a god. He was a prince, son of Atlas, first king of Atlantis, grandson of Poseidon, and he was more beautiful than the gods."

"What was his name?"

Thessaly's mouth turned up at one end. It was the closest to a smile I ever got from her. "I'd rather not repeat such strong talismans. Not here. Let us call him the prince."

She shivered, and I wished I had a complimentary Villa Venus robe to give her.

"When I was a young siren, my father liked to take me to where he grew up as a mortal, before eating the dogstooth. So, we used this dock to go above, and we would fish and swim as he had in his youth in the warm waters of the Tyrrhenian Seas. Our nets bursting, we would descend back to Nibiru where Glaucos would grace the village with his continued presence and kiss my mother in front of them all. She was softer in those days, but even then, she hoarded his love and held it above all else. I adored his presence, because it was the few times that the other sirens left me alone. Now, I know they were merely scared of Glaucos. When he was gone, their little cuts hurt as much as their constant hunts of me. If I were to go anywhere alone, one would always be lying in wait to pull my hair or put poisonous sea slugs down my chiton that would leave welts Grandmother would have to heal. I had no respite. That's why I loved it when Glaucos took me above. To me, Earth was a wonderland, free of my tormentors."

I stayed silent, starting to understand her a little better. I guessed bullying wasn't just for humans.

"Once I got older," she continued, "I would sometimes go without Glaucos to sit by myself, collecting shells and urchins and flotsam from shipwrecks. Sirens are usually only called to sing our songs for the gods' pleasure or sometimes for their wrath if it's to drown a hero. Hardly any of us ventured above for fun as I did. Our days were our own and most of my kin spent it here. It was once a great palace of coral walls filled with amber windows and pearl frames. We were completely submerged in cornflower blue waters."

"But not you?"

"Not me," she agreed. "I craved to be on Earth, the place where my father once roamed. I thought it might please him to see me take to his home realm so well, and he would invite me to live there forever."

"That makes sense. But what about the prince?"

Thessaly's face pinched in pain. "Once, I surfaced during a storm in an attempt to escape my tormentors. A trireme was being tossed between the foamy crests of the waves, its crew slowly drowning. There was one shining face that whisked about the sinking deck, boosting sailors onto boards and securing lines. I watched the boat disappear, swallowed by the sea—and I dove. Despite being the son of a demigod of the sea, he was half-drowned, his face the same blue of the waves, but I could sense a faint tug of divinity. A temple to Poseidon was in the distance, so I pulled him to the water steps and stroked his dark hair from his head so I could kiss him awake as I'd heard in stories my father used to tell me. Finally, when a rosy hue lit his cheeks, I left him for the priestesses to help him recuperate."

"Oh my God. You're the Little Mermaid."

Thessaly turned her purple eyes on me. "I know of this story. I sang once to a marooned sailor sometime during the high years of my curse. In exchange for not drowning him, he promised to write a happy ending the entire world would read."

"Was his name Hans freaking Christian Anderson?"

"Yes."

"Are you kidding me?" I gasped.

"No."

I blinked. "If I start calling you the Little Mermaid, will you maim me?"

"Terribly."

"Noted. Okay, so what happened next?"

Thessaly pulled her long hair over her shoulder and began to braid it. I'd never seen her with a nervous habit, but it seemed to be exactly that.

"After I pulled the prince to safety, I fled. Humans are not tame creatures, and siren young are brought up to be fearful of them. But how could that be if my father was once human, and he was the best thing I knew? I had an insatiable curiosity. Every day, I came back to the temple and watched as the virgin priestesses fussed over him. I glowed with pride, secure in the false knowledge that he would know me as his true savior above all others. Yet I was much too frightened to reveal myself. I simply watched as he healed. When his father came to collect him, I saw his crest and his flags whipping in the breeze. I knew, then, that he was a prince. A prince of Atlantis no less. Atlas ruled the seas from Etruria to the Pillars of Hercules."

Thessaly paused while I digested. Freaking Atlantis.

"You know the Pillars sit at the entrance to the Atlantic, named for Atlantis, of course," she said.

"Uh, sure."

"And on them are carved a warning, *Non Plus Ultra*. 'Go no farther.' Most think it was carved by the gods to warn the Greek and Romans not to venture into the wild Atlantic, or by Atlas himself to keep his people safe. But do you know what I think?"

I shook my head, aware my mouth was slightly open, but unable to stop.

"I think it was carved by the gods living in the far western reaches on the opposite side of the Atlantic. To warn their own people about the Greeks and Romans."

"By the ancient Americas, you mean?"

Thessaly nodded. "It would be safer for them to turn around, go back home against the wild and frenzied Atlantic. The deep, cold ocean was safer than our warm waters with our gods of wrath and ruin."

I had a feeling I knew where this was headed, but then again, the version I knew ended happily with the mermaid married to her prince. Not chained to a rock for eternity and an entire population of demons decimated.

"Over the next year, I grew bolder. I visited Atlantis every day. Usually, the prince stayed near the Pillars where his father's palace was, but sometimes he was sent across the seas to Etruria—or Italy. When I gathered enough courage, I allowed him to see me stooping to gather my baubles."

I pictured Thessaly, her blue hair to her waist, trying to casually admire a sea urchin before plunking it back in the water, looking anything except casual. But I kept that mental image to myself. "Was it love at first sight?" I asked.

Thessaly's marble cheeks reddened slightly. "I might have sung one stanza of one song. Just in case."

"Thessaly! You love-sang him."

She looked defensive, her fists balled up and her eyebrows winging down. "I was scared and young. It just popped out, and I stopped once I realized what I was doing."

"Okay, okay. What happened next?"

"He said my eyes matched the spiny murex snails used to color the royal robes so prized throughout the ancient world. He curled my hair between his thumb and forefinger. He said I was the most beautiful creature he had ever seen as he kissed my neck and unclasped my chiton. So, I became his mistress." Her face grew angrier. "I believed his honeyed words when he said he loved me, but he could not marry me. That he could never be seen with me. That our love would be an abomination to his father, even if it wasn't one to him." Her voice went lower. "Then, months later, he told me he was going to marry the priestess who found him that day on the water steps. The woman who saved him."

I clapped a hand over my mouth. "Did you tell your parents?"

She scoffed. "Of course not. I told Grandmother, though. I told her of a sea witch I had met on Earth and her prophecy. The witch promised me that if I wanted to get rid of my pain, I had to kill the prince and sprinkle his blood on my feet. Only then would I be free of his curse. Grandmother tried locking me in a cell of the palace, afraid of what I might do in my jilted, warped mindset. Afraid of what Poseidon might do if Atlas asked him for vengeance."

"And that's how that story ends?" I asked, hopefully.

Thessaly shook her head. "I gnawed the shackles made of cockles and seaweed and escaped. I swam to Atlantis and watched the nuptials from the murky depths. Then, I followed them to their wedding bed." She stopped talking, and an awful, cold feeling settled over me.

"Thessaly," I said, my heart dropping. "What did you do?"

She turned her eyes back to the dock and the setting horizon. "The sea witch was wrong. I still feel my pain."

"Oh my God, Thessaly. The Little Mermaid doesn't kill the prince in either the Hans Christian Anderson version or the Disney version," I objected. Although, I'd had so many warnings from so many people—*Sirens are still demons*, Aurick had said. Nonna had never trusted her. Still, this new piece of information shocked me.

"The writer told me he couldn't let his heroine kill the prince in his version. It wouldn't play well for feminine beauty. I thought about eating him at that moment, but men give me indigestion. Too much testosterone."

"You *killed* the prince? And the priestess? You killed a demigo—"

Thessaly slapped a hand over my mouth, her purple eyes wide. "Shhhhh," she said. "They're hunting us."

Chapter Five

"LITTLE TESS, little Tess. Where did you go?"

"You always loved games so."

"Yes, come play with us!"

There were at least three distinct voices. Three feral sirens with nothing to lose and a millennia of hurt to avenge. Even Thessaly looked unnerved. She crouched behind the decayed dock and tugged me down.

"We should have escaped immediately. What folly, indulging in my story!"

"You killed a demigod and Poseidon cursed you and your entire village!" I harsh-whispered. "I don't know if I would have helped you if I'd known."

"Which is why I said nothing."

I sagged as the siren voices went up in pitch, probably sensing their prey was near. Us. I shot Thessaly my best "we'll talk about this later" mom glare and then chanced a quick look. On the other side of the dock, three, shining white fish bone spears bounced gaily, their wielders clearly excited to be on an actual hunt. They looked wicked sharp.

I tried to formulate a plan. It didn't help that I was in

shock over the fact that Thessaly had murdered a prince and an innocent priestess in cold blood and then was cursed by Poseidon for eternity. My Thessaly. It was like coming to terms with the fact I didn't really know anyone, not even myself.

"Do you regret it?" I asked.

"No."

"Thessaly!"

She jerked her head toward our hunters. "I think we have more important things to worry about."

"Fine. What can we do?"

Thessaly blinked rapidly. "I'm not sure yet, but whatever you do, don't reveal your powers."

"Seriously? I'm literally worthless in a fight without them."

Whatever pearl of wisdom Thessaly was about to offer was cut off by the whiz of a spear. It struck the dirt between us, sinking three inches deep into the ground. I swallowed hard, knowing how much that would have hurt if it had hit flesh.

"I didn't hear a scream," one of the sirens complained.

"I told you your aim was embarrassing," another scoffed.

Thessaly nodded toward the spear. "Take it and follow my lead."

"If you say so," I whispered back, "but I still think it would be better if I blasted them back to the village. The fresh water alone might put them in a better mood."

"Do nothing."

"Fine." I kept the weapon steady in front of me as we rose. Three sirens, two with spears and one with a fish-gutting knife, stood ready to pounce ten feet away. They looked deadly—and deadly serious. We wouldn't get away alive if they had anything to say about it.

"We were just leaving. There's no need for—" Thessaly began, but the siren with coral pink hair cut her off with a terrifying yell.

And the battle began.

Two of the sirens lunged at Thessaly. One received a foot to the face, and the other got a fist to the stomach. It was good to know that, even among her own kind, Thessaly was a badass. All three of them moved with cat-like quickness, twisting and turning in the air as they battled.

The third siren, on the other hand, moved slowly toward me, giving me plenty of time to study her sea green hair and hate-filled eyes. Clearly, I was considered the weak link, which, unfortunately, I was if I couldn't use my powers.

All the while, the sirens taunted Thessaly, telling her to use her voice. Bring the rains. Spell them. Kill them.

Murderer. Cursed One. Better off dead.

Their taunts rang in my ears.

"Use your magic," I yelled at Thessaly, remembering the way she'd held the sea serpents back with a great plume of seawater.

"Oh, she can't. There's not enough water here. Unless you'd like to take what we just collected?" a siren taunted. "Would you like to do that? Would you like to take your poor mommy's only water to try to drown us?"

My fingers itched to let out a burst of magic. Just something to make them regret all of their bullying over the centuries. I felt it welling up in the center of my being. Blocking the surge of powers left me gasping for oxygen; it was unnatural. I dearly wanted to give Thessaly water to manipulate. Or, even better, I could give them some chaos to choke on.

Coral Pink Demon Barbie laughed, like she had too much plastic in her brain. "Or you could sing to us! What about a nice lullaby? We do so miss our songs. Would you use your song against your own kind?"

I wouldn't have hesitated, but Thessaly faltered, giving one of the sirens the chance to elbow her in the mouth and slash her with her knife, drawing a deep cut across her lips. Thessaly reared back, blood pouring through her fingers. From behind, a second siren gagged her with some frayed fabric, and I winced as Thessaly grunted in pain.

My own siren continued to circle me, thrusting her spear every once in a while as if she were testing my abilities, unsure who—or what—I was. So, she was smarter than she looked.

Thessaly was still shaking her head no, which seemed like wishful thinking. If we wanted to get out of this alive, something would have to give.

The sirens herded me toward Thessaly, cornering us. Their faces were pure menace, salt in their hair and ice in their hearts. "Remember that time Daddy dearest had to save you from the far reaches of Nibiru?" Coral Pink asked. Now that she was satisfied Thessaly was fully gagged, she had a lot more swagger. "Thessaly was so easy to trick. We promised her scraps of our love and she licked our feet for more. That was my favorite trip, though," she said as I gritted my teeth in anger at the glee in her voice. "We tied her up in the desert and left her to dry out. Of course Glaucos found her."

"I still have the scars," the other lamented, sweeping back her teal hair to reveal what looked like the prongs from a trident that had raked down her neck into her back. "What would equal that humiliation?"

"How about being tied to a rock for thousands of years?" I suggested.

"Shut up," Coral Pink snarled. She stabbed me hard in the ribs, and I almost threw up at the pain.

"Can I call the chaos yet?" I begged in a whisper.

"I said shut up!"

The spear knifed a centimeter deeper into my throat, and I didn't wait for an answer because, soon, the pressure wouldn't allow me to speak at all. I pushed forth my chaos magic, waiting for the tingling of my back to ignite and the feeling of losing control to overwhelm me with its darkness.

I was met with nothing.

My hands scrabbled uselessly at the siren, her fangs curving into a demonic smile as the truth hit me. My chaos was gone. The weight that had hung on me had disappeared, and it had been such a relief. I hadn't noticed because… Well, I was wandering through Nibiru while demons tried to kill me.

My vision went black around the edges, and I saw Thoth again, practically pulling my magic from me to overwhelm his body in that tower.

And I knew. He had taken my chaos for himself.

If I had a mirror, I knew my tattoos would be gone, too. Thoth had tricked me, yet again.

Chapter Six

I WAS DYING. I had been speared, and my life force ran from my body in a rivulet of red. That was the only explanation for the unsettling feeling skittering across my skin, burying itself in my ear, and hollowing out my brain. The sound of death was beautifully chaotic, and it wafted in on a summer breeze—a breeze unnatural to Nibiru.

Except, the siren about to spear me could hear it too. She howled in rage and covered her ears.

It was enough. The pressure released from my aorta, and I saw Thessaly's face bright red with the effort of singing through the stiff fabric.

Ok, so I overreacted, but a siren song was powerful magic. And Thessaly seemed different...

Subtly, I bloomed a pair of protective ear plugs, just as any good mother would do. They allowed me to still hear the haunting music, but filtered out all the brain scrambling effects.

Now that I could think again, I rolled to my feet, scooped up the siren's weapon, and aimed it at her heart.

Her aquamarine eyes were hateful as she kept her hands over her ears, her fingers plugging them closed.

With my other hand, I quickly slashed Thessaly's gag. It was like listening to an aria under water until, suddenly, you burst from the bathtub and heard the notes in all of their ringing glory.

Thessaly didn't dare stop her siren song, the only siren left in the world who still had a voice. It must have been part of her curse. Poseidon had painted an even bigger target on her back by allowing her alone among her species to keep their most prized possession: their songs.

No one could accuse the gods of being uncreative.

The other two spears clattered to the ground as the sirens howled, probably trying to drown out Thessaly's voice. I rounded them up, menacingly shoving the spear at their navels and forcing them to sit with their backs together.

Despite everything happening around me, my mind still played a constant chorus. No chaos. No chaos. No chaos. I had hated the heft of it while I'd had it, the weight like an iron yoke across my shoulders, but without it? How could I ever defeat Thoth? Only a god of chaos could kill another god. That was the deal.

The implications were just starting to register.

Thoth was on Earth and I couldn't stop him. Thoth had my chaos magic. I had dew drops and some mothering to keep us safe.

Thessaly's mournful aria overwhelmed my own song of sorrow, and my heart felt like it could burst. I was an even bigger failure than I thought, but all I could do was put one foot in front of the next.

It wasn't until we'd safely tied them together and triple-checked the ropes that Thessaly paused in her song. "I promise I won't kill you. I'm going to fix this."

Coral Pink Demon Barbie had a bitter laugh. "We don't want your help."

"My help is all you have."

"We'd rather die."

The others agreed.

"I don't care. I'm still going to find a way."

"Let's go, Thessaly," I murmured.

She gave one last, haunted look back at her tormentors. I would have told them to go kick rocks, but I guess Thessaly wasn't there yet. She led us to the spot where the worlds were thin. From here, I could hear the waves crashing faintly on the coast above, and I could almost feel the warm Mediterranean sun on my skin.

As we ascended together, I fingered the mark of script that Dido had imprinted on my skin. *Dux femina facti.* A woman authored this achievement. And I would continue to write my story in my own way. I would find a way to destroy Thoth, one way or another, with or without chaos. Whatever that meant.

My feet hit the other side first, but it wasn't solid. Nothing was solid, and I was drowning. Water flowed into my mouth, briny and choking. The shock of the return trip made me infantile.

Finally, Thessaly grabbed my arm and lugged me onto something hard. We were both breathing heavily as I welcomed her beautiful, old hunk of rock. It had never felt so comfortable before.

"Whoa, take it easy," I said, seeing the look on Thessaly's face. Clearly, she didn't feel the same way. "It's just the portal, remember? You're not tied here anymore."

She put her palm on it, her eyes still spooked. I didn't

blame her. She'd been cursed to this rock for centuries, and while I had supposedly broken a portion of its hold, uncurling a few of Poseidon's claws, I was clearly a failure at this god stuff since she kept waking up to find herself back here. There was no way to fully release her from its grip.

"I don't feel the pull as hard," Thessaly said. "It's as if… Nibiru gave me strength to fight it."

"Really?"

"Yes."

"You were pretty incredible down there," I agreed. I shielded my eyes to see Villa Venus at the top of the cliff. It looked deserted from here. "How long do you think we've been gone?"

"Hard to say. Time moves differently in Nibiru," she answered. "Let's hurry. I want off this rock." She dove into the waves, and I was forced to sort of flop into the water and swim after her.

Eventually, I remembered I had water magic, and the waves parted more easily after that until I staggered up the shore. By now, I could hear what sounded like a battle, faintly roaring in the distance.

"Is that Thoth?" I cried, my heart pounding against my fragile, human rib cage.

Thessaly disappeared at the edge of a cave, her liminal highway, and reappeared a moment later.

"No, it's still the Council. It looks like only a few hours have passed here."

"What the hell? I had them all knocked out."

"They probably woke up and recommenced fighting."

Suddenly, the absence of an ominous presence flowed through my veins like ice. "I don't feel Thoth, and I definitely saw that bastard wake up in the crypt."

Thessaly looked grim. "My guess is that he slipped away in the chaos of the Council battle."

I groaned. "Great. Well, let's go defeat the Council, again."

Except, my friends and found family were doing a pretty good job on their own. Thessaly and I ran into the square just as Aurick sucker punched Bruno, right in the temple. The vampire fainted to the ground in a heap of black robes.

I was amazed to see everyone still there, defending Ava and Aradia. Even Jo the Cadmean Vixen had decided to stick around after helping me escape. I knew it probably hadn't been very long by the way her eyebrows tracked down in confusion at seeing us.

"Ava," she said in that luxurious accent, thick enough to spread like clotted cream. "What are you doing back so soon?"

I actually smiled at that. "Trust me, I've been away a lifetime."

A few more soldiers appeared, and Jo sprayed them with super pheromones. Their eyes crossed and their tongues wagged. I felt the tug too, but I only had eyes for one supernatural. I locked onto Aurick as his face jolted at the sight of me. The air sizzled as if touched by a superconductor, and shivers raced down my already shaky legs.

Bruno made a movement like he was thinking about coming back into consciousness, and Aurick barely paused in his strides to aim his boot-heel at the vampire's temple. In seconds, he swept me into his strong arms, where I wilted, letting frustrated tears slide down my face.

"Ava, Ava," he murmured, as I rested my head on his shoulder. "What's the matter?"

Knowing I couldn't indulge, I pushed away from his chest and jumped down. My world felt like it was still tilting at the sight of him, and for one more second, I closed my eyes and let it spin. When I opened them, Aurick's gaze bore into mine, a concerned frown cementing his face. I swallowed hard and Aurick caressed the smooth, vulnerable places down my neck with his thumb.

My voice was hoarse, but clear. "Thoth escaped. He reclaimed his body, and he took my chaos magic."

A collective gasp rose up from the square. Marco shed his lion form just in time to catch a fainting Rosemary in his arms, and Coronis let out a terrified caw. I couldn't help but think it sounded accusatory, although the rational part of my brain told me it wasn't. It was just a shock. Coronis tumbled to the ground and ran straight to Thessaly.

"I'm sorry," I said, choking. "I thought I was killing him with chaos, but it allowed him to die and be reborn. He's already claimed his body and fled Aradia."

I heard footfalls as someone ran to check the crypt, but I didn't need visual confirmation. In my bones, I knew Thoth had come, conquered, and gone.

"It's okay, Ava," Aurick promised. "We'll figure it out. We always have. Let's get settled and decide what to do."

I shook my head. "Wake up Bruno. It seems we have a common goal, now."

"Are you sure?" Aurick asked, eyeing the vampire in disgust. "I think he would rather imprison you first and ask questions later. And you're no help to us in prison."

"They couldn't hold me."

"I wouldn't be so sure. They'll have the same magical wards for your mortal body that they used on the archon."

"The archon," I repeated. "I wonder if Thoth will go to him. Nonna told me it was male. What would you do, if you were only the second god left in this realm?"

Aurick shrugged. "I don't know. I don't know if he'll want to prop up the pillars to Axis Mundi again or what his goal is. Surely he'll have one after so long in stasis."

"Surely. You'd think I'd know it, or at least have some idea. I'm the most worthless goddess you could have on your side."

Aurick took me by the shoulders. "Stop that, Ava. Beating yourself up won't do anyone any good. You're doing the best you can with the knowledge you have. We'll figure this out. Together."

Bruno chose that moment to come to, and he hissed and leapt at the sight of me, going for the jugular if I were to hazard a guess. Aurick caught him by the neck, exerting pressure to knock him unconscious again, but I held up a hand.

"Wait. We're better in numbers. We need the Council's help."

"You shall never receive it," Bruno spat. "We despise your kind. Any offer would only be a ruse from you, anyway. Gods never speak true. We will have you in chains under the Arch."

"What would imprisoning me do? Or even killing me?" I demanded. "I am a goddess. I will be reborn and still be a thorn in the side of humanity for as long as you can imagine. Consider that. Then, consider that I am the only thing as powerful as Thoth on your side. I am the only thing that could hope to counter him."

Bruno's jaw went slack. "Thoth is… here? I don't believe it."

"He's not trapped in Axis Mundi, if that's what you're asking. He's here, and he's got his immortal body."

I decided not to mention the fact that none of this would've happened, neither his body being rescued from the Archon Wars, nor his body being reborn, without me. It seemed piddling, really.

"While you figure out if you want a goddess's help or not, I'm going to actually get to work," I informed him to his outraged scoffs. Very centuries-old mature.

We left him chained in a Gordian Knot and walked out of earshot. Aurick said low, "Let me follow Thoth. I will go slow and gather intel."

"Do you think you can track a god with a good head start?" I asked.

Aurick's nod was crisp and sure. "Absolutely. I was a supernatural bounty hunter in a previous life."

I paused. "You should definitely tell me that story later."

"It was fairly mundane stuff. Mostly skinning supernatural lawbreakers, but I'm grateful to have the skills now." He gave me a hard kiss, devastating me with his woodsmoke scent that I adored so deeply, and took my upper lip between his teeth. I savored it for a moment before breaking away and tenderly brushing back his golden hair.

"Don't get yourself un-un-dead. If that's a thing," I whispered. "Promise me you won't do anything rash."

"Me? Rash?"

I laughed faintly. It was true; he was very organized and calculated. I remembered how it felt like playing chess with him during our first date. No wonder kings and emperors asked him to advise their councils. Still, I worried that if he saw Thoth playing god to mortals or even hurting someone, his honor would compel him to intervene.

"Don't worry. I promise not to engage the god. I'll strictly follow to see what he's up to."

"Even if it's smiting puny humans?" I asked softly, attempting a joke.

"Even if they're the puniest."

I winced. "I'm sorry, that sounded terribly divine and unjust of me. I swear, it's only because—"

Aurick stopped me with a second, longer kiss. "I know. There wouldn't be much I could do to stop a god in an immortal body if he wanted to kill someone. I'd just get myself sent permanently to Nibiru, too."

My heart staggered. "So you could. You could die, in a way. I always thought of you as invincible."

"Don't count me out yet. It would take a lot more than waking you up on the wrong side of the bed to do me in for good." He gave me a wry smile. "Remember, Ava. I believe in you. I always will. You are who you choose to be."

"I hope that's true," I said sadly.

"It is." Aurick unsheathed his bone dagger and was gone, leaving a ragged hole behind him that vanished as quickly as he had. I felt his absence deeply. But then—

A swoop, a crush, and the emptiness filled.

I felt Rosemary's strong, yeast-worked arms and Marco's furry beard. I smelled Coronis's elegant fragrance and felt my eyes prick at Thessaly's cold arms. She was here, helping me, when she really should be stopping me. If it were me, I might want to clear my name and come home a hero. Be someone everyone in my village was forced to look up to for once. I had to admit; it felt damn good doing it here on Aradia. Going from Ava the ignored to Ava the goddess. But not Thessaly. She had more at stake—more heart—in our found family. I only hoped when the time came, I would keep my same convictions. To stop the gods from returning, no matter the cost.

Anyway, the prince probably deserved it. He sounded like a leading-on douche canoe.

After a five minute group hug, we pulled away, and Rosemary inspected everybody. She'd only had a few hours to digest the fact that I was Tefnut, but she took it beautifully. "Goddesses need espresso and biscotti, too," she insisted.

"Wait," I held up her fussing hands. "I don't see Nonna."

"I'm sure she's at the villa," Coronis said and everyone murmured agreement. It was best for someone her age to stay out of the fray.

Thinking of Nonna made me remember Tiberius and my stomach dropped. "Actually, I need to tell you all something else. I think… I think I accidentally killed—"

A flying furball hit me in the cheek and bounced into my arms. "Ava!"

"Tiberius? Tiberius!" I shouted, astonished. "You're not dead. You're not dead!"

Tiberius twitched his whiskers. "I think I broke Ava. She keeps repeating herself."

The tears came freely as I checked him over for wounds. "You're not dead. How are you not dead?" I asked as he winced at a particularly tender spot on his back leg. "Also, you're not a slug."

Rosemary came and gave him a pat. "He just got back an hour before you. Both Mak and Coronis tried healing him, but whatever daemon physiology he possesses is beyond their abilities. Still, he's been trying to convince us to let him go back to Nibiru ever since. I've caught him twice trying to sneak away and do it alone." She waggled her finger at him. "You are in no condition to astral jump to the villa, let alone Nibiru. What good would it do if you killed yourself on the journey there?"

Tiberius still looked miserable. "It's easier without a passenger, though. Especially such a strong one as a goddess. I'm sorry, Ava. When I saw you building up a burst of chaos, I realm-jumped." He hung his head and his tail went limp. "I was a coward."

"Tiberius, I don't blame you. You were literally about to get roasted because I couldn't control my powers, and you were trying to find me even now. You're the bravest daemon I know."

"I'm the only daemon, remember?" Tiberius's whiskers quivered, and I couldn't help snuggling him to my cheek. He finally sighed and stopped trembling. "Thanks, Ava. I don't deserve a goddess's friendship."

"Of course you do! And I'm hardly a full goddess anyway. I'm more Ava than anything."

Tiberius became agitated, flipping his tail back and forth. "Really, I don't. I'm not worth—"

"Shh," I hushed him. "It's fine."

He snuggled into my neck, burying himself in my thick hair until his nose poked out the other side.

"Have you seen Nonna yet, Tiberius? Is she at the villa?"

For some reason, Tiberius froze.

"Seriously, Tiberius, where is she? I need to talk to her."

"Yes," he said, his voice sounding both ancient and nervous. "I guess it's time you two finally had the talk."

Chapter Seven

MAYBE THE ASTRAL projection should have tipped me off. Then again, it hadn't for months. What could I say? I was a slow learner.

In any case, as we approached the villa, I found Nonna's ghostly face hovering somewhere near the broken walnut tree in the front yard, searching wildly for something. I was so happy to see her, I didn't question anything else.

"Nonna!" I shouted. "You're alive! I'm sorry I didn't get a chance to say goodbye before we left."

Her face went from frantic to shocked to relieved before disappearing with a *pop*. I ran into the villa to find her lying on the bed, struggling to sit up at the elbows. She was wearing a sunshine-colored muumuu, but for once, she was devoid of jewelry, like she'd been too harried to get into her usual array. Even her hair was limp.

"Tiberius said we should talk," I said, a little uncertainty flickering through me as I helped her stand. Both Nonna and Tiberius were staring at me oddly. "He's also been acting weird."

I knew the goddess thing was a bit much, but even Rosemary had taken it better than them. Nonna still hadn't said anything. She was staring at me with such intensity, I let out a weird cough.

"Aren't we a pair?" I laughed nervously. "The woman who never forgets and then me. The woman who never remembers."

Then, like a flint struck against a rock, my mind's eye burned with fireworks. Nonna, the woman who never forgets. The *strega* who could astral project. With the familiar who was actually a daemon.

"No," I said, backing up and hitting the wall, my hand scrabbling for the door handle. "Nonna, tell me it's not true."

Her eyes were bright. "Mamma, you should have told me you were a goddess. You never would've needed to go to Nibiru in the first place if you had."

I couldn't stop shaking. And I couldn't even tell if it was fear or rage. "I trusted you."

"You can still trust me. We can work together, just as gods and archons always have. Mamma, this changes nothing between us. If anything, it makes our bond stronger. I will be your servant, my body and powers for you alone. I will swear it now, if you wish. Together, we'll remake the world and bring the gods back."

"Never," I hissed, sparks already licking up my arms. How was I so blind? It all made sense. Only a few weeks ago, I was researching supernatural beings who could astral project in the Library of Alexandria when Nonna literally astral projected to tell us about the sphinx attack. And I hadn't put the pieces together? Her astral face had been staring at me as I read that ONLY archons have this power. Instead, I'd believed it when she told me she spent centuries learning on her own.

She'd sat me down with Tiberius who was a daemon, a being that only worked with gods and archons. I had willfully ignored the facts because they'd painted a picture I didn't want to see: that Nonna was never my friend. That she had been consistently betraying me from day one.

Nonna hadn't stopped talking. "You can go back to your real home. Together, we can prop up the pillars and restore Axis Mundi. It will be as it once was. You must accept who you are. I will help you. I will make it easy. That is my purpose in life."

"How long have you known I was the Runaway Goddess? Since the day I arrived?"

"No, not until today. But Aradia knew. Her consciousness is mine. I have fed her my own blood dutifully for centuries, sprinkled like quicksilver into the mud. She has been calling to you. Looking for any opportunity to bring you home to Thoth. I must admit, even I was a bit shocked when it was that floozy your husband was sleeping with who managed to heed the call. She was your conduit."

I should have known Marla and Jim were going to screw me over, one last time. "And?" I asked tightly.

"And Aradia has been pulling supernaturals to her shores for centuries. Waiting. I knew you must have been something, but it wasn't until that morning at Rosemary's Bakery when you said you had twin boys that I let myself hope. We'd heard over the centuries that Thoth had cursed you. He bragged about it once, drunk on nectar and so very lonely without you."

"What a pretty way to put betrayal. Couch it in terms of hope," I scoffed.

"Mamma, come now. Search your memories. This is bigger than the little games you and Thoth like to play. I want to see Culsans. I want to hold him again before I die.

Only the gods can overcome the Council's power, and you saw yourself how evil the Council has become."

My breath was fire in my belly. Every swallow was torture. "Who is Culsans?"

Nonna shifted her weight. "You met him."

The serpent's tail and horned head trapped in an oubliette under the Arch sparked to mind.

Nonna continued. "He's been imprisoned by those fools. They built that prison merely because they are afraid of what they do not understand. But you do. You are perfection, better than I ever dreamed possible. You understand both sides."

"I refuse," I hissed, backing away from what I assumed was my first real friend on Aradia. No wonder she had wanted me to "burn it all down." All she wanted was her lover. I had been used, tricked, and manipulated again. In what lifetime would I learn?

Nonna's admonishments and pleas seared into my brain, the memories tugging through. Of course she wanted me to bring my boys here. She was constantly mentioning it from the instant she found out I had twins. *Best forget about mummies and men. Think of your boys.* Now, her words haunted me. When I wouldn't do it, she brought them here herself. When I found them wandering in the basilica, it was because she had been stalling me in the kitchen. *What's the rush, Mamma? Here, have some more espresso.* She'd been actively working against me from day one.

Still, she was talking. "You're the Wandering Goddess. Thoth is the great love of your life, exactly as Culsans is mine. Together, we will get them back."

"Nonna, I never want him back. That may have been true millennia ago, but I've suffered for centuries at his hands. I've learned more in the past few months on Aradia as Ava about what I want in life than I ever did as Tefnut. I don't want his toxic energy anywhere near me or my sons."

"Ava—"

"No!" I thundered, the walls around us shaking under the force of my anger.

Nonna's face took a turn. Whatever she was expecting, my anger wasn't it.

"After all this time knowing me as Ava, did you really think I'd want the gods back?"

"Ava is just a drop in the ocean of who you are. Search your true self, Tefnut, and you'll see I'm right."

"So you were just waiting to see if it were true. That the She-Wolf was indeed Tefnut," I pieced together. Before she could confirm it, because of course that's what she did, I demanded, "Show me your true form."

The old woman looked uncomfortable for once. "Do we need all that formality?"

"Yes. Show me."

"As you wish, my goddess." Nonna's true form erupted in brilliant azure and gold. She smelled like crushed herbs. A thin layer of golden fur coated her body, and her eyes were sharp and intelligent instead of rheumy and unfocused.

How did I never notice her serpentine edges? The triangular tilt to her chin and the calculations in her glances? There was nothing human to her. Even her eyes were too bright, too intense, her gaze fastened on me completely.

"You fear nothing, Tefnut. You are life and death, and Thoth made you even more powerful, albeit unwittingly. Now you are a mother a thousand times over. Embrace this." Nonna held out her hand. "Together, we can remake the world as we wish. We get a say in which gods could return. Surely you miss your children, Geb and Nut? As they miss you. It doesn't have to be like before. You know both sides, you can make it as you will. You can make it better. You could strive for perfection."

Nonna was talking faster, afraid I'd try to stop her. "You are uniquely positioned to understand it all. Look at you! You went from being a scorned wife and a forgotten woman to become the one being able to completely change our world order! The power is yours. Let me help you take it, Tefnut."

That name. I shook my head slowly, every bone and sinew crying in pain from my fight with Thoth. "That's the problem. I don't want to be her. I want to be Ava."

Nonna barked a laugh. "A mere woman entering the beginning of the end? Come now, Mamma. Don't be silly."

"My old memories are coming in bits and pieces, and I don't like who Tefnut had the ability to become. Chaotic, vengeful, puffed with self-importance. The gods are not fit for the mortal world. And if you're not with me, you're against me, Nonna. I will sacrifice everything to destroy Thoth, myself included if need be."

"You would sacrifice your own happiness? I love Ava, but I respect Tefnut."

"Everything," I swore. "As Ra's Right Eye, I was meant to bring chaos to the realms. As Ra's Left Eye, I ushered in order to the cosmos. It's in my very veins. I failed then. I will not fail now."

"Tef—"

"Power corrupts. Absolute power?" My ironic smile was a grimace. "Even you must remember the saying."

"Fine. You want a compromise? One pillar. Prop up one pillar and let me and Culsans slip under. None of the other gods would even know, and it would allow us to live forever together, unlike this realm where we age every day.

It's been so very long since I've touched his face or held his hand. I'm dying, Ava, and I'm scared. Don't let me die."

"How can you ask that of me, Nonna?" I felt like I was drowning, begging her to throw me a life vest and save me like she always had before. "We have no idea what may happen if we prop up a pillar. It could potentially unleash all of the gods, and I'm not naïve enough to think otherwise. Look at how the gods terrorized MILFs! Look at poor Coronis!"

"Stop acting like you're above them. You're not. You're one of them. You're a goddess."

Nonna's face splintered and flickered whole again.

"What are you doing?"

"I'm going to get Culsans. I would rather have you on my side, but I can't afford to waste any more time. You were the one who was sad I was dying. Now, you have the power to save me and you refuse. To me, it seems you are more of a goddess than you want to admit." Her voice was bitterness incarnate, distilled and refined into a blistering purpose.

"Nonna, no!" I cried as her face shimmered like an oil slick and was gone.

Chapter Eight

TIBERIUS and I stood staring at each other, slack-jawed. "Did you know she was going to do that?" I asked.

"I knew she was getting desperate, but I thought you'd be able to talk her down."

I ran out of Nonna's room, flipping past familiar photographs and memories. "Tiberius, can you get us to the Arch?"

He didn't answer, and one look at his ragged fur and broken whiskers was enough to tell me the truth. Tiberius had been squeezed through a hand-cranked pasta roller and came out the other side barely breathing.

"Shoot." I repeated myself. "Shoot. Shoot, shoot, shoot. No, this calls for a bigger word. This is shit. This is total and absolute shit."

"Aurick is gone, but what about the Council?" Tiberius asked.

I stared for a minute. He was right. The Council could get us there in no time, if they were willing, which they weren't. Bruno was a non-starter, and Manu's icy glares told me he wouldn't be helping me anytime soon. I wondered if there was a rulebook around here I could throw at his head and knock some sense into it.

At my rotten-egg expression, Tiberius suggested, "How about a little chaos magic to encourage them?"

I jerked at his words. "I can't."

"What do you mean?"

I hesitated. I hadn't wanted it in the first place, but without it, I felt oddly naked. "When I was feeding it into Thoth to destroy him, he was actually absorbing it. It not only caused his rebirth, but he somehow ripped it out of me." I pulled down the back of my shirt. Only the cobra and sun disc remained. The Eye of Ra had been burned away, leaving a trail of raised welts in the shape of the Eye.

I heard footsteps behind me and turned to find Coronis and Thessaly had arrived at the villa. Their faces told me they'd seen my back. Perhaps none of us, not even me, had truly believed our best chance at defeating Thoth was gone, but this absence was undeniable.

Tiberius was horrified. "Nothing?"

I shook my head, shame coursing through me.

Coronis spoke first. "Rosemary, Marco, and Mak have the Council members resting comfortably at the taverna. What do you want to do next?"

I stared at their still-hopeful faces. How was it that I suddenly ascended into the leadership role? I'd felt up to the task a day ago when I'd charged headfirst into Nibiru with only a chipmunk daemon to guide me, but now? Let's just say failure had humbled me. Mistakes had made me cautious. I wasn't prepared to lead this operation. In the grand scale of things, I'd only known I was a goddess for a few hours.

Thessaly stood up straighter, and that mere movement commanded our attention. "I still believe in you, Ava. I would put my life in your hands. Whatever you command, we'll do."

Coronis beamed. "Me, too."

Tiberius jumped on my shoulder and proudly nibbled my ear.

Thessaly continued. "Hopefully, it includes death and destruction, but again, it's up to you."

"Getting more of your wrath back?" I teased.

She fixed me with a pointed stare. "Yes. For those that stick their heads in the sand, a thousand times yes."

As much as I wanted to run straight there, I stood rooted to the spot. I wished I could fly, fight, avenge, but caution held me in place. Rashness had gotten me nowhere fast the last time. My hands balled into fists at the memory.

"Nonna is an archon," I announced to gasps from the women. "Her lover, Culsans, is trapped beneath the Arch, and she was in a desperate state when she fled. She's dying and will do anything to see him one more time. Everything she's strived for over the centuries is crumbling around her. Now, she's cornered. Now, she's dangerous."

"What are you going to do to Nonna?" Coronis whispered through her fingers.

"I'm going to talk to her reasonably. We were both fired up when we spoke a few minutes ago. Let's just say it didn't go well. But there has to be a better solution than bringing all of the gods back. Nobody wants that. Not me, and probably not even her. She said something about propping up one pillar so she and Culsans could slip through. That means she's not totally lost."

"But we can't do that," Thessaly objected. "You have no idea what else could slip through."

"I know. I'll think of something on the way. That's the first problem: getting there. Aurick took off with his bone dagger, so we're going to have to make a deal with the Council for one of theirs. Unless I could steal one?" I ventured hopefully.

"Warded to each user," Tiberius said.

"Right. Obviously, because that would make it so much harder," I muttered, steeling myself to face Bruno and Manu.

"Tiberius, what if Nonna decides to try her luck with Thoth, and he suddenly has access to two archons? Can they prop up a pillar without a daemon?"

The rest of the women looked horrified, but I already knew what he would say. I was just hoping I was wrong. I'd been wrong enough, I should at least get to be wrong on something I wanted to be wrong about. Right?

Tiberius twitched his whiskers. "I only help make the process easier. You should know better than most that, compared to a god and two archons, I'm only a small part of the equation. I'm sure they can figure it out without me."

"Fine. Let's make a deal with the devil to stop a god."

Chapter Nine

BRUNO REACTED WELL. And by well, I mean he tried to gnaw his way out of the Gordian Knot while spewing hate, which, if it wasn't for the time issue, I would have gleefully watched with a bowl of popcorn and a bottle of red wine. As it was, I rolled my eyes and addressed the rest of the taverna full of imprisoned Council members, hoping one of the ostrich idiots would pull their heads out of the sand for a second and listen. My hopes were about as high as a broken kite.

"I know most of you would prefer that I didn't exist, and you will refuse to listen to a word I say," I began to growls and jeers. "You'd also rather die than admit you're wrong. Well, I'm not talking to you. I'm talking to the ones who would be willing to compromise if it meant we all achieve our ultimate goal. Safety and protection for our loved ones and for this world." I had to keep raising my voice until Marco roared and shook the taverna down to its knees.

I thanked him and kept plowing forward, eyeing both the guards in black robes and the townspeople I'd come to love over countless espressos and apertivo hours. Who here would be receptive? Who here would be my foe?

I took a deep breath. "I am Tefnut."

A huge commotion broke out, and I called for calm, eventually yelling, "By all rights, I should be your enemy, and you only have my word that I'm not. I give you my word now that I don't want the gods to come back—"

"Because you want to be top god, pushing us little guys around? Tell me, has all that power gone to your pretty little head?"

I recognized the voice immediately, and a second later, Spyro elbowed his way through the crowd. I tried not to let the hurt show on my face.

He put his hands on his hips, his erection jutting out defiantly as usual. "That's it, eh? You think because you're a god, you can reject perfectly good gifts from my shop? Well I say enough is enough!"

"It's probably your stench, satyr," someone shouted in the back.

Others started yelling too, but I noticed one person who was silent. Before it devolved into complete chaos, I dog-whistled. As much as I itched to use my mother magic and blanket the place in calm, I hardly thought that gesture would go over well. Instead, I zeroed in on the one individual who made the unlikeliest of allies.

Slowly, I approached Manu. The runes carved into his head glowed faintly, and the face tattoos seemed to suck in all the light in the room, but he didn't say a word. He was the only one who seemed to be truly listening. I remembered how much like an abyss his eyes had seemed when I was his prisoner. Now, he was mine, but if we were to defeat Thoth, our interests were better served aligned.

When I reached him, I crouched down to where he was seated with his legs crossed. The Gordian Knot bit into his wrists, and it should have felt poetic, but it didn't. I needed him. Or at least, I needed his trust long enough to use his bone dagger.

"There's another archon. I didn't even realize it myself until a few minutes ago, but she's trying to reach her lover, the one the Council has imprisoned under the Arch. You can choose to believe me or not, but I swore I wouldn't help her, and now she's gone there to release him directly. Do you think your protections in place will hold?"

"They'll hold, but not for long. Not against another archon."

I nodded grimly. "That's what I thought. I'm going after her. I could take the long way, but I'd rather not risk losing all of that time."

"You can't wield my bone dagger. My wards will disable it if it were to leave my possession without my permission."

My anger boiled beneath the surface, and I frantically tamped it down. Was that Tefnut or me? Was there a difference? I swallowed hard, forcing myself to ask calmly, "I know. I'm not asking for you to give it to me. I'm asking you to come with me."

"And trust a goddess?" He laughed without any mirth.

More of that divine retribution, angry and boiling, bubbled to the surface. Luckily, Bruno chose that moment to interrupt, howling that he would drink Manu's blood to the very dregs if he so much as thought about helping me. As much as I itched to pull an Aurick and cold-cock him, I resisted. This was my time to prove I was a tame goddess. As feral as I felt.

"There is already one archon on the loose, and she is probably only moments away from freeing a second archon," I reminded Manu. "That's not to mention Thoth. Tick tock, what will it be?"

Manu swore loudly, warming my heart. That meant he was breaking. "You will swear an oath?"

"I'll swear whatever oath you want," I agreed, suddenly wishing for some of Jo's subtle seductiveness, but my powers were too aggressive and showy for subtlety.

Manu stood and I followed. He still towered over me, but I met his defiant gaze with my own.

"I will get you back to St. Louis, but this is my price. The oath must be done in blood runes."

"Lay it on me, big guy."

"You will either destroy Thoth or die trying."

I tried not to let my surprise show, but it must have anyway, because he added, "I know how much you adore this reincarnation. This will prove to me that you are of your word. You will succeed or you will sacrifice yourself as Ava. End of story."

"You know I'd just reincarnate."

"If this isn't a ploy, it would be one less god to worry about for a few decades. So what will it be?"

"And if I succeed, there will be one less god to worry about with Thoth out of the way. Win-win, eh? I shudder to think what you'll ask me to do to Tefnut."

"Tick tock. What will it be?" he mimicked, quite poorly in my opinion. One thing was certain: Manu and I would never be buddies. He was careful, binding me in this way. I was not careful. I was behaving as recklessly as I felt.

I nodded for Marco to hand me one of his butchering knives. The blade was slick in my hand, my palms sweating slightly in my all-too-mortal body. With a quick slash, my blood welled before running down my wrist. We shook, the blood splattering the iron nails embedded in the centuries-old floor. Our embrace hissed and spit sparks, binding us with runes from Manu's scalp, which smoked like cigar puffs.

"Now that that morbid business is done," Tiberius said dryly, "where is the bone dagger?"

I slit Manu's cuffs and the blue Knot fell to the ground, blinking out of power. Manu reached inside his leather duster and handed me the bone dagger, hilt first.

I accepted it, surprised. "I thought it wouldn't work for me."

"I give it freely. Plus, we are bound now. It will respond to you."

I looked to Coronis. "Are you sure you want to come?"

"Absolutely. What if you get injured? I can still heal your mortal body."

"Okay." I hugged her tight. "Thank you."

"I'm going, too," Tiberius said, woozily struggling to his feet.

"I don't think so, buddy," I told him. Bending to his ear, I whispered, "I need you here to keep a watch on Bruno." I also needed him to heal.

Tiberius crossed his paws and eyed the vampire. "Only because my goddess commands it."

I patted him. "Great. Don't let Bruno hear that sort of talk. I doubt it will endear us to him."

"I'd like to endear him to something," Tiberius muttered, but he agreed nonetheless.

Thessaly volunteered to stay on Aradia and act as watchdog/messenger between the liminal spaces in case the prisoners here got any cute ideas. I had a feeling it would take seeing a vengeful Thoth in the flesh before they realized I was the better option. There would be no believing in my good intentions on their own.

The bone dagger was heavy in my hands. Aurick had made it look simple. A slice through the fabrics of reality and bam! St. Louis. Or bam! Aradia. "How do I use this thing?" I asked, pawing lamely at the air. "Does it have previous city settings like a GPS, because that would —ahh!"

The freeze of astral travel overwhelmed my senses, dunking me in a tank of dry ice. I barely felt Manu latched to my elbow. Coronis screamed thickly, I think, but it could have been inside my own mind.

We landed outside the Arch with a thud. It felt surreal to see it after everything that had happened. The runes, hieroglyphs, and cuneiform wiggled at Manu's approach, shifting and curling in on themselves to create new glyphs. At least this time I wasn't in chains, and in some bizarre twist of fate (although surely even the Fates hadn't predicted any of this), my once-jailor had chosen to help me, a goddess, over the Council.

He muttered under his breath as we passed through the Arch's protections and entered the halls of velvet skies and crushed diamonds.

"Don't approach any supernaturals you see here, and above all, don't tell them the truth. You never know if they might see an opportunity. They may believe that, in exchange for helping Thoth, he will be magnanimous. Many will be willing to take that risk."

Coronis and I nodded in agreement. At this point, we had to start trusting some allies. One of them might as well be Manu.

It reminded me of the sirens in Thessaly's village. Most would have loved to bring back the gods and end their curse. The supernatural world was much deeper and more complex than I realized.

Everything went according to plan, until a little goblin in black robes popped out of nowhere and scared the pee out of me. It was just a few drops, but still, the Tefnut side of me didn't appreciate this new development. She'd always had a bladder of steel.

Fortunately, Manu turned out to be a fairly good liar. "Aradia is secure again," he assured the goblin. "The last of the traitors are being rounded up as we speak."

After that encounter, we sped to the women's bathroom. I barged in first with Coronis behind me and Manu taking up the rear, most likely afraid of someone using the facilities, but he didn't have to worry. It was empty.

We skittered around the corner, barely taking notice of the cleaned up tiles, fixed faucets, and unbroken mirrors from my battle with Mestjet. I zeroed in on my least favorite public restroom stall in the entire world. Scratch that, the entire realms.

The door was swinging from its hinge and smoke poured out of the stall. The back of my neck prickled, as I knew what I would find without even having to look. I bloomed a protective shield of mother magic around me and entered.

Chapter Ten

EVERYTHING HAD TAKEN on a hazy edge, except for Nonna. Her hands were clasped in prayer, and she was staring up at a vaguely humanoid figure. He towered over us by at least two feet, not including his crescent-shaped horns. They nearly scraped the top of the ceiling, except he was staring down.

At Nonna.

She was sobbing, her perfectly made-up face blotchy and wrecked. A fake eyelash was trying to escape down her cheek like a furry caterpillar. Clearly, she'd taken pains to get herself done-up before seeing her lover for the first time in centuries.

I felt the presence of Manu and Coronis behind us. Everyone moved slowly, as if in molasses. No one knew what to expect or how to act. All seemed very freaking lost.

Suddenly, the archon snapped his head to me. I remembered that tail as it smacked the tiles under his oubliette and the sparkling fur that shone along his jaw like a golden beard. Seeing them up close and personal was a very different sensation altogether.

"So, it's true. It's really you, Tefnut."

I nodded cautiously. No reason to lie now.

"It's good to see you," he continued. "Well, as well as I can." His image flickered, and I realized it was only an astral projection of him. He was still trapped beneath the women's bathroom in his oubliette. All was not lost.

My left eye twitched. "I go by Ava Falcetti now."

Was this real life? Was I discussing my name with an archon? Shouldn't I be flinging spells and asking questions later? Yet, I resisted. I wasn't Bruno, and I certainly didn't want to feed the dormant goddess in me. I needed to do this in my own way.

He merely smiled. Nonna got up from her knees, and the creaks echoed like gunshots through the small space. Culsans broke his gaze with me to look at her with concern. I could see how the pair of them fit together like an egg and dart mold of an archway. They really were beautiful.

"Culśu, my heart." He held her tenderly, cupping her chin and tilting her head up.

As I watched, I felt a stab of jealousy. She clung to Culsans in a way I'd never felt before. Perhaps, if I gave it time, I'd feel that way with Aurick. Time was exactly what we didn't have, however. Gods, I missed that man. I hoped he was being safe.

I cleared my throat. "If I may, what is your plan? Because I can't tell if we have a problem or not."

Culsans cocked his head, his horns looming over me. "Do you remember any of your previous existence?"

I did a so-so hand, which felt a little silly in front of an archon of his stature, but whatever. I was over being told how to act. "I believe I asked my question first. What is your plan?"

Nonna burst out, "To survive, of course! You can

understand that, Ava. Free Culsans and let us remake the world as we wish. I have been waiting for you to do this for centuries. Please!"

I felt Manu tense behind me, but I waved him off behind my back. The last thing we needed was another shoot-out.

Suddenly, the door to the bathroom swung open, and a tiny faun clip-clopped inside. Manu's head glowed and in a heartbeat, he was hidden behind a ficus tree in a woven basket. When my eyes shot to the broken stall, I didn't see Nonna or Culsans. Even Coronis had great reflexes, and I found her stooped over the sink washing her hands. I was the only one who didn't move. Instead, I stood there like a tourist visiting the world's weirdest attraction. All that was missing to complete the awkward was bad elevator music.

The faun gave me a weird look as she went into the unbroken stall and did her business. We all waited a beat, and then I did my best to seem busy when she came out, but she still managed to give me one last disturbed glance as she exited.

Everyone let out a sigh of relief as the ficus shimmered back into a mage, and I realized that Manu wasn't hiding behind the plant. Rather, he *was* the plant. And he couldn't have shot me a last second spell and made me a fern?

Rude.

Coronis turned off the water and dried her hands while Nonna and Culsans reappeared in the stall. Despite the interruption, Nonna's face still pleaded with me to help.

"Nonna, I'm sorry—" I couldn't even get out the rest over the absolutely devastating howls my first friend on Aradia released. It was a small earthquake, and the entire bathroom rumbled in response.

Culsans finally stopped her with a kiss, and her anguish

devolved into quiet tears. The archon met my gaze. He seemed fully in control and determined. I had to remind myself he hadn't been set free. Not yet. I still had the upper hand.

"Ava, is it?" he asked.

I gave him a firm nod. "You understand why I can't help. It breaks—"

"Oh right, it breaks your heart more than mine," Nonna interrupted bitterly. "Just like a parent whipping their child as they insist that, 'this will hurt me more than it hurts you.' Well I don't believe it for a second. You're much more Tefnut than you wish to admit, acting like you're the parent and you know so much better. You've remembered you're a goddess for all of a day. There's no moral high ground there. How could you? How could you deny me?"

Hot tears pricked at the corners of my eyes as Coronis came to stand next to me, offering her moral support. "I'm sorry," I whispered again.

"I have a suggestion," said Culsans. He had a deep, vibrating voice. "Let me share a memory with you. Tefnut was dear to me. We have many memories together."

"And what would that do?" I demanded. "I still can't prop up a pillar. I refuse."

Culsans looked down at Nonna with a small, wistful smile at the corner of his lips. "I am not so set on this wild adventure Culśu wants for us. Death is equally interesting to me."

"You don't mean that," she insisted. "I finally get to you, and you say death is fine? It's not. It's not fine, it's—"

He hushed her, murmuring to her in some ancient tongue I had long forgotten, if the gods even knew the language of the archons. Perhaps it was some gift only between them.

I cleared my throat. Time was still ticking, a relentless

march forward. "So you believe this memory will convince me to trust you?"

"Precisely."

"And then you think I will set you free."

"I believe you will, after you begin to remember."

"Ava, that was not part of our agreement," Manu interrupted. "You swore a blood oath."

"To destroy Thoth or die trying," I interrupted. "Yeah, nothing about archons."

Culsans looked up at that. "You would sacrifice yourself? Tefnut—"

"Ava," I said sharply.

"Ava," he allowed with a dip of his head.

Manu whipped in front of me, angry lines and a thin mouth. "You cannot seriously be thinking about setting a second archon free."

I called over his shoulder to Culsans. "How do I know you won't manipulate this memory and show me what you think I want to see?"

He laughed deeply up from his belly. "You're a goddess. You will know. The memory will fit you like your skin. If anything feels off, you can drown me from the inside where I stand."

"Please, trust him," Nonna begged.

"Ava," Manu warned. "Don't do it. Trusting this beast is a mistake."

"Beast, eh?" That got me. It was how Thoth referred to my friends and family. Culsans clearly knew enough about Tefnut to know she had water powers. And this was Nonna. I couldn't believe she would try to hurt me now, just because I was denying her… Okay, it was best I didn't think too much about it and just did it. I held out my hand. "Show me the memory."

"Ava!" Manu shouted, but I cut him off.

"If we're going to work together, you're going to have to put a little more faith in me. I want to see this memory and decide for myself. If we could get two archons on our side, isn't that better than creating an enemy? Besides, it seems to me some great injustice has been done here." I turned to Nonna. "But if anything happens…"

"He won't hurt you. He loved Tefnut. I swear. Take his memory and see for yourself."

I hesitated. Nonna had her fingers outstretched, spanning the distance between us with a pleading look on her face. Thick, black eyeliner dripped down her eyes, and her perfectly coiffed hair was in riots of curls around her face.

I turned to Manu, preparing myself for his fury. "I swear I am not breaking our oath. And I'm not trying to find the loophole."

His teeth ground together. I could see his jaw working from three feet away. "Oh?"

"Truly. I'm gathering allies. I will destroy Thoth. I promise."

"You must. Or you will die."

Nonna made a little noise. "Ava, what did you do?"

"It's just a blood oath. Nothing a little god-murder won't solve," I quipped.

Manu's face resembled roadkill. I had to admit I enjoyed annoying him. If Nonna and Culsans were telling the truth, then gaining allies was the cherry on top.

"I'm not promising I will release him, though," I said, feeling like a jerk. "Only that I'll let you share the memory."

"You'll release him. You two were close," Nonna insisted. "You're the one who got us together."

"I… what?"

She held out her hand. "Come see, goddess."

Like a linked tree, I grasped it, and I saw an island.

Making Midlife Marvels • 73

. . .

I held a beautifully painted red and black oinochoe vase, sweating slightly in the heat. "Would you like some honey-sweetened wine? It's Cretan."

The archon lounging across from me nodded, stretching out his goblet.

"Yes, please."

I poured, used to serving and fending for myself, alone in my self-imposed exile. I never stayed anywhere for long and chose to trust only a certain few. Culsans was one of them.

"Don't they hop over bulls or some rot like that?" Culsans asked as I tipped the pitcher back up, catching the last drips with a hand woven, navy linen cloth.

"I believe they do. They also have a fascination with snakes and bees. But they really do make good wine."

We clinked our goblets and sipped. I had chosen this island in the turquoise waters of the Mediterranean because it was as close as I could get to Egypt without arousing Thoth's attention. I wouldn't be able to linger long, though. Maybe a few months at most.

"Delicious," he agreed.

I leaned back, my jeweled sandals resting on a lion-skin footrest. "Thank you for that hiding spot in Nibiru. Thoth would have caught me for sure that time had I stayed in this realm."

Culsans's smile was wicked. "For being the god of wisdom, he only thinks surface level."

"It does feel good to outwit him," I admitted. "I like to see his tantrums."

We laughed and enjoyed our mezze platter and red wine in goblets of hammered gold from the city of Knossos. The Minoans there might have worshipped Zeus, tragic, really, but they knew how to ferment grapes.

After Culsans assured me that Geb and Nut were able to speak at least one night during an eclipse, he got to the point. "Where next, goddess? I hear Acre is nice this time of year. Or have you considered the Far West reaches? They say dragons roam there. I wouldn't mind seeing a dragon."

I took a small sip. It was best to always keep my wits when on the run from such a formidable enemy. *"I was thinking of shaking things up."*

"Oh?" he said. *"Somewhere cold? Because I really didn't enjoy that place with all the white stuff."*

"Snow?"

He snapped his fingers. "That's the stuff." He shivered.

"Actually, I was thinking I'd let him catch me."

Culsans shot to his feet, alarm evident in his dilated eyes and the bristling of his fur. A warrior on his toes.

"Don't do that, Tefnut. You'll play right into his game. You were there. You know he survives anything, including regime changes. Somehow, he even manages to thrive. Despite being Ra's most trusted advisor, he switched allegiances to Horus, Isis, and Osiris without anybody thinking a thing was amiss. That shouldn't happen. He should have been thrown out with the old sun god."

"That's because he helped birth them and gave Isis the spell to put Osiris back together. As a favor for me. It's not surprising they trust him. I'm sure he whispered in their ears about Ra's senility and how Egypt needed someone great again. Those sort of snake thoughts are just his type. I'm afraid my grandchildren would have loved to hear how young and virile and better they would be for Egypt."

Culsans's face darkened. "There is always an ulterior motive with him. He could have been planning that from the beginning. What if…" He got a faraway look, and I waited for him to fit things together. To see the full picture that I'd already grasped. "What if he told Ra to fear the Demon Days, then manipulated you into trusting him by offering to gamble the moon? He created the problem so that he could solve it. And, in the end, garnered the trust of the new god-babes. It made both of you trust him as well. Win-win-win."

Maybe I was weary of all the games, but I didn't so much as lift an eyebrow. "It would not surprise me."

"So don't trust him. Keep running. This life doesn't look so bad."

I glanced at the beautiful furnishings I had commanded the locals to create for me and all of the offerings I ordered them to bring to me. To honor me. Unfortunately, I went through mortals rather quickly, as none could be allowed to live after seeing me. I came like a scourge to every new place I hid, and I left no survivors. I embodied chaos, but it was beginning to tax me.

"True, but it's not everything. It's not my children or my homeland. I miss the smell of the silted Nile and the taste of desert sands on the wind. And I was thinking…"

"I don't like the look on your face," Culsans said.

I laughed. "Probably for good reason. Thoth has those tablets. The ones he bragged about for so long."

"He has what? Thoth doesn't strike me as the bragging type."

A ghost of a happy smile, a happy memory when we loved each other, threatened to pass my lips, but I held it back into a grimace. "He bragged to me in our bed. Deep down, there is that little boy that craves love and affection. He needs petting and constant attention. I gave it to him for too long, a part of me proud to be the one who tamed the great Thoth. Of course he bragged and whatever is in those tablets is the key to his undoing."

Culsans didn't look convinced. He flipped his tail in agitation.

I gave him a fond pat. "I'm tired of running. I want to go home. But I will not be controlled by Thoth any longer."

"So you'll let him find you." Distrust lined his face.

"One can't wander forever."

Culsans snorted. "That's just a lack of imagination."

"We're of different kinds. You love the unknown of Nibiru and all that its nooks and crannies have to offer. I do as well, but sometimes, the comforts of home call to me. Just the simple ones. The feel of Egyptian cotton, the softness of the linen. The taste of honeyed dates grown in the Oasis of Siwa. I want to scoop that sand between my hands and let the grains sift through my fingers."

Culsans got to his knees and took my hands in his. "If you insist on this course of action, I promise to aid you in times of distress. If anything happens, I am yours to command."

I stood over him. "I accept your loyalty. Thank you, old friend. Now tell me. How is wooing Culśu going? Have you managed to find something that doesn't make her roll her eyes or wince in mutual humiliation?"

"Would you believe it? I think I have. She mentioned some new thing called pasta that she wants to try…"

As we came out of it, emotions I hadn't felt in centuries swirled around me. Other memories of Culsans began to coalesce. However, I gave the archons my poker face. "I trusted you, it seems."

Culsans bowed low. "You did. I alone knew of your whereabouts during your self-imposed exile."

Still, I hesitated.

And then he knelt before me. "I swore I would always help you and find you. I failed. Thoth cursed you with those damnable tablets and I couldn't locate you. I tried for centuries, but I never found a trace because you weren't you. You were human. Yet, my allegiance has not wavered. I still serve you, and this time, I will not fail you."

Nonna cried, "No!" and began sobbing again. She flung herself on Culsans, and his astral image flickered and bent. "How could you? How could you?" she kept asking, banging against the tiled floor.

"Sometimes, the greater good comes first. This world will not be a better place with the gods back in it. I firmly believe that."

"But humans and supernaturals are hardly better. Look how they've imprisoned you in this tiny cage!" Nonna's fists balled together. This had been her singular goal for centuries, and it was crashing around her at the moment of her victory. I felt her devastation, but I could disagree with her at the same time. I was only thankful Culsans seemed reasonable. It was important to have one of those around.

Culsans stood from his kneeling position, bringing Nonna with him. "My heart, we are together at last. No more tears on our behalf. We have loved long, and we have lived longer. Now, we will help Tefnut and ride off into the sunset, as they say." He wiped a tear falling down her cheek and licked it. "Tastes like new hope," he teased her. "And a hint of sage."

I thought it was weird, but Nonna snorted a laugh and pitched her arms around him again, crying silently. My heart was breaking a thousand times, as I was essentially ordering them to go die. But we couldn't prop up a pillar, not even for a second. Dark things lurked on the other side in Axis Mundi, their hate fueled for centuries, and they were waiting for such an opportunity to spring back to Earth. I turned my head so Manu wouldn't see me cry.

"Tef—Ava," Culsans corrected himself.

I turned back around, quickly wiping my face with the back of my hand. "Yes?"

"There are little polished jewels I have kept hidden in the recesses of my mind, as imprisoned as I am. I will release one now, into your keeping."

"Thank you, Culsans. I will take whatever help you choose to offer me."

He nodded. "You, Ava Falcetti, have an immortal body to find."

"You know where Thoth went?" I asked, hope flaring in my chest.

Culsans's tail flipped wicked fast. "No, not his body. Yours."

Chapter Eleven

"MINE?" I said incredulously, kicking myself for not realizing that, of course, I had an immortal body somewhere.

"I'm sure the rest of your memories will be found within your immortal body, locked in eternal slumber. It was Thoth the magician who helped Isis reanimate her murdered husband, Osiris. I'm sure Thoth's spell pried your Ba from your immortal body, leaving behind your memories of Tefnut still inside of her."

"Shit," I said, feeling my control slipping from my grasp and pouring into my word choices. "No, I didn't know that. Or, I forgot that, I guess. Oh that's bad."

"Ba?" Coronis asked, giving me a nervous look. "We're not familiar with this concept in Greece."

Culsans turned his luminous eyes upon the crow shifter. "The five concepts of the soul. The Ba is a soul's personality. The other four encompass a soul's secret name, their physical body, even their shadow. But it was the Ba that Thoth would have taken, ensuring all of those mortal bodies had a similar personality to Tefnut. Every one of her previous lives would have been some form of her."

Meanwhile, I had begun to pace as two archons and a shifter looked on in some concern. Manu had taken to banging his head against the wall, probably debating all of his life choices since meeting me.

"What is it, Ava? What are you thinking?" Coronis asked.

I stopped. While it was gratifying to know every one of those badass women were indeed some part of my innate personality, my Ba, something Culsans had said worried me. "Thoth gave Isis the magic to reanimate Osiris?"

Culsans nodded once.

"Even if I figured out how to use chaos to kill him, for real this time, wouldn't it stand to reason that he would simply perform some anti-death spell again that puts himself back in stasis?"

They all considered it. "If he has enough time and foresight, I don't see why not," Culsans agreed. "What do you want to do?"

I wrung my hands. "What can I do?"

"Rely on your friends," he advised. "You always wanted to do things alone. Your burden was yours alone. It never worked out for you then. It won't now. Take everyone's strengths and combine them into a megaweapon."

"Is that a technical term? Megaweapon?"

Culsans grinned, and I was suddenly hit with a wave of déjà vu. I'd seen that grin before. Culsans was fun to be around. We had fun together. Once.

"It really should be one," he said.

Manu's face, however, resembled sour grapes. The idea of learning there was a second immortal body here on earth must've been painful, but to know it was mine? He was in a living nightmare.

Join the slumber party, buddy.

Not only had I *not* stopped Nonna from releasing her

archon lover, I was going to do it for her myself, because I trusted him. Thoth had escaped Aradia, and I'd sent Aurick into danger to follow him, because of my mistakes. Yes, a banner day.

"Are you going to go look for it?" Coronis asked.

"It might be the only way to fully combat Thoth as an equal," Culsans pointed out.

"I would have no idea where to find it, though."

"We'll help you," Coronis said confidently.

While I admired that, I had a feeling it wouldn't be so easy. It wasn't like I could feel my senses tingling or something comically supernatural like that.

"First things, first. Are you busting me out?" Culsans asked.

"Oh right. Hang on."

I joined hands with Nonna, and instantly, I could feel the power humming between our fingers. "Do you know where you're at?" I asked Culsans.

"No. I don't know where exactly, but I'm not far from here. The dungeons are deep beneath the Arch."

"Then why is the illusion you created over the centuries in the women's bathroom?"

"Because I found projecting through a toilet to be the most convenient to access. Something about pipes."

"Oh. Sorry, I asked." I turned to Manu. "Any ideas Mr. Council Man?"

To my surprise, he nodded. "I can take you to where we keep the most dangerous creatures." Then, he added, "I hope I don't live to regret this."

We worked quickly, using Manu's status as a high-level lackey to find Culsans. A few key words, a few head scans and boom. We were standing before his door.

As the last bolts fell away, everyone stood back. Culsans stepped out of the darkness and into the dull glow of the dungeon's torch-lit hallway. I couldn't help but tense up as he emerged, his golden furred chin lifting into the light and his intelligent eyes blinking at what must have felt like a sudden onslaught.

And then came the crush. He dipped his head to Nonna, and she flung her liver-spotted arms around his neck. "You're perfection, my heart," Culsans murmured as he brushed her hair for real this time.

They embraced, tears shining on every face, and we turned away for a few minutes, although Manu scowled the whole time. For a long while, they merely held each other. No one spoke or shuffled their feet or coughed. It was a moment of the purest silence.

Finally, Culsans pulled away. "What's the plan, Tef—Ava?" he said, not so smoothly transitioning into my new identity from the only one he'd ever known. I decided he'd need a bit of a grace period.

"We find my body. Easy as pie."

"That must be some American saying," Coronis mused. "Because pies are not easy."

"And neither will this be," I laughed. "So I guess it fits."

"Yes, but if anyone can do it, it's you, Ava."

Manu, like a dog with a bone, said, "After we find it and kill Thoth, we kill it, too."

I looked at him with a raised eyebrow. "Would you like to make a blood oath to that, too?"

"Actually—"

Coronis cut in smoothly. "Ava has always put others above herself. She hardly needs to spill more blood to that effect."

"But—"

"How about we shake on it?" I stuck my hand out. Manu looked like he might want to bite it off by the way his jaw was ticking, and a huge vein pulsed across his forehead. His runes lit up, too, but I took his hand and put it in mine and mechanically bounced it up and down a few times. "Great. I'm glad we're all on the same page. Let's get going. Do you think he hid my body in Egypt or is that too obvious?"

We took two steps towards the exit before Manu exploded. "This is ridiculous! I will not stand by as we release archons and more gods into our world. I simply cannot."

I watched him for a moment, knowing in my heart I'd rather die than let Tefnut take over who I had become as Ava. If Manu needed another blood oath, it was no skin off my back. Unlike him, I truly believed the only way I could seriously destroy a god was if I was also a god. Whether it was a true death or not… I didn't know. But a mortal attempting it? I just didn't see how it was possible.

In a blink, I pulled his bone dagger from my belt and slashed my palm. Manu stared at the dripping blood. "Care to join me?" I asked, gritting my teeth against the pain.

Quickly, Manu enacted another oath, binding us tighter together. I either destroyed the gods, one way or another, or I lost Ava forever.

Coronis muttered ancient Greek curses about dissolving innards and organs as she healed my wound, but Manu merely shrugged. "It had to be done."

Nonna took out her clam compact and was attempting to re-glue an eyelash when she shut it with a snap. "I could probably figure out some tracking spell for your body."

"Too easy," I said, giving Coronis a grateful squeeze. "Thoth would've cloaked it."

"You're probably right. We should go back to Aradia and look at my grimoire, although they've already yielded more secrets to you than they ever did for me."

That made me pause. "Speaking of which, how did you get Thoth's tablets?"

Nonna gazed fondly up at her archon lover. "After you told Culsans about their existence, we decided to go searching. Basically, you let Thoth find you, and then you disappeared off the face of the earth forever. We hoped the Emerald Tablets would reveal his secrets. Or, at least, tell us how to find you. They never did, but I consider it one of my greater joys to have disguised it and myself over the centuries, showing it to worthy mortals who helped me decipher its secrets. I'll admit, after the Archon Wars, it was easier without Thoth constantly searching for them. I got old and staying on Aradia was so very lovely. That's why I decided to make it my home base and feed it my blood."

"Calling supernaturals to its shores, you said."

She nodded. "Exactly. I was hoping eventually it might be strong enough to call you. And it was."

"Through Marla. Isn't that weird?" I mused, an unease skittering up my spine. I really hoped my ex-assistant didn't have anything to do with the supernatural world.

"Thoth was livid that we stole them," Culsans laughed. "Remember that one time in Rome when—wait. That's it. Rome!"

"What's it?" I asked dumbly.

"Rome. He found you there after you'd managed to turn into the She-Wolf. It clearly frightened him that you had done something he hadn't anticipated, so he put a second curse on you. What if your body was there, too? It explains a lot. His fear, his anger."

"It's worth a try." I turned to the mage. "Are you coming with us, Manu?"

His monotone voice brooked no disagreement. "I feel

duty-bound to watch your movements and prevent your baser instincts from controlling you."

"Well, I'm all warm and fuzzy."

Manu nodded in a non-ironic way while Coronis turned a laugh into a cough.

"I have always been your loyal servant," Culsans said. "We will go, too, and help you search."

I took the archon by the hand. It felt weird and familiar. "No. I need someone to protect the pillars. Until we know what Thoth is up to, we must guard them at all costs, and you two are our best hope."

"Didn't she just say she wanted to lift the pillars?" It was Manu again. "And you're sending them to guard them. What if Thoth shows up and they turn on us?"

I closed my eyes and counted to ten so I didn't accidentally liquify his liver. "Manu, I have given you two blood oaths. Now, I need you to trust me. I have known these two for longer than you have been alive."

"Far longer," Culsans said with a devious smile.

"Not helping," I said. I turned back to Manu. "It's clear I have trusted these two with my deepest secrets and my very life. They have always been loyal to me. I trust them without reservation."

"Well said," Culsans added.

Manu didn't seem to share his opinion, but he kept his mouth closed.

"Thank you," I said to them both.

With that done, the two archons bowed from the waist, making me shift uncomfortably at the display. "As always, we will fulfill your command. We will also gather shades while we are there."

Nonna added, "Many should be antsy to fight a god."

"I know a few who can help," I said with a grin as I

pictured Cat, Gianna, and Queen Dido. "They're pretty badass. If anything happens, project to our location."

"Now that I have found you again, I will not lose you, Ava Falcetti." Culsans squeezed my hand affectionately. Then the two of them turned, made a small motion with their hands, and were gone.

Outside, the fresh air felt nice, although it also carried the smell of the Mississippi River, the industry of St. Louis, and a flood of memories. I'd spent my life here without knowing anything, and it made me wonder if Marla would eventually see the grass wasn't greener where I was standing. She was still young. She could get out. This time, I wasn't thinking that to get back at Jim. I don't know why I cared what happened to her, but I didn't want her to suffer in an unhappy relationship like I had. And perhaps, being far away from supernatural central St. Louis would be good for her.

"Are you ready?" Manu asked, bone dagger in hand, although his face was still pinched.

I nodded, and a moment later, we found ourselves in a loud, honking, bustling city. Over my shoulder stood Trajan's Column, and to my left, a cute café and terrace bustled with tourists. The yellowed stone buildings glowed in the warm sun.

Rome. Although I'd never been here before, not as Ava, it still felt like a homecoming of sorts.

My skin skittered, and I turned my head. As if by thinking about her I had conjured her, there stood Marla.

Chapter Twelve

"WHY DON'T you have your cell phone on you?" Marla asked, her eyes wide and frantic.

"Uh," I responded.

She tapped her long, pink-painted nails on her cell phone, practically cracking the screen. "I keep calling and you never answer. Are you mad at me?"

"No, of course not." I shook my head to clear the crazy. "I don't carry my phone anymore since it doesn't work on Aradia."

"But that doesn't fit into the plan," Marla said.

"What plan is that?" I asked. I couldn't stop staring. "How are you here? And how did you know that I was going to be here?"

"Good fucking question," growled Jim. "Why don't you tell me, because I'd love to know why I was dragged out of a very nice meal at a trattoria to find my ex-wife while on my supposed vacation from her bullshit."

I was too stunned by this recent turn to even respond. Jim. Jim and Marla were standing in front of me in Rome. Jim and Marla were standing in front of me in Rome, waiting for me. At least, Marla was. She waved her lit-up phone under my face. "I'm supposed to be here. Right here for you."

Coronis and Manu exchanged glances. Subtly, he slipped his dagger back in its holder, probably remembering how impotent Jim was from the times he dropped me off at my old house, aka jail. Coronis raised an eyebrow. She seemed equally unimpressed with her first impression of my ex.

Jim whirled on Marla, and I got a good look at his widening bald spot. Stress was not nice to him. He used to be the man every woman turned toward in a bar. The master of his domain. Let's just say, his Italian getaway had not worked the same wonders on him as it had on me.

"You," he pointed at her. "You gold digger. You squeezed a trip out of me to meet up with Ava? Please explain the logic because I'm about to lose my mind over here."

The protective side of me burned red, and for a second, I feared what Tefnut may do to this man. Crush him and then turn him to ash? Marla had been my assistant for the past few years. She had been my responsibility. When she failed, it made me wonder if I'd failed. Now I knew I had, but something else drew me to her, and I didn't want to fail her again.

To her credit—and my relief—Marla completely ignored him. She shoved him to the side and waved the phone in my face. "See? The messages? You need me."

I looked. Her entire phone scrolled with messages from me to come to Italy and wait right here. If I ever thought it had been a coincidence that Marla found Aradia for me, that notion was gone.

"I don't understand," I said.

That's when Marla's shadow moved.

Marla hadn't.

"Did you?" I broke off as the shadow moved again. Not only did it move, it beckoned. It crooked its finger, begging me to follow.

"Marla… who are you?"

She blinked and ran her hand through her curled hair. Her shadow imitated her—a beat too slow.

The crowds around Trajan's Column weren't exactly thick. It was, after all, Italy in late winter. But there were enough stops and quizzical stares that I felt compelled to move our group. Marla kept repeating herself as we meandered through the maze of Rome. I chose not to tell her, or Jim for that matter, that I was actually following her shadow.

"Seriously, Marla, who are you?"

"I'm just Marla. Who are you, Ava? Why do I keep getting messages that I have to help you?"

"That's why we booked this trip?" Jim exploded. "You promised me—" he cut off sheepishly. I really did not want to know the sexual favors she had to promise for this. I had a few ideas, as I was married to the man for two decades.

"Sometimes I should get to decide things, you know," Marla responded.

"No. You're twenty-five. You should barely be allowed to decide dinner."

My She-Wolf fur was ruffled now, but Marla handled it. "You always think you know best, but you don't. You don't even know how to run your own company. It's falling apart without Ava, and you know it!"

That shut Jim up for the moment. He glowered at the two of us as we passed gelaterias, antiquarian shops, and ruins from a hundred centuries. My mouth practically watered at all of the delicious things to see, eat, and do, but my mind knew we had a singular purpose. There was no time for a Roman holiday today. Sadly.

Bending to Coronis, I whispered, "Can you distract Jim? I want to have a conversation with Marla alone."

Coronis winked. "Ciao, Ava."

Just as Jim was gearing up for his next verbal assault, Coronis snuck behind him and transformed into a crow. I narrowed my eyes, wondering what she had planned and also thinking how cute she was bouncing in that way crows do when they walk, except she was the size of a Prius. With ease, she nipped Jim's wallet out his back pocket and cawed rather loudly. He stumbled, his eyes wide and unblinking.

Then he fainted.

Coronis immediately transformed back, her eyebrows pulled down in surprise. "That wasn't exactly what I had in mind, but does that work, darling?"

"Uh, yes. Thanks."

Marla, meanwhile, was shaking. Her phone fell out of her hands and dropped to the cobblestones with a clatter. She knelt, feeling around for it, never taking her eyes off of Coronis while her shadow stood tapping its toe with its arms crossed. A rather rude shadow, to be honest.

So perhaps, Marla wasn't as magical as I suspected. She seemed genuinely shocked by Coronis's transformation. I held up my hands cautiously, trying to show her I meant no harm.

"Marla, I know that was… odd." Coronis puckered her lips at me and I mouthed sorry. "But we're not going to hurt you. In fact, I think I can help you."

An idea had begun to coalesce. Culsans had mentioned the five Egyptian aspects of the soul. My Ba was with me. But my shadow? Fair game. It's sassy behavior certainly fit the bill.

I balled up my mother magic, my one constant, the feeling of contentment that I relied on the most, and I jetted it at Marla's shadow. Even if the shadow wasn't mine, it didn't feel right. It didn't belong stuck onto Marla.

The shadow lurched, but it didn't try to escape. It clung to my offered threads. Hand over hand, it used my magic like a rope to pull itself out. With a great gulching sound, it sucked free, like unsticking a boot from man-eating mud. I pointed another finger at it and commanded, "Speak."

Marla was trembling from head to toe now, her eyes blinking rapidly.

The shadow, now completely separate from Marla, put both hands around its throat in a rather dramatic representation of being speechless.

Coronis whispered, "I don't think it can."

I rolled my eyes, a thousand percent certain this was mine now, and sent it another bloom of mother magic. The shadow gave me a thumbs up and cleared its throat.

"It really is you, Tefnut. I always suspected, but I can feel it clearer than ever now. Soon, we will be complete."

"Girl, you better tell me how long you've been in Marla and what you've been doing. Also, it's Ava. Thanks."

My shadow tsked. "For now. But together, we are Tefnut."

My heart somersaulted at a horrible thought. Had my shadow made Marla want to be with Jim? Had my shadow essentially made that poor girl sleep with an older man? More awful scenarios flipped through my mind, and I knew without a doubt that my immortal self, the goddess in me, would have had absolutely no problem using a mortal like that. The goddess in me would easily use and throw away mortals to fit her end goal. The mother in me wanted to hug Marla and ask for forgiveness, but my shadow cut off the wallowing.

"I only guided Marla. I don't have the ability to control her. My powers lay in the dark shadows and recesses of the mind. I helped get her application to the right office where you worked. I helped her say all the right things and get her eyelashes to flutter at the right time to woo Jim. I helped her book the trip to Aradia. But I didn't make her do anything she didn't want to do. Although I am surprised, Tefnut. Does that matter?"

"Of course it does, and I told you, I go by Ava now. Also, stop reading my dark recesses," I growled at my shadow.

If Manu's normal state of being wasn't grumpy-ass, I had a feeling he would be enjoying this.

I turned to my ex-assistant, feeling a sickness in the pit of my roiling stomach. "Think deeply, Marla," I urged her. "Would you have been with Jim? If you could go back and do it all over, what would you choose?"

Her mouth worked open and close, and she had to swallow a few times as the information crush nearly trampled her. Finally, she nodded. "He was wealthy, handsome, and attentive. At first, at least. It made me feel special. It made me feel good, even equal to you, in a way. And I'd always looked up to you, so that was special in itself."

I closed my eyes. Yes, Jim could be all those things. He could also be dismissive, belittling, and ugly when you looked deep enough.

She continued. "I'm sorry, Ava. I don't know if I would have succeeded without your shadow, but I did find him attractive." She looked down at Jim who was still passed out. "But I think our time is over."

Oh God, she was going to leave Jim in Rome.

"It's okay. You're allowed to find a man attractive, but

you don't have to stay with him. I don't mean that as a jilted ex-wife, either. I want you to be happy, to make your own choices, and to live freely. Honestly, if you want to stay with Jim, that's your choice. You're a grown woman. But if you ever need my help, financially or otherwise, I'll always hire you to do…" I grasped around for something that sounded legitimate. "…something. I'll always find something for you to do."

Eh. I'd worry about it later. The important thing was that I supported her. I mean, my shadow had influenced her life, whether the desires and tendencies were there or not. I'd save my lecture about sleeping with married men for the next time.

My shadow slow-clapped. "Can we find our body now? I've only been waiting for thousands of years."

I ignored it. "How are you going to get home?" I asked Marla.

She shrugged. "I have my ticket. I don't imagine it will be the world's most awesome flight back to St. Louis, but maybe I deserve that."

"Marla—"

"No, it's okay. And anyway, I want to get the drinking cup you gave me from the house. Then I've got to figure out what I want to do with my life. Maybe grad school."

"The drinking cup I gave you? That's what you want out of that relationship?"

She looked at me a little shyly. "I've always admired you. You seemed to juggle it all."

"Well, I wasn't. I was miserable."

"You made miserable look pretty cool."

"Thanks, Marla. If you need letters of recommendation, let me know. And uh… if you feel any earthquakes or sense anything odd… make sure you get somewhere safe."

I didn't want to alarm her about a possible world war with ancient gods, but I had to admit the prospect was possible.

Marla rolled her shoulders back. "I feel light. Like I could do anything." She gave me a fierce hug, not noticing how I'd winced. She did, after all, feel light because one fifth of my immortal soul wasn't dragging her down. "Good luck to you, too, Ava. I'm glad you're happy."

Coronis, back in woman form, tossed Jim's wallet onto his belly, and patted his cheek rather hard. He flinched and his eyes began to flicker open. I wished I could be a fly on the wall when he went to his therapist and explained that one. Alas, I had more important things to do. Like follow my very cheeky shadow to my immortal goddess body.

Chapter Thirteen

CLEARLY, Manu was hanging around us far too long. His morals were slipping. I barely needed to get the request out before he zapped Jim with something that made him shake our hands while his eyes crossed. After that, Jim and Marla were safely on their way back to St. Louis without a peep. It was amazing what a little rune magic could do to a guy.

Everyone seemed to enjoy themselves, except my shadow, which stood with its arms crossed, tapping its imaginary watch. "Fine," I said. "We're coming."

We had to practically run to keep up as it darted from shadow to shadow, borrowing the long fingers of trees and the squatty outlines of café tables. It even hitched a ride on a human here or there as it bounded through the Arch of Titus. Each time it quit a human, they stumbled, as if they'd stubbed their toe.

When we reached the Palatine Hill, whispers of memories ruffled my hair and spoke in beguiling voices. *My shaggy belly full of milk. Twin boys humming in their sleep in the cave. The vengeful god at the entrance.* But it wasn't anger. At least, that's not all it was. It was also fear. Just as Culsans had said. Thoth had been afraid here.

My shadow kept saying it was under the hill, which wasn't exactly helpful. "There are seven, you know," I finally snapped.

"The only one that ever mattered to you," it snapped back.

"Does anyone have a phone?" I called, exasperated with one-fifth of myself.

"I do," Manu said gruffly, pulling it from his demon-catching leather duster while we all gaped at him. "What?" he shrugged. "I have another life, you know. A regular life."

I closed my mouth first. "Right. I knew that. Do you also have high-speed internet?"

"I don't live under a rock, Ava. I just work under one."

And that was my cue to know the world really was about to come to an end. Manu had made a joke.

I took his phone and googled the She-Wolf's cave. Immediately, I got a hit. "Bingo," I said as beautiful mosaics came up. "Excavators found a cave. Whoa! Not until 2007. It was on the Palatine Hill under the Palace of Augustus, and they call it the Lupercal. Some archaeologists think it's where the She-Wolf nursed her twin boys, but it's not open to the public, and they still haven't found the entrance. All the images of the mosaics were captured by wire and drone cameras."

"Wow," Coronis said. "I bet no one has been inside since Thoth sealed you up. He put Tefnut there pre-Roman times, you found it as the wolf, and then he caused it to cave in. No wonder the Romans built over it and worshiped it. There was literally a goddess inside. Even if they didn't know that specifically, the ancients felt its sacred purpose."

I jerked my chin at my shadow. "I'm guessing you don't know how to get into the cave without an entrance?"

"I could get in. You can't."

"Helpful."

Suddenly, Thessaly's face blinked from a bottle of water in a tourist's hand. I yelped, and Manu and Coronis immediately tensed. "It's okay," I said. "It's only Thessaly."

She mouthed the words "Aurick" and "incoming" before disappearing.

An instant later, a rip sounded from behind a hedge of Roman trellis flowers, and Aurick stepped out, dusting himself off.

He smiled at me first before locking eyes with Manu. "I had to see it to believe it," he said. "Thessaly told me you had agreed to help Ava, but this is quite the turnaround."

Manu's face barely registered his surprise. "I hold myself to the same principles you do, Aurick of the Tarim Basin. The Council of Beings serves the people. We don't serve the beings on the Council. It just took a little reminding."

"Also a blood oath. You got to admit that helped you trust me," I said.

"You did what?" Aurick demanded, moving a foot closer to Manu, his fingers closing into a fist. It was quite the sight. His eyes narrowed, and his muscles bulged under his t-shirt. I could watch the way his eyes dilated and his body readied for a fight all day.

"Just a little blood oath." I waved it away, trying not to lick my lips. "Don't worry. I plan on getting rid of Thoth. Because if I don't... well, I hope you liked me for my personality and not this body in particular."

Aurick spun on Manu. "You made her swear to die if she doesn't perform the impossible? Are you always this murderous or just on days that end in Y?"

"Ava agreed willingly."

I stood between them while my shadow did some rather spectacularly rude gestures toward Manu. Aurick breathed heavily through his nostrils, making them flair, and his blonde hair came out of its perfect wave. I smoothed it back, and he caught my wrist, pulling it to his lips. It didn't take much to guide his attention away from the mage and onto me.

I let myself melt into him, ignoring the gagging performance my shadow was now putting on as it slipped into Aurick's shadow. I flailed my hand, but it was too late. He must have felt something slither across his skin, because he jerked back. "Did you feel that?" he asked.

I sighed. Cock-blocked by my own shadow. "Aurick, meet one-fifth of myself."

AURICK WAS STILL DIGESTING as we stole through the ticketed entrance onto the hill. Besides the cave over the Palace of Augustus, there were tons of other ruins, including temples, stadiums, and imperial baths. It was full of cypress trees and felt very secluded. Yet it offered spectacular views of the city, the ancient overlaid with the modern. I breathed in its unique smell. I loved Rome. No, I adored Rome.

"So you let another archon go free," he repeated. "And Manu was fine with this?"

Manu nodded once.

"Whatever you're giving him, give me double," he whispered.

"There are no hallucinatory drugs involved," Manu said. "Thoth is the vengeful god. The archons agreed to leave the pillars alone. Ava is bound to help. We must find her immortal body and take the battle to Thoth. Surprise him before he gathers too much strength and too many allies in our realm. The solution is simple when laid out so. And you? What did you find out, Death Walker?"

"Death Walker?" I interjected.

"It's a mummy thing," Aurick said. "I caught up with Thoth, but I don't believe he realized he was being followed. Then again, I didn't need to follow him for long to get the general gist. He is indeed gathering allies."

I wrinkled my nose. "Whatever he promises them will have a catch."

"Agreed," Aurick continued. "I returned as quickly as I could to Aradia where Thessaly told me you were in Rome. She's been following your movements."

"And Bruno? Is he still tied up?"

"Yes. Marco had to put a gag on him, and Rosemary might have subtly suggested to Spyro that he should 'sell happiness' and peddle his wares to the Council members. Their horror alone was worth watching for a few minutes."

I couldn't help it. I snorted, picturing the scene, and it felt good to laugh since I knew nothing good was about to come next. Aurick sobered, too.

"Thoth has allies on the ground already. They are the demons without names. Sons of the soil. He's calling them up, binding them to his cause. He is the god of magic and MILFs used to pray to him to receive spells to protect against these very demons in this life, and the next. Of course, the mortals didn't realize he knew the protection spells because he was intimately acquainted with all of the demons' vices and foibles."

"That sounds distinctly not good," Coronis commented.

Apparently, whatever ability I'd given my shadow to speak had long ago worn off, which explained why it'd been so quiet. It was now trying, rather ineffectively, to pull me toward the Lupercal cave. It made me feel better that my shadow clearly couldn't force anyone to do anything. Not even me and it was a part of me. Otherwise, I had basically ruined Marla's life and not the other way around. It would have been hard to live with myself if that was the case.

"So what do these demons do? Can I blast them?" I asked, jerking my head in the direction my shadow wanted.

"Yes, you'll be fine."

"Great. In that case, I'll lead the way." And off on the weirdest sightseeing tour we went.

I wished I could've stopped to smell the flowers, but once in the Cave of Hypnos was enough to convince me that not everything in the ancient world was as it seemed, and despite the modernity of Rome around us, the ancient world was as much here, a palimpsest to be uncovered, as I was.

We finally made it to the top of the hill. The Palace of Augustus and the House of Livia, his wife, as I knew from my Cleopatra memories, were not major tourist attractions like the Colosseum. Which was a shame. The mosaics alone were breathtaking!

In the off season, they were even less crowded, and we had the place to ourselves. The complex was huge with multiple levels to explore.

"Where do you think the body is?" Coronis whispered. Despite the palace being empty, it didn't feel right to speak loudly. This was some of the most sacred ground in ancient Rome.

"I doubt it will be labeled," Manu contributed gruffly, eyeing a few of the *trompe l'oeil* frescoes.

We descended lower along the guided route into more rooms, more frescoes, some with gruesome looking stage masks that reminded me of grotesques, others with brilliant columns festooned with pine boughs and pine cones. Even the ramp room had beautifully painted coffers, instead of real ones.

"Do you feel anything?" Aurick asked.

I shook my head in sync with my shadow and a chill passed over me. That was seriously creepy, but it merely shrugged and kept examining the niches.

The rooms got significantly colder as we descended into the lower, protected levels, which were surrounded by blocks of concrete and rocks. Dew drops peppered the back of my hands. I turned them over and the drops raced to the center of my palms. "I have an idea," I announced.

Five minutes later, I had everyone stationed along the caved-in part of the wall. There were little cracks, but nothing to suggest an opening or a large cave beneath us. "Look for any place where the water flows," I ordered. Then, I called on the flood.

Okay, not in an ancient and stunning location like that. I didn't want to damage anything. It was all very controlled. The water ran from my fingers and swirled in eddies and rivulets, bumping against the walls, but never finding its way. The palace was silent, and the weight of Rome's ancestors blanketed us all as they watched our efforts impassively.

Suddenly, the water sluiced away, and we could all hear the echoing drips as they plunged into a new section of the palace.

"The cave!" I said excitedly. "Can you guys open it up without damaging anything, like these beautiful mosaics or my immortal body?"

Manu pulled out his bone dagger and grunted.

"Great! Let's go see what I've been missing my whole life."

Manu took Coronis through and Aurick took me, while my haughty shadow decided to wrap its arms around Aurick's thick neck and make exaggerated kissing lips against his throat. I did my best to ignore it. The last thing I needed, as I went to find my new body, was to get jealous of my own shadow.

We ripped into the abandoned cave and gasped. Since I had last been a resident, it had indeed been turned into some sort of shrine. Offerings lined the floors and drawings of the She-Wolf peppered the cave walls. If I was a betting woman, I'd say Thoth got antsy about all the interest I had generated and collapsed it himself.

What a jerk.

Unfortunately, as Manu snidely pointed out, there were no arrows or neon signs to lead us to my body. I wasn't getting any feelings of familiarity, either, and my shadow kept sniffing the walls, which wasn't super comforting.

I wandered to a broken column and sat on the drum base, closing my eyes and evening out my ragged breath. With each inhale and exhale, I connected more to myself and let my awareness shift around the hidden chamber. I could almost picture hiding here, my paw over my snout in sleep.

I didn't realize I was walking, following something, until I stumbled over ancient debris and a strong arm caught mine. I didn't have to peek to know it was Aurick keeping me steady as I followed the trails to a deeper part of the cave. My eyes still closed, I sent out tendrils of probing mother magic. I doubted Thoth even realized what he'd accidentally gifted me when he cursed me that second time. The gift of pure motherhood.

"Duck," Aurick said. "The ceiling is getting low here." We took a few more steps. "Actually, we're going to have to crawl."

I got on my belly and slithered forward, certain I was heading in the right direction. Either that or I was about to get a face full of rock. I could hear Aurick grunting behind me, struggling to squeeze through the tiny opening.

Then, just like under the basilica, the air changed and all sound seemed to disappear, as if this spot had been sucking everything into its essence so as not to be found. I cracked open an eye and saw a huge cavern yawning before me. "This is it," I breathed.

Coronis crawled out behind Aurick and hugged me while Aurick kissed me hard, his eyes bright. Only Manu retained his aloof composure, merely brushing pebbled dirt from his duster.

"Wow, it's really me," I murmured, moving around the slab holding Tefnut's immortal body. It didn't look real. Nothing in this world should look like that. It was preternaturally beautiful in a way that makes your neck tingle and your nervous system blare warning signs. In this case, I froze. So much for fight or flight.

Coronis broke me out of it with a squeal of delight. "Wow, look at the workmanship on this fabric! Can I touch it? Is that weird, Ava? It's so delicate and sheer, but it looks like linen. That must be something from Axis Mundi. There is no way this is from Earth."

I snorted. Soon, I was full-blown choke-laughing. It was all so ridiculous. Jim and Marla were in Italy. I wasn't a failed housewife, domestic or feral, and a crow shifter was gushing over my immortal body's dress. I had to admit, it was gorgeous, and I was never much for fashion.

The pure white sheath dress had one shoulder strap and pleated folds down to her bejeweled, sandaled feet. It was diaphanous with gold thread woven throughout the fabric, like images I'd seen depicted in tomb paintings. It was also very revealing, and I wanted to shield her bared breasts from lingering eyes, but Manu and Aurick both were pointedly not staring. Also, they were perky as hell. Gifts of a supernatural life, I guess. Matching violet amethyst scarabs in a gold filigree bracelet encircled her delicate wrist and both biceps.

Tefnut still had a full face of makeup, black kohl lining her eyes, ground green malachite eyeshadow, blackened eyebrows, and lead white paste for concealer. A ribbon of white encircled her natural, black, lustrous hair. I must have lost my traditional wig and cone of incense somewhere along the betrayal.

Like Thoth's body under the Basilica of Aradia, hieroglyphs seemed to be etched onto her body. They also seemed to move. And this time, I knew what they said. They were magical incantations to preserve the stasis, places where the missing pieces of my soul could enter.

I caught my shadow by the arm as it tried to dive back into one of the hieroglyphs. "No. We do this together."

It pouted, tapping its toe with its arms crossed, but I wasn't going to be pushed or rushed into anything.

But I knew. All I had to do was reach out and touch.

I could hear the shifting of weight and a slight rise in tension as I stared at my body, fearing what I would lose if I gave up Ava. What if I never got her back?

Make no mistake, this goddess on a slab was a monster. She wasn't human. And yes, I was curious what secrets her mind held, but I was also terrified.

Finally, I turned to Aurick. "Catch me when I fall?" I asked.

"Always," he said, not quite understanding me. He'd understand soon. He was quick like that.

With a nod to my shadow, we reached out to press fingertips to hieroglyphs. Ribbons of black smoke wrapped around both of my bodies. They felt insubstantial—until they tightened. The ribbons sunk into my eye sockets and rolled my eyes into the back of my head. I saw nothing but the darkness. I felt nothing but the darkness. All was black and I couldn't move.

Vaguely, I heard my friends and they sounded frantic. Aurick in particular had a keening voice that made my heart ache.

"I'm okay," I wanted to reassure them, but I couldn't. I didn't know what I was, but okay didn't seem quite it. The ribbons of darkness had invaded my mouth, and my body was on fire. Golden ichor carved through my veins like an ancient bedrock blasted with dynamite.

Then came the real pain. It was thunder and lightning, blasting through my flesh, pushing me to my limits. But like a summer storm, it was there and then gone.

Chapter Fourteen

HELIOPOLIS, Egypt
 Middle Kingdom
 Tefnut

MARRIAGE WAS A FUNNY THING. Why did the gods conduct it? I knew of no pair who remained faithful forever, except, as rumor had it, the new gods of the Greek Underworld. Supposedly, Hades and Persephone's love was the brightest thing in their gloomy afterlife. I'd like to see how long that lasted. The gods in Greece couldn't even keep their power, let alone another's love. Already the Titans were overthrown by their children, the Olympians, and it was hardly a handful of millennia since I'd gone to their spectacle on Mount Othrys.

I had chosen my twin brother, and I never regretted it until now. Now, I wished to burn him, to throttle him with my bare hands, to rage against him as I did the barren lands of Egypt. I wished to be chaotic.

That, however, would not accomplish my goals.

The way Shu's eyes had blackened into nothingness as he held back the earth and the sky, ignoring their screeches of pain and anguish—our own children! Their pain was mine as I hung onto his implacable arms and begged him to let them be together.

"When they are together, there is no room for others in Egypt," he said impassively. "Ra commands it."

"Have you no heart?" I demanded, the winds whipping my tears into a cyclone around us, the lands drenched with my sadness. A flood for the ages. The first Inundation of the Nile. After this flood, my poor son Geb would ask his friend Hapi, the flood bringer, to recreate my act of grief every year. I think Geb hoped Nut would watch it from the sky and know he was mourning her.

"My mind is greater than my heart, dear wife. Now step aside." And he'd shoved them apart forever as I screamed in harmony with their heartbreak—

"Shu literally pushed them apart with his hands?" A voice interrupted my recounting of my great love affair with Shu and his betrayal.

My anger flared as bright as Ra's noonday rays. "Be quiet, mortal seed of Ra! Do you dare call me a liar?"

"I'm so sorry, my lady. Forgive me," the priestess murmured. Her name was Mestjet, I believe. Descended through Ra, although many times diluted, even tainted some would say, by mortal blood. It was such a macabre red. So thin and quickly their blood flowed through their veins. Like dirty river water.

Mestjet was of some use to me, however. She was writing a series of texts that would be stored forever in tombs. I wanted my story, in my own way, to be recorded for all of eternity. So I employed the priestess to hear my tale. I found priests, with their arching eyebrows and pursed lips, filled the empty spaces with too much commentary and condescension for my liking.

"Yes. Shu broke apart our children, my babies, and forced them to live apart forever. I have never been witness to a love as pure as theirs and will never again."

The scratch of her reed quill on papyrus was an itch in my ear, but I let her continue. "What happened next, my lady?"

"I left him."

The scratching quill stopped. Mestjet glanced up at me, surprise evident in the furrow of her brow.

"We are still married, of course. That cannot be put asunder. But I desired to spend my nights with someone new." *Here, I had to swallow down a hard lump of bitter regret.* "Thoth had begun to court me in various, quiet fashions, as was his wont. I didn't think much of it when he told me Ra had requested my presence. At least, I didn't think much of Thoth's role. I only thought Ra would want retribution for the Demon Days."

"Demon Days?"

I played with the crystal rim of my goblet, the ruby red wine not as tantalizing when I thought about that moment. "Yes. The five days that Thoth gambled for the moon to pause its orbit so that my daughter and son could birth their five children. Five children destined to overthrow Ra."

"I didn't know the days had a name."

"Yes, and a new world order was precisely what occurred. But were they not magnanimous? Ra merely went into retirement. He was getting a bit senile, wasn't he? My children are nothing like those Greeks with their eternal punishments in the depths of their Underworld."

"Of course not, my lady. So he made you into his Eye in punishment for the Demon Days."

I took a deep drink, draining my goblet in spectacular fashion. "Yes. I tried to outrun it at first. The moment he bestowed chaos on me, I fled the great halls."

"Where did you run?"

"Everywhere. Nowhere. With the seductive power of lessened control, I raged across the lands. It was the first time I ran, but not the last."

"Was it the reason you became the Runaway Goddess?"

"I've had many names. The Runaway Goddess. The Wandering Goddess. The Distant Goddess."

"Of course."

"But that was not the reason I earned these names. That came later. After Ra gifted me his Eye, I ran, but I came back." I sighed, rubbing a hand over a vulture pectoral around my neck. *"I am tired, mortal seed. I wish for you to leave my presence."*

Mestjet bowed her head, quiet murmurs on her lips.

I beckoned her with a bejeweled hand. "I will grant you a token. A gift. It is hard to judge mortal years at times. It would do no good to come back to finish my story only to find that you have been dead for a hundred years."

I admit I took some small pleasure in seeing her flinch. Death was so very interesting to me. I watched her keenly as she swallowed that pronouncement in the way mortals must.

Reaching around, I unclasped my ornate pectoral, enjoying the way it gleamed in her eyes. They widened even bigger as I placed it upon her breast. "With this vulture, I give you the life of the gods. Immortality is yours, Mestjet, daughter of Ra. Begin to tell my story and tell it well. I will return to you soon to finish it."

The black-eyed priestess bowed her head, her hands clasped in prayer and reverence for her goddess.

Chapter Fifteen

I WOKE up on my hands and knees, gasping. But at that moment, I also realized I didn't need to. I sat up and stared. My eyesight was precise. More than perfect. I could see a dust mite crawling out of Manu's pore on his bald head.

I squeezed my eyes shut, but that just made me realize how perfect my hearing was, and it was all I could do not to wail. I could hear insects burrowing in the wall and my heart beating in my chest. It was me, but it all felt unnatural.

I had everything. My memories, my recollections. My whole history with Thoth, Culsans, Shu, and Ra. It was all there. I was uncovered, bare and naked before myself.

It was so much more unnerving than being naked in front of a man. I was forced to see my many faults. They shone like stretch marks across the skin, blemishing the perfection of a goddess. That was the great secret the gods didn't want you to know. They were far from perfect.

I was cruel.

I was emotionless.

I was immortal.

There was not a scrap of humanity in Tefnut, and if it wasn't for dragging Ava's memories with me at the last moment, I might have stayed that way.

Cautiously, Aurick called my name. I couldn't help but see him flinch when I turned my gaze upon him. I knew how inhumane it was from the mirror on the barge memory. And I also knew how it made my body purr when my gaze caused Mestjet to flinch. But right now? I hated it.

"Don't be scared," I said, choking a little at the deeper tones of my voice.

"I'm not scared for me," Aurick said firmly. "I'm scared for you."

I could read the lie in his eyes, but his voice was true. He was both—scared of me and for me. Yet, he wasn't giving up on me.

"How do you feel?" he asked.

I turned my hands over, all traces of sunspots gone. Even the vein in my left hand, the one that had gotten more prominent lately, had vanished. It felt crass to say, but I was physically perfect. Unfortunately, that didn't help keep the growing feeling of superiority stay dormant. I shoved it away, mentally locking Tefnut's memories in a vault and focusing on Ava's.

Please, focus on Ava!

I took one look at the hall—the acanthus columns, the braziers sparking with cassia incense—and I let the chaos consume me.

What I mean to say is, I ran. And I didn't look back.

As my feet beat a tempo across the hot desert sands, I could only feel. I thought nothing. Ra had bestowed his Eye upon me, and I was supposed to accept it as a good, faithful daughter. This was a twisted punishment meant to look like a gift. How could I refuse?

My rage blew across the desert, scorching everything within my wake like a tsunami of fire. Villages were incinerated and rivers were vaporized. And then? I hit something hard.

Thoth.

He had grabbed me, pulled me out of thin air and wrapped me in his arms, shushing me. I let him as Ra's rays sank in the horizon and the moon rose over the blackened dunes. I let him for many days and many nights.

"Do you remember our first date?" I asked desperately, pulling myself back to the Palace of Augustus and the hidden Lupercal cave. My memories fought for domination. The first time I ran. The way Thoth wooed me after that. Our life together, shunning Shu for centuries upon centuries. My growing suspicions of Thoth's motives. My final run when Culsans helped keep me hidden. Until I decided to let Thoth catch me. Until he cursed me.

I had lived for *centuries* with Thoth between my two runs. Pinpricks of heat and lust poked at me through the veil of memories. He was right. I had loved him, in the way that immortals can. Which isn't to say very well.

I yanked my gaze back to Aurick.

He watched me with pain in his eyes, as though he knew what I'd been remembering. Of course he knew Thoth would be there in my memories. Aurick was the most intelligent human being I'd ever met.

"Our first date? Under the lemon trees behind Marco's?" I begged.

Aurick jerked at my question, and a smile tugged at his lips. He ran a hand through his hair, sticking his reddish gold locks on end. "Every detail. You accused me of being a closeted serial killer, and when you tried the savory zabaglione for the first time, your eyes dilated and you licked the top of your lip with the tip of your tongue."

"I implied you could be a serial killer," I said, lightness suffusing my bones at the memory. "Never outright accused. That would be silly." But warm gooseflesh covered my arms at his recalling. The way he had watched me, fascinated, was enthralling. Could I say I'd ever truly felt that way with Thoth as Tefnut?

"What else?" I asked.

Aurick let himself fully grin. I loved seeing that grin. "You pushed back on all of my subtle probes to determine what you were. You were classy and beautiful and intelligent. It was captivating to watch you maneuver around my questions."

I remembered thinking how it felt like he was playing chess while I was skipping checkers across the same board. Maybe I never gave myself enough credit. I returned the grin, feeling more secure in myself. Tefnut was not the endgame. I would figure it out. "If we had known then, I doubt either of us would have believed it."

For the first time, I remembered what I was wearing. I crossed my arms over my chest. Coronis and Aurick seeing my boobs? Fine. Manu? Not fine. Not fine at all. The rest of Italy would probably think I was some performer or street artist that wanted tourist money for pictures. There were tons of gladiators walking around the Colosseum, posing for photographs and kissing their biceps.

"Here, darling," Coronis said, offering me her fashion scarf from her neck. She helped secure it around my breasts and took me in. "You look ravishing."

"Is that a synonym for ridiculous? Because that's how I feel."

"Don't be silly. You are divine in every sense of the word."

"I don't actually want to be divine," I said quietly, staring at my Ava body. She was on the ground, her eyes wide open, unblinking, unseeing. A husk of nothing.

"Close her eyes, they're creeping me out," Manu said gruffly, breaking my moment with myself.

I knelt and placed my fingers over my eyelids and pulled them down. They popped open. I did it two more times. Finally, I threw my hands up. "This is too weird. I can't do it. Coronis?"

She closed them a few times, too, with no luck.

What can I say? I always was a feisty bitch.

Manu rolled his eyes and strode forward, probably about to blast my body to bits like he'd wanted to do for so long.

I held up my hand. "Hey, leave my body alone. It can't hurt you anymore."

"I wasn't going to—"

"Uh huh. I saw your trigger finger getting itchy. Leave her alone." I turned to Aurick. "Can't we do something? It feels wrong to leave her here." I pushed away a stray piece of gray hair and tucked it behind my—Ava's—ear.

"Oo, we could pull a Weekend at Bernie's!" Coronis exclaimed. I wondered vaguely if she'd acted in that, too, or if she'd already left Hollywood by then.

"That's not exactly what I had in mind."

"A shrine, darling?"

"Well, no," I said, "but… maybe… someday I could figure out a way to go back inside her?"

"You want to give up immortality?" Manu asked, clearly astonished.

"That was always the plan. Remember? I'm supposed to destroy the gods. I don't plan on sending myself with

Thoth, so I was hoping to find some cool magic trick to stick me back in the old flesh prison here."

Aurick watched Ava thoughtfully. "Actually, she is the one who did your blood oath. Tefnut is under no such obligation."

Manu's face was a delight to watch as he worked out this new twist, which he couldn't have seen coming. Finally, he pushed out his response like he was birthing a kidney stone, "But Ava will always be under oath to me, so if you want back in her, you'll have to adhere to it."

I was tempted to pat him on the back, but settled for a finger gun motion. "Don't worry, big guy. I am a woman of my word. Even if it was only part of me that gave it."

Aurick gently lifted Ava over his shoulder, but it was still painful to watch her head loll helplessly. My butt stuck in the air and I cringed. Were my hips really that wide? I mean, I knew they were, but from this angle... Tefnut's on the other hand. Well, I could safely squeeze into a size zero if I wanted without breaking a sweat or getting a hernia. It was annoying to be in a body that was a perfect doppelgänger—no, a perfected one. This face and body was me created in the cosmos, and I couldn't help recoiling a bit. Thanks to the memories of my many lives, I had too much humanity in me now to not shiver at the sight of immortal perfection. It was unnatural, and it scared the human in me.

Aurick said, "I'm going to take her back to Aradia. I know some mummy magic involving linen bandages from Egypt. I'll nip over and get some to wrap your body in and keep it in stasis indefinitely. It will be fine." He gripped one of my shoulders while his other arm flexed to steady my Ava body. "*You* will be fine, I promise."

"Thank you," I said gratefully, knowing that it was one

of the most appreciative things to come out of Tefnut's mouth. I paused. "Wait. Did anyone hear that?"

Everybody stilled, shaking no slowly. I cocked my head, aware my ears were infinitely better than theirs. Then I whispered, "Something is coming."

Chapter Sixteen

"I THOUGHT you weren't detected, Death Walker," Manu shouted as he flung runes at the sons of the soil.

"I wasn't. Thoth has already tracked us, or more likely, he has sent them here to guard Tefnut in case she returned."

Coronis shifted into an attack crow, and Aurick flung glass globules with one hand and slashed with a dagger in his other. I guarded my Ava body, and now, I clutched her, afraid to do anything. I hadn't had time to test how much power my immortal body held, but I thought it was safe to assume it would change how I wielded it. I didn't want to accidentally flood the whole cavern and kill every living thing.

As for the monsters, there wasn't any other way to describe them. Their bodies consisted of crumbling mud, as if they'd been poorly formed of red clay, and their beady black eyes seemed incapable of blinking. Despite that, they moved with a speed that was hard to capture with a human eye, and Manu kept throwing runes a few beats too slow.

When their blows landed, Aurick and Manu managed to knock the onslaught backwards, but only a little. They were made of rocks and dirt, after all. Wherever the molten glass hit, sprays of pebbles flew off wildly like shrapnel. The monsters barely noticed. They continued their advance, a hundred of their bodies blocking every escape. The entire cave shook with the force of their lock-step. Dust and flakes of ancient paint fell onto our heads from the mosaics above. Future archaeologists were not going to like that.

Coronis's beak was no match for their bodies of sunbaked brick, and I yelled at her to come protect my body. She swooped down and covered it with a wing while I stood and dusted myself off, my hands clenching to sucker punch any monster foolish enough to get close. The first went down like a concrete balloon.

Aurick whooped for me, but the truth was, that wasn't going to work. Perhaps, I could eventually stun them all or even kill them with my inhumane strength, but their sheer numbers would overpower my friends before I got to them.

Clearly, Thoth was scared. He really didn't want me to find this body. I said a silent thanks to Culsans as I hemmed and hawed. Which was worse? Letting demons kill my friends or accidentally doing it myself? Perhaps I could control it. Shouldn't I at least try?

"Stop being scared to use that power and help us!" Manu shouted.

"Ava, you can do it!" Coronis cried, and that name unhinged my fears. I let the waters flow.

Like a cold, dark lake, the drops swirled from my fingers and smashed into the sons of the soil. They were swept off their feet and jumbled together, heads over end as they smashed and collided into cave walls, while I kept an invisible dam in front of me to protect us.

The sons of the soil disintegrated into bits of rubble, and I let my waters recede. It evaporated to reveal their bodies, now merely mud, slathered thick on the cave floor. Except for one. I'd let one monster live. He had some things to tell me that I was sure to find interesting.

The still standing demon took one look at us and fled. Aurick shouted, "Don't let him escape! He'll tell Thoth about us finding your body."

I didn't want to chase a demon through the tourist-filled streets of Rome, possibly endangering humans, so I took off, sprinting across the uneven and slippery cave floor, and tackled the monster with a flying leap. The son of the soil went down hard, dust blowing up from his body.

"Holy hell, Ava!" Aurick cried. "You could play in the NFL if you wanted. You could be your own team."

"Thanks," I said, holding my demon to the floor. His eyes were flint hard, and I could feel the hate in them.

Honestly, I was beyond caring what a monster thought.

"You have information we need," I said.

The monster glared, not very forthcoming. I slammed my foot down on his misshapen arm and smashed it into bits like broken pottery.

The monster howled and tried cradling the stump, but I struck his other arm. His cries were deafening, but it was already too late. My immortal body remembered exactly how to hurt him, the exact weight and angle that needed to be applied. I knew how to be brutal, and it felt seductively good. It felt powerful.

Aurick shouted, but it was little more than a tunnel echo, easily ignored.

"Now you will tell me where Thoth is."

The monster gnashed his jaw and stared with those eyes.

I only waited two seconds before smashing his leg.

"Athens!" the monster shouted. "An old friend to the gods is there."

"Another god?" I demanded.

"No. Half a god. A demigoddess."

Before he could beg for clemency or twist any words, I bludgeoned his head. The monster was dead.

So were the rest, but this one was different. I pushed away from his quiet form and rose. My three companions were watching me with various degrees of horror on their faces, and I saw myself through their eyes. I must have looked uncontrollable to them. As if I were the monster.

Aurick stepped forward first, his hands outstretched, some pretty lie on his lips about trusting me as he always had when I could see the truth plainly on his face. Anger whipped through me. They could never know what it was like to be at war with their many sides! They hadn't lived the hundred lives I had. Their fate and the entire realm's fate was on my shoulders alone. I carried the burden and it was heavy. If they wanted to be saved, I would have to continue dirtying my hands.

"Ava, it's okay," Aurick said.

And that simple sentence broke down my defenses as easily as my own flood waters. In a few steps, he reached me and held me tight. "Shh, it's okay. You were protecting us. This isn't who you are."

"Maybe it is. Maybe I'm doomed. I fear the ichor in me has replaced all my warm blood. I should have killed Tefnut and stayed Ava."

Aurick laughed, which stopped my wallowing immediately as threads of indignation shot through me. "Excuse me? Is this a laughing matter?"

"If you think you could have killed Tefnut, I guess I adore your confidence."

I let the heat in him burn away the chill of my fears. In

a way that Tefnut had never done before, I let him comfort me. I felt his strong arms wrap around me and leaned into his desert-tinged scent. He was my oasis, although not even Aurick could completely extinguish the chills that winged through my body.

This inhumane thing inside of me was not finished.

Chapter Seventeen

BEFORE HE LEFT, Aurick made me promise to take a brief rest at a local café before returning to Aradia. I sat and watched the world pass before us, jealous of the tourists' care-free attitudes.

If I were still mortal, my hands would be trembling. As it were, they were perfectly still. Only my mind jumped around like a rabbit on pixie dust. I realized I hadn't even broken a sweat, and I wasn't sure if I still could.

It was dinnertime, and as hard as it was to believe with all the realm and time zone hopping, it was still the same day I'd returned from Nibiru. At this point, I didn't care if it was past espresso time. I needed some uppers.

The waiter sat down a plate of petite white cups with a thick lip of foam, but they spilled as he stumbled, the coffee bleeding all over the table. He stammered, staring at me and then averting his eyes, then staring again. His entire body shook as he apologized in halting Italian, his very voice failing him.

Clearly, Tefnut was too much for this world. I waved the waiter away, as Coronis got up to order at the bar.

Manu crossed his arms and sat back.

"You don't like what I did," I said.

Manu pursed his lips and watched a couple argue before embracing. "You know exactly how dangerous the gods are. I hardly need to explain that."

"And you still trust me enough to back me over Bruno?"

For a moment, Manu paused to consider all sides. Thankfully, it didn't take him too long. "We need the fire power. Eventually the Council will see that, but you will need to learn to control your godly urges," Manu said matter-of-factly.

"I don't know if I can kill him without chaos."

"Why? Because in some old myths, that's what happened?"

"Myths are real," I reminded him. "Set killed Osiris with chaos."

"Set wants you to think he killed Osiris. But didn't you say Thoth brought him back? What if it wasn't what it seemed at all? What if Thoth was pulling strings as usual and gave Set something else?"

"Like what?"

Manu shrugged. "Some spell that would merely make it look like Osiris was dead. If there's one thing I've learned about the gods, it's that they prefer tricks over substance."

"And then what? Thoth gave Isis the counter-spell to 'revive' her husband?"

"Isn't that what you would do?"

"He was chopped into pieces," I reminded him. "Pretty hard to fake that."

Manu gave me his stoic look. "You don't think magic could make it appear that way? I thought Tefnut would be smarter."

Anger laced up my fingers, but before I could do something rash, Manu continued. "I also considered that it was a spell that actually killed Osiris. If it were chaos, any chaos beast could kill a god, and that doesn't make sense."

I was taken aback. Manu had a point. "If anyone in all the realms knew a spell for that, it would be Thoth. And it would be in his Tablets."

Manu let me sink into my thoughts as Coronis came back with a round of espresso and biscotti. What if Manu was right and we didn't need chaos? What if we just needed the right spell? It certainly sounded like Thoth, the puppet master magician.

Ever since I'd lost chaos and set Thoth free, I felt impotent, like I was a burden to my supernatural friends. Now I felt hope. I had an immortal body and a lead.

Coronis noticed my smile as she handed me a cup. "Either you've gone mad or you know something I don't know."

"Hopefully the latter." I breathed in the creamy foam and took a long sip. "Poor ancient Egyptians. They never knew Italian espresso."

"Or apertivo hour," Coronis said. "I can't wait until life is normal enough to do that again."

"I wouldn't count on it," Manu interrupted.

"You don't have to rain on our parade," I told him. "You're the one who just gave me a clue."

"And yet, we sit here. We know Thoth is looking for old allies or to cement new ones. There are plenty of demigods and priestesses who would consider the gods coming back a good thing."

"You always have such a dreary view of humanity," I noted, although I noticed Coronis turned a little pale at his words.

"How can we stand against an army of demigods?" she

asked, and I could feel the fear dripping in her voice. I also heard something else: the silent accusations that I never should have gone to Nibiru. That I brought trouble to their paradise. That I was the problem.

She gripped my hand. "I can go to the other supernatural islands. Remember the Scottish selkies I told you about your first night on Aradia? Let me talk to some old friends. We can gather our own army."

And just like that, the spell of my suspicions was broken. I shook my head as if to break the last gossamer threads. Tefnut's millennia of betrayals and lies were getting to me. If I really thought Coronis was blaming me or against me, then they were winning. I had to keep fighting Tefnut, or maybe the answer was more simplistic than that. I just had to hold onto Ava. I had to hold onto my humanity. How Nonna loved me. How Rosemary welcomed me. How Coronis saved me. How Aurick held me. The smell of a bubbling Sunday sauce. And above all, the sound of my twin sons' laughter. Everything that made life wonderful.

"Let's all go back to Aradia and form a plan. I can't help but feel we're being reactionary right now. Like we're on the defensive."

Nobody answered.

I looked up from my espresso. Coronis was frozen with her cup halfway to her lips. Manu had a biscotti sticking out his mouth, crumbs falling from his lips. They floated motionless in the air. I glanced around the square. The fountain had stopped flowing. A couple were paused in a dramatic dip. The waiters ceased their swirling dance.

Rome was frozen.

I was almost tired of saying the words, but I did it anyway like some ritual that needed to be completed. "Show yourself, Thoth. Let's get it over with."

He rippled into view, a curve to his lips. "You are a vision, Tefnut."

Inside, my body strained to strike, like sails snapping in a storm, but I couldn't risk an all-out assault around all these people. Better to find out what he wanted first. I had a feeling he wanted to see for himself if it was true that I was Tefnut again.

"Funnily enough, I still prefer Ava," I said. "But you! Look at you. All not dead and performing magic again. I recall you did this from stasis when my boys turned eighteen."

Thoth smiled. It was leonine and majestic and utterly abhorrent to me. "That was a great party, wouldn't you say?"

"I've thrown better. I assume you're strong enough now to pause the entire city of Rome if you chose?" I shrugged. "It's a little one-trick pony for me."

"Master of time, you remember," Thoth agreed, not rising to my dig at his creativity. "However, those that discounted your wisdom were always fools."

"Yes, I was always good at figuring things out."

"Like what?"

"Like how you're currently in Athens with that Daughter of Ares." The words came out before I even realized what I was saying, but the moment I spoke them I knew they were true. My Tefnut memories confirmed it. Thoth's face confirmed it, too, but he recovered quickly.

"So, you have found your immortal body and discovered my hideout. What else have you accomplished this afternoon?" he asked, a smile playing on his lips.

I kept my mouth shut. I wouldn't encourage him. He was here for a reason, and for now, nobody was in danger —beyond the fact their lives were trapped in some great game of the gods.

Thoth circled Manu and Coronis, and my heart fluttered. He glanced at me, but I remained silent. Until he cupped Coronis's frozen face.

"Don't touch them," I snarled, rising from my chair.

Thoth gave me the funniest look. He cocked his head, and I could imagine a long-beaked sacred ibis staring at me. "So it's true. Mortals matter to you now."

"Don't you dare hurt them," I threatened.

"Why would I want to do that? All I want is you, Tefnut. Really, the equation is simple." He caressed Coronis's white bobbed hair and separated a single strand. Without taking his gaze from mine, he pulled.

Her face was frozen, but something shifted in her expression. He was hurting her.

He plucked two more before I could slam my hand into his face, hoping to shove his nose into his brain or something of that regard, but he anticipated my attack.

Thoth tsked. "That could've hurt, were I not a god."

We both stood on café tables now, porcelain and plates frozen in mid-air from where our brief fight had flung them.

"You have the ability to stop this, Tefnut. Our love is waiting to be reignited. Join me and we will rule this world as we did before. All you have to do is one thing."

"And what's that?" I asked, genuinely curious about his terms.

"Let yourself fall into our love again."

My eyes did a full circuit in their orbit, a diva sized eye-roll fit for a goddess. "Don't act like this was about love. It hasn't been about love for a very long time. This is about power."

"One day, my love, you'll see."

"And you will keep killing me until I do? I guess I foiled that plan."

Thoth's eyes turned flinty for a moment. Me finding Tefnut was not in his equation, although I was certain he had a contingency plan. The Archon Wars weren't part of his equation either, and he still managed to escape.

"I won't lie. I am impressed to see you whole. Don't you feel more complete than you ever could have imagined as that mortal woman?"

My silence was enough of an answer.

"You truly are a marvel and my only equal, Tefnut."

I scoffed. "I'm so much more than you."

And with that, Thoth was gone. Rome was alive. Plates clattered to the ground where they split into pieces. Coronis cried out in agony.

"Are you okay?" I asked desperately, sinking to my knees in front of her.

She rubbed her shoulder blades, not her head. "I feel… plucked. Like someone was pulling out my feathers one by one."

I told them about Thoth's visit, feeling sick the whole time. I had never realized how obscene a bare neck looked when compared to an immortal. Now that I was Tefnut, their necks looked so very breakable, so exposed, their blood pounding under a thin layer of veins and skin. It would take only a glance and a twist of my wrist. I would hardly notice I'd done it before they were gone forever. I shuddered. It didn't feel like a homecoming, jumping back into Tefnut's body. It felt like a home invasion, except I was the invader. The misfit. The unnatural thing.

"Is it permanent?" I asked.

Coronis's eyes welled up. "I don't know. I can't seem to heal myself, and I doubt I can fly."

"I will kill him." I stood. "Manu, take me to Athens right now. Alone."

"No!" Coronis stood to meet me. "We do this together.

Remember what Culsans said? We're stronger as one. Let's all go back to Aradia like you said. We'll think of something." She put her hand on my arm, pleading with her eyes. "Please. We don't even know if we can kill a god. Don't go."

My hair was still bristling, but I relaxed an inch.

Manu slowly pulled out his bone dagger. He looked extremely disturbed that Thoth had been here. "I agree with the crow. We go back to the island, for now."

Chapter Eighteen

ARADIA WAS QUIET. I didn't like it immediately.

Manu pocketed his bone dagger while I helped Coronis limp into Rosemary's Bakery. Before I'd even closed the door, Thessaly somersaulted over the lintel and raced to her. If I were to guess, she had been watching and already knew what had happened. Their reunion was loud and exuberant. It was also tinged with fear.

"I'm going to find Mak and see what he thinks," I announced, wanting to leave them to their peace.

Protectively, I reached out and touched her bobbed hair, but Coronis flinched, and I pulled back, trying not to feel hurt. I'd brought the gods back into their lives, and here they were, menacing and hurting them again. Here *we* were. An existential crisis had nothing on what I was going through right now.

I heard a rumbling chatter in Marco's Taverna, so I headed there first. Candles smoked on the scarred tabletops, and a fire still blazed in the large wood-oven behind the bar. It'd been going since Marco started the place in the thirteenth century and nothing would put it out. Nothing, except total war coming right to Aradia's shores.

Bruno sat in the center of the room, raising a racket about being imprisoned. Through bared fangs, he hissed all of the horrible penalties he was busy dreaming up for us. And here I thought vampires didn't dream.

Rosemary sat next to him in a flour-covered lemon apron, fear and uncertainty pulling her lips into an unfamiliar frown. I made a bee line for her, but before I could tell her about Coronis, she screamed. "Ava? Is that you?"

I closed my eyes briefly. "Yes, and also no. I found Tefnut's immortal body."

Rosemary reached out to touch my face before squeaking sorry.

I grabbed her hand and held it cradled to my cheek. "Don't you ever apologize, Rosemary. I don't plan on keeping this body. I'm Ava, first and foremost."

"Darling, I don't think that's how it works," she said.

"Sure it is. What's the use of being divine if I can't do whatever I want?"

Rosemary smiled weakly, and I quickly changed the subject. I gave her the rundown on Coronis and Thoth. My friend's face dropped in horror, and she quickly ran over to the bakery, grabbing Mak by the arm as she went. With those two on it and Thessaly guarding her, that was one less thing to worry about.

Meanwhile, I had to summon my general skills and bring this grotesque game with Thoth to an end. "Tiberius?"

The chipmunk sailed through the air, and I was pleased to see how much stronger he looked already. "Yes, my goddess?" he bowed.

"Tiberius, cut that out. Can you summon Nonna and

Culsans back from the pillars in Nibiru? I'm switching tactics."

"Sure, but why are they there?"

"I thought Thoth might try to prop the pillars up and release the gods again, but now I'm positive that's not what he wants. Other gods would only get in his way."

"Of what?"

"Absolute power."

"What should we be worrying about, then?" He twitched his whiskers because, of course, there was always something to worry about.

"Demons and other supernaturals," I said grimly. "Ones loyal to Thoth. He hasn't been awake long in this realm, but he's already building an army. We need to stop him before he gains too much support."

Tiberius nodded. Then his eyes bulged and his body disappeared. I would never get over the mechanics of realm jumping.

As if we were standing in the middle of an astral highway, a tear opened up in the air and Aurick stepped into the room. In his hands, he held Egyptian cotton wrappings with colorful hieroglyphs on them. We locked eyes, and I followed him to wrap my Ava body, ignoring Bruno's threats at my back.

"Where did you put her?" I asked, very aware how weird it was to ask about myself in the third person.

"Where do you think?"

"The crypt?"

Aurick smiled. "Ava deserves better than that. She's comfortably resting at Villa Venus."

The moment I walked inside the spare bedroom, hot tears welled up in my eyes.

Aurick caught one on his fingertip. "I didn't think

goddesses could cry," he said lightly and blew the teardrop as if it were an eyelash and he were making a wish.

"I assure you, gods can cry, but this is my human side. Thankfully, I still have it. My Ba remembered it all."

"Have you let yourself sink into the memories?" he asked. I could feel a frisson of tension on the surface of the question. He knew as well as I that Thoth would dominate my goddess memories.

"Only the one when my souls re-connected," I said. "Actually, I was with Mestjet. It seems I granted her immortality."

Aurick's eyebrow quirked up. "Now that is an interesting twist."

"Yeah. I gave her the stories for her Coffin Texts about my marriage to Shu, the birth of my grandchildren during the Demons Days, and how I decided to run away from Thoth a second time. Apparently I ran in agony when Ra first bestowed the Eye on me, but this second time I left for centuries because I was done with Thoth. That was when Culsans helped me hide. But Aurick?"

"Yes?"

"I was horrible. I made mortals help me. They brought me luxury items in my exile and then I killed them so Thoth wouldn't have a breadcrumb trail to follow. That's all here." I tapped my heart. "I can feel it constantly fighting. What if I'm not the good guy I want to be, because Tefnut is just too dominant?"

"You are who you choose to be," Aurick said firmly, taking me in a familiar hug. He still towered over me, even in Tefnut form. "Ever since you jumped into your immortal body, you've only been worried about your friends and if you're still a good person. A selfish goddess would not worry about such things, just as Tefnut did not worry when she killed mortals to benefit herself. But you? You care."

In response, I snuggled deeper into his chest. We were alone, and I desperately wanted to let him worship me in other ways, but that would be selfish and I was sort of trying to prove the opposite.

He kissed the top of my head. "What's more? I believe in you."

"Thank you," I whispered.

After a few moments together in peace, I helped lift my old body as Aurick wrapped it, quietly intoning spells and charms to keep it safe and preserved. Then I tucked her into the spare bed. Finally, I changed into my comfortable old blue jeans and a plain black t-shirt, delicately folding and storing Tefnut's beautiful Egyptian dress.

"Do you have a plan?" Aurick asked as we took Nonna's familiar lime green Vespas back into the town square.

"Only the seeds of one, but maybe that's a good thing."

Aurick gave me a raised eyebrow.

"Every time I've had a plan, Thoth has outmaneuvered me. Maybe it's better to…"

"Wing it?"

"Not exactly. I want to call everyone together for a town hall meeting. I've learned my lesson. We're better together, and someone may have another seed of an idea that will sprout into the answer."

"A town hall," Aurick said, smiling. "Only you would think up something like that."

"I'm hoping that's how we defeat Thoth; by coming together as a town and relying on our humanity."

"It's as good an idea as any," he said.

The taverna had turned into a makeshift war council. Marco set out acacia wood bowls heaping with various red and white pastas and fresh salads. We all needed to "keep up energy and morale" he boomed, slinging a huge scoop of boar Bolognese onto a plate and forcing it on me.

It would've been quaint if it wasn't for Bruno throwing another fit about his treatment. I didn't hold it against him. Honestly, for being imprisoned by his worst nightmare, he was acting fairly lame.

"Take his restraints off," I told Aurick.

"Are you sure?"

"Yes. He's basically defanged as it is. He's no danger to anyone but himself."

Aurick spoke a command, and the Gordian Knot unwound itself and dropped to the ground. Now that he was free, Bruno's complaints grew louder, so I turned my luminous eyes on him and pushed tendrils of mother magic into the air to soften his angry demeanor. This might have been our last meal, and I wanted to eat it in peace. I ignored the little voice telling me this was exactly what I'd refused to do as Ava before I left. Use my magic on others for my own benefit.

Everyone grabbed a plate and a glass of wine as I stood on top of the bar and called for attention. The faun sisters in their blossom gowns sat with Spyro. The recently returned archons were practically inhabiting each other's space in a darkened corner. Thessaly held Coronis's hand as Mak shot me a thumbs up. A pressure eased in my chest to see Coronis smile again. Even Mino, Mae, and Jo sat together, waiting expectantly as they swirled and sniffed their wine. Everyone I had come to know and love were here, looking to me to lead them. I only hoped their trust wasn't misguided.

I cleared my throat, but the right words were snagged somewhere along the way. Only the fire crackling in the hearth made a sound.

Finally, Spyro broke the silence. "I'm not getting any younger, Ava. You may have gone and gotten yourself immortal beauty, but some of us have to sleep still."

The room broke out in laughs. I could always count on Spyro to be an inappropriate icebreaker.

"Right. I'm sure many of you have questions and I'll be happy to answer them. I am Tefnut of Egypt, but I'm not on the gods' side now, nor will I ever be. And I plan to prove myself with my actions."

Someone shouted in the back, "Did you fight against us in the Archon Wars?" It was a boar shifter that liked iced lemonade in the mornings. Briefly, I wondered what he thought about our dinner selection.

"I was stuck in my mortal death cycle during the Wars, but at one point, yes. Thoth conscripted me to fight for him. At the time, I didn't know who I really was, or what he was. I was a human pirate queen by the name of Jeanne."

There were low murmurs that were hard to read. Hastily, I clapped my hands. "I have been fighting Thoth for almost my entire existence. Nothing will keep me from finding a way to get rid of him for good. I swore a blood oath to Manu to that effect."

Manu nodded, and he was even nice enough not to mention the loophole—that technically only Ava had made that oath—which I appreciated.

"Currently, we have a few loyal shades still in Nibiru watching the four pillars to ensure they stay down—"

Instead of reassuring Aradia, my announcement sent

the townspeople into an uproar. I got the feeling they didn't realize the pillars could be propped up again. Marco had to roar to get everyone quiet again, while I sent out more tendrils of calming mother magic.

"It won't happen," I promised loudly. "Tonight, I brought everyone together so we could brainstorm. Thoth is surely gathering allies and so must we. Coronis has begun reaching out to other supernatural enclaves to warn them and to see if they are interested in providing support. Does anyone else have any ideas?"

Donatella, the faun, raised a hoof. "We can provide oleander blossoms to the cause. While deadly to MILFs as they are found in nature, with a little earth magic, we can make a potion that would be deadly even to supernatural beings."

Her sister Hilda added, "Some of Napoleon's troops died from roasting their dinner on spits made from oleander branches. And those were normal ones." She smiled savagely.

You could hear a pin drop. Who would have thought the cute little fauns were capable of brewing deadly tea?

Mak blinked a few times and stood, looking shaken, but impressed. "I can have my bees make honey from the nectar of the, ah, *enhanced* oleanders, to add to your potions."

I stifled a laugh. "Should I just invite Thoth to a deadly tea party?"

The fauns tittered. "We don't pretend to be powerful enough to kill a god by ourselves, but the potion could be deployed as a deterrent to those who join him."

"Yes. I also have a few plague powers from my progenitor, Apollo," Mak said. "I would be honored to fight for you, Ava."

"Thank you," I said, my chest tightening.

Rosemary jumped to her feet, a mamma bear expression on her face. "I will stand with you." Marco joined her and let out a roar. One by one, the rest of the town got to their feet, pledging to help.

The only one who didn't was Bruno. He glowered in the corner, his wine and food untouched and his arms crossed petulantly against his chest. I caught his gaze and held it for a minute, letting his red eyes mull over my new body, before deciding a confrontation in front of everyone wasn't worth it. I was working on being the tame goddess. Or, at least, appearing to be one.

Afterwards, I mingled and answered questions for a bit from the curious townspeople—"Yes, Spyro, these are natural. No, Spyro, they don't droop." Many had never seen a goddess before, and they were still shocked to learn that one was here the whole time serving them biscotti and espresso.

Luca was last in line. While still his normal, broody self, he looked miles better than the last time we'd talked. The bags under his eyes were gone, and his skin wasn't so sallow. Aradia had worked her sea-side wonders, or perhaps it was just the fact he'd been re-accepted by the citizens he'd betrayed.

"It's funny, isn't it?" I began.

"What?"

"You tried to steal my body, and as it turns out, I had a back up."

He winced at that. "Yeah, I'm still sorry about that, you know."

"I know."

"I'd like to go back to my old haunts in Siberia and see what interest I can drum up there. Or at least, try to get some assurances they won't support Thoth," he said grimly.

I stared. "You think necromancers are going to be cool with group projects?"

"Won't know until we try. I'm not sure what else I can offer."

I gave him a hug, which felt anti-Tefnut but just right as Ava. "Thank you, Luca. Oh, I should tell you something."

He pulled away, his dark eyebrows knitted together at the change in my tone. "Good or bad?"

"I met Gianna. In Nibiru."

Luca staggered back two literal steps. His entire face lit up, and his eyes were bright. It was a Luca I didn't know but wished would come out more often.

"She was as great as you said. She's safe, hanging out with Queen Dido and Caterina Sforza. She said she's waiting for you, but as you know, time moves differently there. Don't worry about her. She's having a ton of fun in the meantime, kicking shade ass."

Luca's head bent over my hands for a minute and his shoulders were shaking. When he looked up, tears shimmered in his eyes. "Thank you, Ava. Thank you."

With the crowd gone, I finally headed over to Nonna's table where she was engaged in a full-on make out session. Culsans managed to stop sucking her earlobes long enough for her to sheepishly say hello.

"Are you sure about the pillars, Mamma?" Nonna asked, a hickey the size of my fist on her wrinkled neck. One of her gold hoop earrings was caught in the tangles of her waved up-do. It threw me off-balance to see her like this, but she looked decades younger, if not centuries. Grief could seriously age a person, and now the shroud of hers was lifting. I was happy for her. Desperation had driven her to do terrible things, but in the end, she was willing to sacrifice herself to help us. What someone did at the very end was what counted the most. No matter how long it took them to get there.

I nodded resolutely. "It's a gamble, but I am willing to take the risk. He doesn't want the other gods back. He wants us to rule together as one. Other gods would just get in the way of his plans and lead to more civil wars between them."

"Between you," Culsans corrected.

I waved him off. "It's a good thing we go so far back."

"Indeed," he agreed. "You have always valued my honesty."

"Yes, I can see how it has its value despite being so annoying," I said with a half-smile. "Anyway, what's more, he can't be sure what alliances and truces or disagreements have flared up between the other gods in the centuries since getting locked together in the Axis Mundi. He won't want to risk losing his grip on this realm with all of that uncertainty. If there's one thing I know about Thoth, it's that he doesn't like uncertainty."

"Smart thinking," Nonna agreed. She leaned in, almost whispering. "I didn't want to mention it in front of everyone, as you never know who might be a Thoth spy, but we should try the Emerald Tablets again now that you're a goddess. They might reveal more to you."

My heart thumped in anticipation. "Absolutely. And there's one ghost I know who would love to help."

"That old dog?" Nonna complained. "Even his lute playing is atrocious. It's an attack on true romance."

I laughed. "Oh yes. It's time to face the music."

Chapter Nineteen

WE ALL SHUFFLED into my room at Villa Venus, a curious melange of characters—a goddess, a mummy, two archons, and a chipmunk daemon. I sat cross legged on the bed with the scrolls in my hands. Night had fallen by now, the room dark, and it felt like one of those awkward childhood sleepovers where you try to summon a ghost. Only, this time, I knew one would appear.

"Piero, are you around?" I called. "Piero?"

A brittle wind swept through my room, ruffling the lace curtains and doilies. Everyone else shivered, but I no longer felt the cold of it. My Renaissance Romancer popped into view a moment later, already crumpled into a deep bow with his lute held forward. He straightened and began to strum a popular medieval love song as he sang.

"*Sei la cosa più bell ache mi sia mai capitata. Resta con me per sempre, mia dea*! You are the best thing that has ever happened to me. Stay with me forever, my goddess."

"Yes, lovely to see you, too—" I was cut off by an ungodly screech as Piero's fingers got tangled in the strings.

"Ah," I said. "You haven't seen my new body in the flesh, have you?"

"My lady, of course you look divine—no, *scusa*, but of course you are divine, a vision, a rose among thorns—"

Nonna let out a disgruntled snort at that, and I hastily waved away his scattered compliments at seeing me as Tefnut in a pair of blue jeans. "We're actually about to open the Emerald Tablets. I thought you might like to help.

"*Certo, mia dea*. As long as I don't have to incant anymore."

"I don't think you will," I promised as Piero drifted to the foot of the bed, scowling at Aurick the whole way, who looked faintly amused.

"Are we ready?" I asked. Everyone nodded, the whole vibe in the room muted as we held our collective breath.

As if reacting to my divinity, the scrolls shook the moment I laid my hands on them. Something dark roiled over the cover. "No one move," I commanded. "Thoth's curse is still trapped within the pages."

"Can you disable it?" Aurick asked in a hushed voice.

I closed my eyes and hovered my fingers over the papyrus. I could sense the malignant force just below the surface, like a crocodile waiting for its prey to get too close. As Tefnut long ago in that lemon-scented room, I was simply too excited, too hungry to see its secrets. Now, I'd learned caution the hard way.

Ideas flitted through my mind, but I couldn't find any way to get rid of it. Only Thoth could do that. Just like with Thessaly's curse, only the god who set it could undo it. Finally, I dropped my hands.

"No," I said with a sigh. "We could probably access what we have before, but not the deep secrets, the parts Thoth wouldn't want us to see. Unless…"

"I like the sound of that," Nonna said at the same time Aurick said, "I don't like the sound of that."

"Hear me out. I think I could use my protective mother magic to hold the curse at bay for a bit. Maybe twenty minutes? Thirty at most."

"Wouldn't Thoth have predicted that?" Aurick asked.

"No, I didn't have that power when he made this book. It's something I've gained through my many years of suffering at his hands."

"Do it," Nonna said.

Aurick looked conflicted, but that told me he really wanted us to find Thoth's secrets, and that was good enough for me.

"Get ready, everyone. You're going to have to speed read."

I let familiar curls of power surge over my forearms and down into the Emerald Tablets. The malignancy fought me at first, a darkness jetting around, looking for entrance into my protective bubble, but I held it at bay —for now.

Script that was previously invisible welled up in golden ink, bleeding across the papyrus. There were spells for memory, divination, invisibility, even a spell to dispel someone else's invisibility. Everything Thoth had learned about magic was in these works. It was breathtaking. Some were very cruel, including a charm one could write in myrrh on a bat's wing to induce insomnia in a woman. The poor woman would die within a week from lack of sleep. Death was too good for Thoth. He needed complete and total humiliation first.

"I only scratched the surface," Nonna said in awe. "I recall letting an Egyptian magician use the scrolls once. He suffered terrifying hallucinations every time he opened them. I always thought he was playing it up, but I guess they really were cursed."

"Oh look," said Aurick. "A spell to make your enemies—or your wife—appear to have a donkey nose. How useful," he said wryly.

"Ah, let's see. All you have to do is wait until nightfall, take a lamp wick, and dip it in donkey blood. Then light it when your target arrives. Or rub your wife's mirror with donkey tears." I looked up from reading. "Do donkeys cry?"

"Concentrate," Nonna barked. "Anything about souls?"

I kept scrolling through spells to call daemons, spells to make a wife manageable, which made me almost shatter the bedpost when I gripped it in anger. Fortunately, there was even a spell to restrain rage, which I totally could've used to counter it.

Suddenly, a shadowy image emerged from the book. Thoth was handing another god a rolled up piece of papyrus. I recognized him immediately from his sly eyes. Set, the god of chaos, the one who slayed Osiris.

"That's not my memory. I saw some of mine in here before. But this is definitely Thoth's. Why aren't we seeing my memories again?" I whispered as Set went to his knees with a bowed head in thanks.

"If I were to guess," Nonna said, "they held the resonance of the last moment you touched it. The moment when Thoth cursed you. Otherwise, they are his memories captured between the pages."

That seemed to ring true. Thoth was with me in the other memories I'd accessed, such as on the barque. "After I touched these tablets in their cursed state, I only remember what happened to my mortal selves, meaning he must have used the curse to strip my Ba from Tefnut. That began the death and rebirth cycle with a mortal body. I don't have any memories of him taking Tefnut's body to Rome because my Ba wasn't in that body—it was in my first incarnation."

"What was your first incarnation?" Culsans asked, his voice tinged with guilt.

It was strange to know exactly what had happened without any help, such as astral travel or Thoth's nightly invasions. Now that my soul was complete, I could recall everything in perfect detail. Supernaturals may slowly forget, but that wasn't the case with gods. No wonder their grudges were so old.

"I had two lifetimes before the She-Wolf. My Ba was so disoriented, I merely let events wash over me. The first was around the Ninth century BCE, a simple fishing woman, and the second was more of the same. Thoth probably hoped to humble me. Then, I hid myself as a wolf. Of course, Thoth found me immediately, scared I'd discover my body in Rome, which I almost did. He cursed me anew, and I spent the next few centuries as *lupas*, prostitutes, although it only took a handful of lifetimes before I became Cleopatra, the classic whore, who wasn't really. He liked to come to me then," I said, recalling the cat and mouse game Cleopatra had to play. "But my twins and I still died, so I tried to turn away from everything. It wasn't until Jeanne, when I agreed to help Thoth, that my reincarnations started remembering their power again. Then, as an explorer in Brazil in the Nineteenth century, he managed to take it all back. Until Aradia. Until Ava."

"I can't believe he put you through all of that," Culsans said. "I want to gut him like a guppy."

"Let's see if there's any information about the spell he gave to Set. Then we'll decide the best way to shank him," I said.

We continued through the scrolls, and I saw my name. Tefnut. It was part of a spell to separate a man from his wife. "He had supplicants invoke me to cause discord between spouses."

"I bet he used it on Shu," Culsans said darkly. "We archons always were astonished that Shu betrayed you for Ra as he did."

I remembered something Piero had once told me when we first examined these together. "You told me the secret to immortality was here. That's why they were so fabled."

Piero nodded, his fingers gliding up and down his lute. "*Sì, mia dea*. Everyone thought it was some potion they could create and consume."

"What if it was and Thoth gave Set a spell like that to preserve Osiris even in death?"

"Then it would strengthen the idea that Set never truly killed Osiris, which isn't good. It was all a set up."

I bit my lip. "Aurick, what happens if I can't fulfill my blood oath?" I had been so sure, so steady about it, that I never worried. Seeing these shadowy memories wedged a little crack into my confidence.

Aurick put a comforting hand on my thigh and shivers emanated from his touch, even through the thickness of my mom jeans. "We have time. Manu didn't put tight restraints on it or a deadline. For everything he is, he isn't a madman. We will figure it out."

"Or I lose Ava."

He nodded, his eyes grave. "Yes."

Nonna took notes on a charm for victory that she could brew up for the residents of Aradia, while Culsans copied one for restraints that would be handy in battle.

For the next few minutes, everyone was busy reading through separate pieces of the scrolls. I could feel my bubble starting to degrade at the power of Thoth's curse, but I kept coming back to a few lines that seemed innocuous at first. The more I thought about it, the less sense it made. Why would a spell about separating spouses, with my name no less, be next to one about weighing souls? More temptingly, it was here that the memory of Set accepting something from Thoth had first appeared. There were still shadowy memories playing out over the looping script, the hieroglyphs mingling together with Demotic Greek and Latin. I could make out a fierce battle between Set and Osiris and the keening wail of Isis as she gathered up her husband's body parts. From the looks of it, there was indeed a deception spell involved because I found one on the next page. It only *appeared* as if Set had dismembered Osiris. That did not bode well for my whole "destroy Thoth forever" plan.

But perhaps…

"Did you find something?" Aurick asked, looking up and seeing my expression.

"Maybe. I'm not sure. Thoth took out part of my soul, right?"

Aurick caught on quickly. "He separated one part. And the rest?"

"If you combined these spells, could Thoth separate all five parts of the soul? Is that possible?"

"Good question. Here's another," said Aurick. "What happens to the body once you remove all of the soul? An immortal body, I mean. Is it still immortal?"

"How could it be if the soul is the source of…"

I felt a crackling along my scalp. My hair stood on end. The protective bubble was beginning to disintegrate.

"Everyone, stand back," I warned. My arms were straining from the force of keeping it intact. "The bubble is being ripped apart."

"But it's only been a few minutes," Nonna protested. "Ten at most."

"Get back!" I shouted, heaving shut the Tablets.

A noxious cloud belched from the papyrus, sending us all into coughing spasms until I trapped it in a bubble of water and dissipated it.

Aurick rubbed circles on my back as we pondered what we'd learned. "How long do you think before we could try again?" he asked.

I shook my head. "I'm not sure."

"Was it Thoth?" Nonna wondered. "Could he sense us?"

"I don't think so. I think I just underestimated his protections around this particular spell. It must be important. I wonder if it's the actual spell he gave to Set to 'kill' Osiris? Do you think—get down!"

I blasted a surge of water over Aurick's head and decimated the window, spraying shards of glass all over the yard. Screams of pain followed.

I grimaced and got to my feet. "Take cover, everyone."

"What was it?" Aurick asked, jumping up to join me.

"Sirens. And they're nothing like Thessaly."

Chapter Twenty

THE SIREN BLEEDING on the ground outside of my window didn't look familiar, but the hatred in her eyes did. She was from Thessaly's gods-forsaken village, and she wanted revenge.

"Why have you come now?" I demanded, holding back at least four sirens with branches I'd borrowed from the walnut tree, twisting them around their bodies. They shook their technicolor hair as more sirens crawled up the cliff-side and across the yard on their bellies. Their fangs were bared and their eyes zeroed in on me. They dragged seaweed from the coast that they had so long been missing in Nibiru. I had a feeling they were quite adept at using it for all sorts of dangerous things, even if they hadn't practiced in centuries.

None spoke. They just hissed, as if waiting. Finally, I saw what they were waiting for—or who.

"Acantha." I narrowed my eyes. "What brings you to Earth? Surely you're not here to make amends with your daughter?"

She laughed, and it was like seashells scraping together.

"So it's true. My daughter hid your true nature, but here you are. A goddess." Her eyes gleamed at me like a lean, winter-starved predator.

"Thoth sent you," I said matter-of-factly.

She bowed her head slightly. "I've been approached."

"But you're hedging your bets and willing to work with either one of us, depending on which one gives you the better deal?"

Acantha's face became pragmatic. "I want a life. A real one. You saw how we live. Only the god who cursed us can lift it." When I stayed silent, she prodded me. "What would you do if you were us?"

"I would want a better life too, but at what cost? What did Thoth ask you to do?"

She bared her teeth, and I saw her eyes flicker towards the town. I attuned my new ears and picked up screams rising from the square. Immediately, I grabbed Acantha by the throat. Her salt-rimmed lips were turning blue, her wrinkled skin dappled with broken blood vessels. "What else came with you?"

She choked and gagged, but I didn't lessen the grip. It felt good to do something physical.

Too good.

I released her and watched her stagger back, my divine retribution side warring with my human, mothering side. For now, the mother won.

"The town is under attack," I said, turning to my friends. "Everyone, go to the square and protect the others. I'll deal with the sirens."

Aurick tried to protest, but I threw up a protective bubble around him and the others to prove my point. I was the least vulnerable among us. Only Thoth could take me down, and I planned on gutting him first.

As they left, my friends made the craziest looking

calvary—ancient beings on their mint green vespas covered in a glowing bulb of light. Some sirens were silly enough to test the strength of my protections, and they received a nasty shock for their efforts.

The other sirens tried creeping in a semicircle around me, but I repulsed them with my mother magic, fearing they'd be able to use my dew and water magic to gain strength.

"Let me make myself clear," I said once the others were gone. "I am a goddess in full control of my powers, and I do not negotiate with terrors."

The siren from my window spat out a glob of blood and laughed. "Which one of us is the terror?"

I glanced between their feverish eyes. They looked drunk, like they had imbibed too much salt water as they ascended to this realm. Acantha had to have known where Glaucos came from and used the same portal. But what did they want from me?

"Does Grandmother know you're here?" I asked sharply.

Acantha showed absolutely no fear. She peered around Nonna's yard, examining the broken Venus statue pointing over the ocean. "Grandmother is not your concern. You are not our family."

"True, but one of you is part of mine."

As if called by my words, Thessaly suddenly dropped down from Nonna's lintel and stared at her mother.

Acantha spoke first. "Daughter. It's impolite to not invite your family to see your new home. Are you ashamed of us?" She laughed. "Wouldn't that be funny? Seeing as we were ashamed of you this whole time."

"Ava speaks true. She is my family," Thessaly replied. "I swore to help my village, but I will gladly go back on that promise if you hurt her or anyone in this town."

"Speaking of which, what's going on there?" I asked under my breath.

"Sons of the soil. They're handling it."

That did not make me feel safe. I needed to be done with these sirens and go destroy demons. Surely Thoth knew they didn't stand a chance against my powers. What was his game?

"How could you possibly help us?" Acantha scoffed. "Only Poseidon can lift this curse. Thoth has promised he will bring back all of the gods, including Poseidon and Glaucos."

"Thoth lied to you."

Acantha's head snapped to me. "No."

I gave a derisive snort. "Thoth has no intention of bringing back the other gods. He doesn't want the competition. Does that sound wise to you? Does that sound like something the god of wisdom would do?"

By the looks on their faces, the sirens understood what I was saying. It made a hell of a lot more sense than Acantha's deluded hopes.

I pressed my advantage. "I'll be upfront. I have no intention of bringing them back either, but I will still aid you. While I can't give you back your singing voices, I can create a space where you will be safe, fed, and watered. I can't bring back the glory of your old castle, but I can give you the means to create a new one. I can't bring you the gods, but perhaps you will find other supernaturals as Thessaly has."

The others looked at Thessaly, and she nodded.

"You only had the word of one god that you could create new life with them alone," I continued, "but doesn't that sound suspicious? It feels a little self-serving to me."

There was some movement, some uncomfortable

glances exchanged, a seismic shift in the feeling of the crowd.

"There are stories," one siren said, hesitantly at first, "of our kind having babies outside of divine mating rituals."

Acantha spun and hissed at the siren, making her shrink back. But it was enough. Rebellion was in the air.

"At the end of the day," I shouted, "everyone wants the same basic things. Food. Shelter. Love. I can offer you the first two and give you the means to find the third."

"And in return?" a siren asked.

"In return, you will not help Thoth in any way. You will not provide aid or comfort. I will not require you to fight alongside me, but I will require that you go back to Nibiru immediately."

"No, we refuse," Acantha said.

"You don't speak for everyone," I replied. "Sirens are free to make their own decisions."

The younger sirens had heard enough. A teal-haired one grabbed Acantha while a dreamsicle orange-haired one produced a length of seaweed rope. They bound her, kicking and screaming. I could see her throat working as her instincts were to sing and save herself, but nothing came out.

I could feel her pain, palpable and thick. There was no other solution, however. She would have to live without Glaucos. Whether she believed Thoth would actually keep his promise was her decision, but at least I was upfront and honest about it. The painful truth was better than a pretty lie. "I'm sorry, Acantha. This is not what you wanted to hear. I know it hurts and I truly wish I could give you everything. The sirens have suffered for long enough."

"You couldn't possibly understand my pain. Gods take

whatever they want and think nothing of it," Acantha said bitterly. "You have to know true loss to know true pain."

I said nothing. Arguing wasn't going to make her magically feel better. I could tell her about the loss of my mortal children or how my immortal children, Geb and Nut, could never see each other. Gods knew loss. But pointing that out wouldn't make her feel any better. It wouldn't make her own pain go away. I realized that Acantha spent her existence feasting on her memories of her lover as if they were exquisite morsels. It was what sustained her. That, and the hope that he would return. Without that hope, I saw how emaciated she had become.

Thessaly's voice was quiet at first, but everyone stopped to listen all the same. "I miss my father. I miss him every day. You know our bond. If I thought it was at all possible to safely bring him back, don't you think I would, Mother?"

Acantha was silent. Thessaly crouched down to her mother and bent her head. They sat in the yard with closed eyes for a moment before Thessaly whispered, "I will always be here to remember him, if you want that. I remember how his eyes lit up the moment he saw you. I remember how he always made sure to catch a sea scallop to bring back to you during our trips above and how he twisted kelp together to make rings for your fingers. I remember his love for us, and even if I didn't realize how rare it was for a god, I never took it for granted."

Acantha sagged against the seaweed bindings, defeated and small, as if a hole had been torn in her bag of anger and all of the wind released. She muttered to herself, but I sensed a change in Acantha. For the first time, she was letting herself be held up by her family. It wasn't easy to let go of something she'd clung to so tightly, but, like a grain of sand rubbing the inside of a mollusk raw, perhaps this hurt would become her pearl.

Chapter Twenty-One

IT WAS DISCONCERTING how often the sounds of battle resounded from Aradia's town square lately. This wasn't normal; it couldn't be normal. I wouldn't let it.

After the sirens left, Thessaly immediately jumped back to the town, and by the time I arrived, she was already holding back sea serpents, the same primeval ones that had attacked us so long ago. With Coronis by her side, she tangled them together like they were pieces of rope and not ancient dragons. It heartened me to see how much easier it was this time. She had grown stronger, and together, they threw them back to the sea.

Manu's head blazed with rune magic as he fought sons of the soil. All around us, there were demons and monsters that thought life would be better with gods. They believed they could go back in the open and send humans quivering and shaking underground as the hunted ones. I was here to make it clear that wouldn't happen. Not ever again.

Except, Thoth had clearly given his minions a few new tricks. I remembered some of the nastier spells he had in the Tablets. Like Nonna, I had barely scratched the surface. There had even been a charm to gain friends, which at first glance seemed sad, but now it felt sinister. How many times had Thoth used it to win gods and supernatural beings to his side? How many more times would he use it?

His soil monsters weren't just throwing clods of dirt anymore; they were flinging spells meant to maim and kill. There were no fewer than fifteen spells to cause "evil sleep." Now I saw what that meant. Where they struck, townspeople fell to the ground, eyes closed, but their bodies twitching and flopping grotesquely.

While it was clearly a coordinated attack between the sirens and the sons of the soil, it didn't feel like the main event. It felt like an advanced guard—one that was meant to probe our defenses or, perhaps, our stomach for fighting.

Okay, I'd make it clear how feisty I felt. My hair flew behind me and rains gathered in my fists. "Enough!" I thundered, releasing the flood that would sweep the demons back into the sea.

The bulky sons of the soil didn't stand a chance against my onslaught. A few demons with scorpion tails clung to trees and the cracks in the cobblestones to avoid the flood. In their defenseless positions, Aurick and Manu easily finished them off.

One of the sons of the soil threw a last rock in his dying moment as the waters took him. I blasted it with destructive mother magic and rose up to my goddess height, towering over the flood waters.

"Tell Thoth to stop sending others to die for him. This is between us," I commanded as I let the demons wash away with my cleansing rains. Coronis cheered behind me as she helped up the last victim of evil sleep.

"That includes you, Daughter of Ares," I said, speaking to an odd shimmer near the fountain.

With a silent look of hatred, Enyo stepped out of her invisibility spell. She was dressed with a bronze cuirass, etched with images of her immortal brothers, Phobos and Deimos. Fear and Panic.

I recalled from my goddess memories that she was just as cowardly as Thoth when it came to actually getting her hands dirty. She thrived off of war and discord, but neither Ares nor his offspring were much good at hand-to-hand combat.

"You are not welcome here," I said. "You have already proven where your allegiances lie."

In response, she made a complicated series of gestures with her hands. I didn't understand what she was doing, but I didn't like it, so I blasted her off the island, her body turning end over end through the air until she landed in the sea with a splash. When I blinked, she was gone.

"Everyone okay?" I asked, turning back and searching the crowd for Aurick. He nodded stoically, his body rippling with restrained violence.

"Good. Let's regroup and discuss potential allies now that we know for certain what Thoth is doing—Manu? Is something wrong?"

Manu looked at me strangely. He took a step and stumbled.

"Manu?" I asked, confused.

"I release you, Ava Falcetti." His voice was rough as if it were a struggle to speak.

"Manu?" I asked again as the mage tumbled to the ground.

Something thick vibrated through my body and then snapped, like a taut string snipped in the middle. Manu had severed our blood oath.

I looked up from his body and finally understood. Enyo had distracted me while a scorpion demon stood over him snarling, readying another stinger-full of death magic with his foot-long tail in attack position.

"No!" I threw myself at him, just as any mother would, and the scorpion's body ripped apart with the force of my anger.

I whirled back to Manu, my former jailor, my enemy, and now, part of my family. Aurick and Coronis already knelt beside him, working frantically on the mage, but I could tell it was a lost cause. Black spiderwebs of poison had already consumed most of his body, stiffening him into a weird contortion.

"I will still honor your oath. I swear to destroy Thoth or die trying," I promised. "Better yet, I plan to kill him."

But his eyes were dark, and the runes on his shaved head had faded to black. His hand floated lifelessly in my receding waters.

Manu was gone.

Aurick entered the taverna, carrying his colleague's body gently as if he were cradling a newborn. My heart clenched with sadness but also pride that Aurick cared so deeply for a man that was constantly undermining him. At the end of it all, they both were trying to achieve the same thing. And it was the very thing that Thoth wanted to break.

Peace.

When Bruno saw the poison-streaked body, his fangs lengthened and hatred tinted his eyes. I knew it wasn't over any great love for Manu; I had been around men in power long enough to see what it was. Another power play. In a world where men like Manu died and cruel creatures like Bruno lived, would anything make sense again?

Bruno pointed his finger at me and tried to corral everyone's attention. "See?" he shrieked. "We can't trust a goddess. She's taking us out one by one. Her sinister game goes even deeper than we can imagine. Return me to power, and we will prevail without her insidious help."

I resisted the urge to let him know even puddles had more depth than him, mostly because I was a ball of rage. Manu died protecting these people, the ultimate sacrifice, and now Bruno wanted to act like he was tricked into helping me. I stalked closer, pulling the hard goddess around me. "You are a little man whose compulsions don't even work anymore. I can sense you trying them now."

The tug immediately ceased, I noted, and I spoke over his next words. "I don't respect you. I think you're a bad leader, and you've maneuvered the community of supernaturals into an untenable position. You've left them too weak to counter actual threats."

"I've handled threats more menacing than a forgotten goddess turned middle-aged woman."

"I'm still speaking," I said smoothly. Bruno slumped back, the power of my being easily overtaking his little vampire tricks. "After this is over, because it will be over and I will prevail, the supernatural community will choose a new Council of Beings. They will clean house from top to bottom and put those who deserve it in positions of power. You will not be on the ballot."

I spun on my heel and walked away before he could say another word. Nonna and Culsans watched impassively, sipping their wine. It was past ten, and most of the townspeople had begun to limp home to try to sleep, but I had a feeling the archons thought life together was too precious to waste it sleeping.

"How are you feeling, Mamma?" Nonna asked, clinking her wine glass to mine.

"Everything. All of the emotions. Devastated, anxious, angry. I'm a blender and all jumbled up."

"Yes, but focus on the hope. It's there and we must nurture it."

"Where's the hope, Nonna?" I asked miserably. "I feel like a failure and a liability. Maybe Bruno is—"

Nonna silenced me with a terrifying look. "Hush."

"But—"

"I said hush, Mamma. Words are talismans, and that bloodsucker could find a wrong in a pile of rights. We figured out plenty from those Tablets. Now, we've just got to figure out how to use it properly."

"Like what? Thoth stripped at least two of the five parts of my soul before, but I don't know how to use that information practically."

Nonna's eyes gleamed. "You leave that to me. I haven't been just playing a strega for centuries. I also picked up a thing or two. But Mamma, what about you? It's safe to say Thoth knows his own book of spells. He might try to strip your soul again."

"You leave that to me," I said grimly, repeating her words.

I caught Luca's eyes and motioned for him to follow me. We took a quick walk near the basilica under the moonlight. The place where it all began. I remembered our last walk on our date. Well, I was on a date. He was on a body-hunting fact-finding mission. Now, it seemed absurd, but it was pretty frightening at the time.

"Tell me what I can do for you, Ava."

"I need your help," I admitted. A wild idea had been forming in the back of my mind ever since we had explored the Tablets again. Maybe a little too wild, but it was worth a shot, and if it had any chance of working, I'd need a necromancer's help. Specifically, Luca's.

"Name it."

"Forget about Siberia and the other necromancers," I said, steeling myself for the possibility that I could die for good along with Thoth if I did this wrong.

Quickly, I ran through a few questions, but he stopped me, already seeing where I was headed. "Yes. Absolutely. Give me a day to gather what I need."

"The time is yours, but hurry."

He caught my arm. "This is only a backup plan, right? I mean, I think I can do it, but I'd prefer not to. I've never caught anything that powerful before. You know that, right?"

"Don't worry too much. If all goes to plan, we'll never need it."

Chapter Twenty-Two

WHILE MY FRIENDS SLEPT, I wandered. My new body didn't need the rest, so I sifted through my memories. I'd avoided it thus far, but it was time. I needed to know what my life was like with Thoth and why I'd run from him. I couldn't keep doing this. I couldn't keep waiting for random attacks as he sussed out my strengths and weaknesses and killed my allies. I needed to get him to truly show himself, and not merely as an illusion. I needed to destroy him, if such a thing was possible.

But first, I needed to understand him.

Closing my eyes, I laid on my bed and let myself sink deeper into my past, deeper into my lives as fated, mortal women, prostitutes, and mother of twins. I sank into the part of my past before I was even the Runaway Goddess. When I was merely Tefnut and in love with Thoth.

The smell of juniper and sandalwood hit me as I remembered.

. . .

I wore a violet amethyst scarab in a gold filigree bracelet. It had two fanged, royal cobras inlaid with jasper, lapis and gold. I wore nothing else. I knew Thoth's eyes would drink me in and his guard would be lowered in his greedy gaze. And for just that moment, I would be able to tell his true mood.

Thoth confused me. He made me want to pick apart his pieces and examine the puzzle one at a time. We sat and talked until my father's rays touched the tips of the waves and sunk into the sea. Our conversations were as varied as the fish leaping beneath us, but there was always a restless energy to him. I could trace the lines of frenzy even as we lay tangled after making love. And then, there was the darker quality simmering beneath the surface. He enjoyed pain. He looked upon it like I looked upon him; a puzzle. Something to be figured out like any other secret. He examined it in his methodical way, but he never could grasp it. It was too abstract.

Years ago, I thought it was interesting to let the young god worship me. I thought I was in control when I made myself interesting to him, and I took his pleasure at my witticisms as breadcrumbs to hoard and devour. I have learned much about men, and more about Thoth, since then. It is through sheer will that we learn anything. Women know much about will. I saw it was what got mortal mothers through hardships, unreliable partners, feasts, and inevitable famines. Although mostly, it was the men in their lives who consistently let them down. Only their wills held them through.

Now, I watched Thoth's thick shoulders rise and fall as he examined my nakedness—this wasn't nudity. He kept his shock of loose, black hair tied back with a gold ribbon, and he appraised me in his silent, knowing way, and found me exactly as he wanted.

With an outstretched hand, my fingers beckoning, we went to my bedchambers, and I let him feel the pain that made his face scrunch in wonder. Sometimes, I thought he might make me pause to jot down a quick note on a particular sensation in the middle of it all, but I never truly hurt him. For all of his swagger and grandeur, Thoth couldn't take true pain, but I don't believe many gods could. They say

Prometheus of the Titans took true pain daily, but I hadn't seen it to confirm. No, the pain I graced upon Thoth was simple and quick, gone in a flash. It was merely a taste, so he could pretend at being mortal.

On those days, there was nothing I enjoyed more than bringing the great god of wisdom to his knees. The rest of the days I filled with my supplicants. I hadn't brought chaos for a long while, but I still brought cleansing rains.

Daily, Thoth stood by Ra's side as my father sat on his throne of stone, flanked by his lions. It was implacable and immoveable as was the word of Ra.

Once, I came looking for my father and found Thoth sitting on the throne. Our love was never the same after that.

With his measured grace and studied approach to all things, even the smallest problems, I thought Thoth would make a good and just king. Until that day when our eyes met and he watched me coolly. He did not jump up guiltily. It wasn't his style. He devoured the most minute details of my facial reaction, and I was sure that's what gave me away.

I had been surprised. He had caught me off-guard because, in that moment, I saw his unbridled, bared ambition.

We still took long walks around the buzz of mortal lives, discussing their various failures and peculiarities. Thoth was much too smart to leave me then. He had to keep me close. But he let more and more of his true nature shine through, as if testing me. Did I have the stomach for what he wanted?

I found that I did not. Yet I found it even harder to leave.

Chapter Twenty-Three

I DIDN'T THINK I was crying, but my door squeaked open, and I touched my wet cheeks. "Ava? Are you okay?" Aurick's voice was soft, and I detected the worry in it.

For all his love, I don't think Thoth ever worried about me. Not as a goddess or as a mortal woman. What would be the point of that? For him, life never ended. I sat up. It didn't end for Aurick either, but here he was, full of worry. For me.

The bed sagged where Aurick sat and reached for me in the dark. "What can I do?"

"Just hold me," I whispered back. "I want to hear you fall asleep."

Aurick laughed softly in the darkness.

"What?" I asked.

"And you thought I had a stalker-serial killer vibes when we first met."

I wanted to roll over, feeling a little miffed, but Aurick gripped me tighter. I couldn't hear the steady pounding of his heartbeat, because he was dead, of course, but there was a quality of aliveness to him that hardly any human I'd ever met could match. I let him snuggle me under his chin and pull us back onto my pillow. Perhaps he was right. If we couldn't joke now, when could we? It was the opposite of lying next to Thoth where every movement must be interpreted and reacted upon. This was bliss.

I might not have needed to physically, but I fell asleep all the same.

Nonna was cutting fresh squares of fig and rosemary focaccia covered in flaky sea salt while Culsans drizzled aged balsamic syrup over the tops. Surreal? You better believe it. She handed me a cup of coffee. "Here you go. Drink up, Mamma."

I glanced at her suspiciously. "It's just coffee, right? No Nonna strega stuff?"

"Not today, but maybe tomorrow," she quipped. Culsans handed me a square, which was still warm from the wood-fired oven. Aurick accepted his own, and the four of us sat down to eat. That morning when I woke up, it wasn't me watching Aurick, but his grinning face staring down over mine.

"Morning, sunshine," he'd kissed me. "Looks like you slept after all."

"I had been feeling comfortable, but now it's creepy."

Aurick laughed and pinned me to the bed, nuzzling my neck and earlobe before kissing every inch of my jaw. We'd already agreed that I wasn't comfortable taking it further with him in my Tefnut body. I wanted my first experience with Aurick to be Ava's or—well, not at all. But I hoped that wasn't the alternative.

"I need to go see Coronis and check-in on her," I said,

swallowing the cup of scalding liquid quickly. I barely registered the pain. "She was so distraught."

Nonna handed me another square of her delicious focaccia. "You should also talk to Mak."

"Why?"

"Yeah, why?" Aurick repeated.

Nonna cackled. "Still jealous, I see, you old bag of bones."

Culsans rolled his eyes in exasperation at Nonna. "We've been discussing the history of god-punishment, and we keep coming back to Ouranos."

"And Mak has the scythe," I finished.

"Exactly."

"But it didn't kill Ouranos. It just cut off his balls."

"Yes, but the scythe helped bring down Ouranos long enough to face punishment. It weakened him, broke his grip on power. If we use a soul-stripping spell on Thoth, it will separate his body and soul, making them both vulnerable. Then we strike with the scythe. It's powerful, chthonic magic on its own."

"From Ouranos's story, we know it can harm a body, but his soul too?"

Nonna had an evil smirk about her. "Has anyone tried hitting an immortal soul with a hammer?"

Now it was Aurick's turn to roll his eyes as he got another cup of espresso. Culsans, however, seriously considered it. "No one's seen Ouranos in thousands of years. Who knows what those sadistic Titans did after they whipped him?"

"You're all forgetting something important," I reminded them. "Getting Thoth close enough to spell him and use the weapon. I doubt he'll come if I call."

"You underestimate his obsession with you," Nonna said.

"That's our play?" I asked, my stomach curling into unpleasant knots. "Draw Thoth into hand-to-hand battle?"

"We'll have the upper hand on Aradia," Nonna replied.

"But we might destroy the island," I protested.

"I hate to admit it," Aurick said, "but Nonna's right. You won't endanger any MILFs here, and I don't think you want that worry on your mind when it comes to a showdown."

"Why does it have to be a showdown between the two sides? I don't want anyone having to fight our battle for us. This is between Thoth and me."

"Not anymore, Mamma," Nonna said simply. "You're our family. So now? It's personal."

"Thanks, Nonna. But let's hope it doesn't come to that."

I left for town and went straight to Marco's Taverna. It smelled like leather and simmering pizza sauce with big handfuls of basil and parsley thrown in for depth. It smelled like home. The bottles of homemade limoncello glowed on the back wall and Marco's lion-like presence put everyone at ease.

Coronis was eating leftover pasta for breakfast as Rosemary sat next to her, coaxing Thessaly to try a bite. There were even helicopter motions and sounds involved.

"*Buongiorno*, Ava," Coronis said, her smile full of life again.

"How is everyone?" I asked. Like a hole in a favorite blanket, it was hard to ignore that our town had taken a hit. As much as it felt like home inside the taverna, things were missing. People were already gone in this war.

"We'll survive. We always do," Coronis said.

Rosemary added, "How are you? Any leads on how to banish or kill Thoth?"

I nodded. "Actually, yes. I need to find Mak."

"He's at his shop, I believe. The faun sisters got him a few jugs of their special oleander mix for his bees to drink and make honey."

I gave them all hugs and thanked them for their help. Thessaly even let me wrap my arms around her. "*Perfecto. Grazie per l'aiuto, sei un angelo! Ciao!*"

I hustled over to Mak's shop and took in the sweet scent of honey as the bell rang over the door. His shelves were still stocked with a thousand varieties of tantalizing flavors and concoctions, and the warm glow from half of them put me in a cozy daze.

Mak sat at the desk, his head bent over pots of delicate, white oleanders. He was wearing a headband with a microscope as he examined the flowers in detail. A gentle buzz emanated from somewhere behind him.

He looked up, his left eye magnified to cartoon levels before taking off his headband. "Hey, Ava. I was just finishing up." He saw my eyes flick to the scythe, and he came around the desk to look at it, too.

"You know," I said. "The last time I was in here, Rosemary had to tell me what the scythe represented. Now, I actually have memories of watching the Titans punish Ouranos."

Mak knit his eyebrows together. "They punished him? That's not in our mythology."

"Right, he basically gets his balls cut off and then fades from history. But the Titans threw a party and invited all of the old gods, including my father Ra and me, to see their spectacle. We watched as they whipped him."

"Did they? That sounds awful."

"It was, but to his credit, Ouranos didn't cry out once. We left before the feast, and it was a big slight, but Ra thought it barbaric. I was glad to go, too. It felt obscene to watch a god endure punishment. I think it made us aware of our limitations, and that made us uncomfortable."

"So what happened to Ouranos after that? Where is he?"

I patted Mak on the back. "It's weird that I suddenly know more than everyone. It's going to take a while to get used to this sensation."

"Enjoy it," Mak said. "You've earned it."

I paused. "Except in this case." I shook my head, trying to remember. "I'm not sure what happened to him. There were rumors that Kronos made a deal with Eastern magicians. All I know is that the scythe is key to breaking an immortal's hold on power."

"By itself?" Mak looked doubtfully at the scythe. "It's powerful, but there's no weapon that can do that alone."

"Agreed. Nonna is also cooking up some strega stuff using a spell from Thoth's own tablets."

"So what's the plan?"

"To find the right combination to do the same to Thoth that he did to me—and that the Titans did to Ouranos. They destroyed him. Of course, it wasn't a true death, but Ouranos has yet to make a comeback. As for Thoth, I'm looking for something a tad more permanent."

Mak gave an involuntary shiver. "You're going to cut his balls off?"

"In a manner of speaking. I believe this weapon can kill his body and hopefully, do some serious damage to his soul as well."

"So you truly need the scythe," Mak said, his eyes tracking to it.

"If that's okay with you."

"Of course. Anything for the cause." Mak went towards it but froze, his fingers inches from the weapon.

"What's wrong?" I asked, studying the flaking bits of dried ichor gleaming in the light of the honey jars.

He smiled with one side of his mouth. "Funnily enough, I didn't remember most of the details of how I came to have this scythe until Coronis and I ate the honey for you. Our memories are not like gods' memories. They're faulty at best, and they become less reliable the further back we go."

"What do you remember?"

"I know my mother gave it to me. She sent me a coded message to find her once the tide seemed to turn for the supernaturals."

"I remember you told me your mom was banished to the island where the scythe was held."

"Ah yes. On our complete failure of a first date."

I gave him a little shoulder bump. "It was always Aurick for me. I'm sorry about that. But you said you wielded this in the Archon Wars?"

"I did, and I just remembered how much it hurts to hold. Only a god can truly wield it, and I am only part-god. It's forged in Gaea's anger and grief, dipped in her molten tears. This is a formidable weapon, and if you think you have a spell from Thoth to add to it, I have complete faith we will prevail."

Mak had a faraway look in his eyes as he remembered his mother. Finally, he sighed. "She was banished with the rest of the gods, but she made me promise to stay on Earth. I fought against my great-grandfather at one point with this scythe. I beat him back with it."

"Apollo," I breathed.

He nodded. "I didn't know gods could look so betrayed. His laurel crown had slipped over his ears, and his shining hair had lost all of its luster, but he was so afraid of the scythe in my hands that he fled. *Sua sponte*."

I translated the Latin. *Of his own accord. Willingly.* I knew Mak was going through a complicated bit of mental gymnastics there. Apollo had ended up displaying only cowardice, which was a hard thing to come to terms with, but self-preservation was a powerful thing.

"You saved the world," I reminded him.

He put a heavy hand on my shoulder. "As you will now, Ava. Please, take the scythe. I choose never to touch it again." Mak went back to his oleanders and bees as I gazed at the heavy weapon.

"Hey Mak?"

"Mm?" he asked, his headband contraption already back on as he fiddled with the lenses.

"You meant heavy figuratively. Didn't you?"

"Unfortunately, yes. If anyone has the strength, though, it's you. Good luck, Ava."

"Right." I steeled myself and met my own eyes in the polished gleam of the handle. Grief and rage. I was familiar with the concepts.

Chapter Twenty-Four

TYRE, Phoenicia
New Kingdom
Tefnut

The daughter of Ra had a certain preternatural look to her. It was in the way she lifted her chin and how she met my gaze without flinching. It must have been many mortal lives since I last visited her for the priestess to look so at ease in my presence. She practically felt divinity in herself now, but I could hardly begrudge her that. Power made mockeries of us all. Perceived power, warranted or not, even more so.

As it was, recent events concerning Thoth and my grandchildren had occurred, and I needed a scribe. For so long, the truth did not matter, only the whims of men. I would not change that reality. I didn't have that power. But I could bear witness to it, in my own way.

"Sit, daughter of Ra."

Mestjet bowed her head to her papyrus, her reed quill in her hand, as I began my tale. "My lord Thoth was untouchable," I began, and we sank together into my memories.

I FUSSED OVER THE TABLE, something I rarely did. The correct wine, the most delicious morsels, the most favorable flowers—everything needed to showcase my own perfection. Any blemishes would reflect on me alone. It was all I had left as the great gods Ra, Shu, and Thoth decided the fate of the throne.

After Set had murdered him, blue-skinned Osiris judged the dead in the Great Below. Isis mourned, but secretly groomed their son Horus to take the throne of the gods. But she was not the only one plotting. Set still lusted for the throne, openly and wantonly. And all of them came to Thoth for advice.

After I caught him upon the throne, Thoth no longer hid his role in their machinations from me. He would give his thoughts while we lounged on cushions of silk in verandas over the Nile. Isis begged for advice on how to help her son, and she had no shame to do it in front of me, either. I was, after all, her grandmother.

Eventually, a contest was decided.

Whichever of the two gods could last underwater the longest in the shape of a hippo would be deemed worthy to sit on the throne of Ra.

I never said it was a good contest.

Smugly, Horus and Set shifted into the great beasts and sank beneath the river in bouquets of bubbles. I couldn't blame Isis for her antsy fingers; I would hardly want my destiny in the hands of a child, either, and certainly not a foolhardy one such as Horus. So Isis magically speared Set with a copper harpoon. No one could say why she missed, except that she did, hitting Horus by mistake. Quickly, she recast and struck Set who emerged from the river in a rage so great that even Isis, Mistress of the Stars, quaked before him and removed the harpoon. Horus emerged next and cut off his mother's head for her betrayal. And still, the winner was undecided.

Thoth paced in our chambers, pulling the great doors shut when I tried to enter, as he conversed with Horus. Finally, it was decided that Thoth would reanimate Isis, and he took her head to a mountain to perform his rituals. Even a beheading couldn't kill an immortal one. In the meantime, Horus took refuge on a mountain and slept.

I begged Thoth to stop playing with the lives of my grandchildren, but I was rebuked as a woman formed from weakness. So I watched, warily, and spoke nothing as Set, disguised as a raincloud, snuck up the mountainside and gouged out Horus's eyes. I spoke nothing about Set entering into Thoth's confidences and asking me for dew drops. I merely simmered, giving him what he wanted, and waited. How Thoth enjoyed toying with their lives as if he had nothing better to do.

Set then proceeded to violate blind Horus and claim ultimate supremacy over his nephew. Except. Except.

Horus had been forewarned, again, and he caught Set's semen with his hands and frantically took his recently reanimated mother into his confidence. Together, they deposited Set's seed in the marshes of the Nile, and caused Horus to ejaculate into a clay pot. I watched as Isis poured it over the leaves of the lettuce that Set so preferred, lettuce being an aphrodisiac to our kind due to its phallic nature. I watched as Set consumed it. I watched as Thoth watched.

Today, the old gods would sit in judgement and decide which of the two should be proclaimed king in place of Ra. Each of the gods thought they knew something special. That they were privy to the utmost truth. Set was smug while Horus could barely contain his grin as the man-child he was. Only I knew what everyone else did not. Only I saw Thoth sitting in the middle of the woven web around our throne.

Set approached first, bowing to Ra, but addressing Thoth as the arbitrator of disputes and fountain of all wisdom. "Let me be awarded the office of ruler, for I have performed the labor of male against him."

Heads swiveled ever so slightly to peer at Horus who reddened at the insult. "All that Set has said is false," he boomed, his voice too loud in his anxiousness. "Let Set's semen be summoned that we may see from where it answers, and my own be summoned that we may see from where it answers."

Gravely, Thoth approached Horus and laid hands on him. "Come out, semen of Set."

The hall waited, breaths held and anticipations rising. Thin as a reed, the semen of Set spoke, not from within Horus, but from the marshes. A long sigh loosed from the crowd as Horus looked down on us in triumph.

Thoth turned to Set, resting hands on him next. "Come out, semen of Horus."

Swirling with the consumed lettuce leaves, it answered from within the depths of Set's stomach, damning Set no matter what trickery he claimed had occurred. The proof was in his body. Thoth demanded it emerge, so it did, slithering out of Set's ear and forming a golden disc on his brow.

The hall of Ra gasped with delight at this grotesque display, and Horus delighted in the pronouncement. He handed the golden disc to Thoth, who gracefully glanced at me before placing it on his own head. I met his gaze with stone eyes and a heart of poison. Was there no one else who saw his thumbprint on every event? Even now, he accepted the gift of the gold disc while Ra willingly crowned Horus king of the gods.

I left, my gown swishing against my legs as I stalked from the festivities. Thoth didn't deign to chase after me. Running after mistresses wasn't a part of his plans, and it might reflect poorly. The hall was set according to my specifications. It was perfection, whether I was here or not. Watching Set and Horus, both of my blood, as well as Osiris and Isis before them, suffer for his games was enough.

I fussed over the table because I was powerless. It was galling, and today I would take no more. At the moment of Thoth's triumph, I would make a mockery of him. I would reject him. I would run again. They say I am quite fast.

He might have helped crown Horus as the new king of the gods, and thus become his confidante, but he would lose me.

A cool breeze flitted across the veranda as I chose a few items to take on my new adventure. It took a while longer than I expected for Thoth to come to me.

Finally, the rosewood door opened. There he stood, blocking out all light as he always had. He had even been able to block out Ra's rays in order to sit so close to the throne.

"You left the feast early."

"I felt ill."

"Surely not from the food. You prepared it yourself."

"Not from the food," I agreed.

Thoth watched me carefully place a few silks in a lion-skin bag. "You have been watching me," he said.

"Only as you watch others."

Thoth exploded. "This is for us!"

"No," I said firmly, locking in on his gaze. "This is for you. I refuse to give you the ultimate honor of having me condone it or stand by your side as you play your sick games."

"So you're leaving."

"I feel chaos bubbling in my veins," I replied. "I am merely letting it out for a walk."

"Where will you go?" he asked, pulling my hands from their packing and gripping them tight enough to hurt.

"Nowhere of your concern."

"I will always find you," Thoth said, the loving words a threat in his voice.

"Good," I said, relishing the word on my tongue. "I look forward to the game."

I let out a snarl of chaos magic, clouding his vision and replacing it with an image of a village on the edge of a little oasis. And then I walked away for a very long time.

It turned out, I didn't even have to run.

· · ·

Mestjet finished recording the story of how I came to be the Wandering Goddess, the Runaway Goddess, the Distant Goddess, and set down her quill. Finally, she appeared sufficiently spooked, although brave enough to ask the obvious.

"Will you kill me now, my lady?"

I raised an eyebrow at her. "So you've heard."

"I don't dream I could continue living, not now that I've seen you and completed your tale. I have served my purpose." Her head was still bowed, and my vulture pectoral glittered on her breast. I traced my fingers along the feathered lines of gems and precious metals before tilting her chin up.

"No, daughter of Ra. You may continue to live. I have decided I would like to see more of the world, and so you are in no danger of revealing my hiding place for I will leave, too. First, you will go to your king, Ramesses, and present him with my texts. Ensure that the priests of Thoth hear my new tale. Then, we'll see what he does with that."

"Right away, my lady," she murmured. "Would you like me to read the last line?"

"Go ahead."

She intoned as the spell came to life on the papyrus, revealing the flaming footprints I left in the sand as I strode away, my shoulders back and my eyes focused ahead.

"I am the fiery Eye of Ra, who went forth as the terrible one, Lady of slaughtering, great of respect, who came into being as the flame of the sunshine."

"I am the Eye of Ra," I repeated. I sat back, a smile at my lips. Now, let us see your move, Thoth. I pictured his rage and it tasted sweet.

Chapter Twenty-Five

THE SCYTHE SAT in a corner of my room, glaring at me. Okay, it was probably my own gaze reflecting back, but just like Mak said, the scythe painted grief and rage on everything it touched. Aurick kept offering to help shoulder the load on the way back to Villa Venus, but I couldn't let him. I refused to do that to him. Now, we just sat exhausted, staring at it.

"I know you're tired, but we should try to read the rest of that spell," Aurick said. "Nonna is working on the first part, but she'll need the rest soon."

I nodded. "Yes, might as well. Time is of the essence." I let out a deep breath and retrieved the Emerald Tablets.

Holding them in my hands felt like holding a nuclear bomb. There was great power here, and it pulsed under my goddess touch, as if sensing I was more than human.

"We're going to get in and get out," I told him, hovering one hand over the whole bundle. "I don't want to give the curses any extra time to mess with us."

Aurick's gaze was heavy on me. "I should take this burden. I'm dead already."

"No. We've already established you can be sent permanently to Nibiru, so don't worry your pretty little head. You just get ready to memorize."

"We still should have at least ten minutes, right?"

I lifted my shoulders and dropped them. "No idea. One would think." I cracked my fingers together and wiggled them over the papyri. "Are you ready?"

"Open Sesame," Aurick replied.

The Tablets melted open under my touch, revealing themselves, but seeming a little pissed about it. I felt an immense resistance yanking and tugging on me.

Thoth's dormant power flowed over me as I searched the script for the spell I'd only seen in begrudging bits and pieces before. Where was the image of Set and the last few memories imprinted from the soul spell?

I let my senses guide my fingers, instinctually slipping past evil sleep spells and love spells, of which there were a disturbingly large number, to find what I wanted. What I needed. It felt like wading through tar, thick and goopy and toxic, and it got worse the further we went through the Tablets. They were on guard against me.

Then came the shadowy remnants of Set and Thoth. There was a tang of ancient magic, metallic and acrid on my tongue.

"Hey. You okay?" Aurick looked up for a bare moment, his eyes crinkled as he scanned the ancient texts.

I shook my head free of the dark thoughts. "Let's just find this spell."

Again, came what felt like light fingertips, brushing and caressing my neck and spine. The curses... They were looking for a way in. They were looking for a way to break me. I clenched my teeth and kept going. I would find what I needed to save Aradia.

The wispy images of Set and Thoth shifted into Set

and Osiris. Blazing red light rained down upon Osiris as Set smiled grimly in front of him. Osiris had one hand around his own throat as he gagged, his other hand reaching for his brother. In their desperate bids for power, my grandchildren grew to hate each other.

I willed the images away and tried to decipher the text. It felt like grabbing at kite strings in a storm. They didn't want to be read. They knew.

I doubled my concentration, like blinders keeping everything dark at bay. My excitement grew as the spell finally revealed itself.

"We can strip his soul. All five parts," I said, stabbing at the words with a finger. "It's never been done before. Set only took one part of Osiris's soul and Thoth only took two of mine. But it's all here. It can be done."

Aurick scanned the spell and committed it to memory as I struggled to maintain the protections around us. Something sinister crept along my scalp, up from my spine. It was more intense than before. Downright bone-chilling.

I was about to close the Tablets when I saw Thoth again, this time with Kronos. Was Thoth the Eastern magician that taught Kronos how to destroy his father? It seemed plausible, for it was exactly the kind of machinations Thoth would have delighted in.

Suddenly, as if spurred on by the image, the intensity of the curses increased tenfold. It felt like I was sinking to the bottom of the ocean, and for the first time since I became Tefnut, my skin grew cold and goosebumped. Even Aurick could feel it. His fingers turned blue and then tinged black.

But I had to press on. I had to go even deeper. I pulled forth everything I had, as Ava and as Tefnut. I combined our forces and sent tendrils forward, looking for the spell Thoth gave Kronos.

"It's fighting me," I gritted out.

"Ava, get out," Aurick shouted. "It's too dangerous."

"But we're so close."

I continued to search the text, as the full force of Thoth's magic bore down on me. I screamed. I could feel my essence being rent apart by curses, my mother magic barely holding me together.

Finally, I felt it, tugging at the end of one of my tendrils. I recognized it by its absence. The only place in the text where nothing existed, which meant it was where the most dangerous spells were hidden. I was sure of it.

I pushed forward, risking everything. I had never encountered anything so strong. I only hoped my protections would be enough.

Slowly, the text appeared, letter by letter. "Oh god. Oh god, oh god, write it down. Write it all down!" I hissed as the pressure grew to titanic proportions. I had twenty, thirty seconds at most. It had to be enough.

Then I heard it. An alarm of sorts buzzing below the hiss of competing magics. "He can feel me," I said suddenly. "He has more than protections embedded here. There's something else."

Suddenly, Thoth's face wavered between the Demotic script and the margins, his face twisted in hatred. I couldn't decide if it was an illusion or a memory. His hands moved in a complicated gesture and his mouth spoke, then his eyes met mine.

"Shit!" I slammed the Tablets shut and flung them across the bed, encircling it in another bubble lest more noxious gas—or something worse—emerged.

Aurick watched it warily, a crease deepening between his eyes. "Ava, what happened?"

My chest was heaving and panic trilled through my fingertips all the way to my toes. "It was him. The here and now him. Thoth knows we have the Tablets and that we're studying them."

"Does he know what we found?"

"I don't think so. Only that we were there."

Aurick's face held steady. I knew his emotions must be rising like mine, but he didn't let it show. "What does that mean?"

"He's mad."

"That's all?"

"No. It means he's coming. Ready or not."

Nonna and Culsans were in the kitchen, brewing up something foul smelling as Tiberius gave advice from his nest by the oven. The three of them looked up when we entered, sensing our dismay.

"Thoth will be here soon," I said, feeling more exhausted than I had yet in my immortal body. I almost felt like Ava again, and that also made me feel nostalgic and sad all at once.

The archons accepted that without a word. Tiberius twitched his tail, clearly remembering his last encounter.

"Did you get the rest of the spell?" Nonna asked, sticking her pinky into the mixture and holding it up to the light. At my nod, she said, "That's all that matters right now. Good job, Mamma."

I reeled off the remaining steps. "Good, good," she kept repeating. "I like it. I'll brew extra. You never know when some may come in handy."

"Having extra soul-stripping potions around doesn't really feel workplace safe," I began, but she stopped me.

"You always need back-ups."

"If you think so," I said, a little dubious. "Nonna, we

found something else. There are two spells you'll need. One to strip his soul and the other to disseminate it."

"Disseminate?" Everyone stared at me.

I nodded grimly. "You can't kill a god. Not really. But what Thoth gave to Kronos was enough to spread Ouranos's soul so thinly, it's been thousands of years and he still hasn't returned. It wasn't the scythe, not alone, anyway. It was this spell. Thoth's masterpiece."

Nonna's eyes glowed. "And you got it?"

"Every last line."

"Well, what are you waiting for? Go, go, go." She shooed me out of the kitchen. "I don't have a second to spare."

I waited in my room, trying not to think about the upcoming battle until, finally, Culsans knocked on the door.

"Nonna's ready," he announced solemnly. "Prepare yourself."

"For what?"

"You'll see."

When I went back into the kitchen, Nonna was naked from head to toe, except for dark vines of ivy wrapped around her head. The attire didn't leave much for the imagination.

"Here," she said, handing me a small vial. "This is the first spell. It will separate his soul from his body, weakening them both."

I jiggled the liquid and it glowed faintly. "I can't believe this is the same curse he used on me."

"It's not. It's more powerful."

"Great. How am I supposed to spell him again?"

"Sprinkle it on him."

"Right."

"Or put it in his wine."

"Do you have any other ideas?"

"Use your water powers to shove it up his nose." Nonna clapped me on the shoulder. "Come on, Momma. You've got to help me to the roof for the last bit."

"Now I know you're joking."

"She's not," Tiberius moaned.

"You want to stand naked on the rooftop in the middle of the day?" I demanded.

"What's the use of getting old if you still care about stuff like that?"

I opened and closed my mouth a few times. What indeed?

Clutching a linen cloth and a cast iron pot full of her potion, we went to the roof together, leaving the male species behind to clean the kitchen. All in all, not the worst set-up in the world.

I put my face near the caldron. "This is the disseminating spell?" I asked, wrinkling my nose and managing to contain a cough. The salve stained the air sharply with its herbs and acrid-sweet smell.

"Yup." Nonna licked her thumb and felt the direction of the breeze. "Don't get too close."

"What's in it?"

"Wild laurel, horehound, and chicory bound together with beeswax."

"That's it? I thought it would be more complicated."

"I didn't mention the last part yet. We'll have to add a sliver of your own soul to activate it."

"Excuse me?"

"It shouldn't hurt too much, and you'll barely miss it."

"Define 'barely'."

Nonna fluttered her hand at me, not answering the question. "Also, don't get comfortable yet. We'll need the scythe."

"Now you tell me."

"Eh, you couldn't have held all of it at once."

"You do know I'm a fantastically powerful goddess now, right?" I said as I climbed back down in search of the scythe. I really did hate holding it. Gaea suffered to create it, and I could feel her sacrifice in every ounce of its weight.

With a sigh, I put my hands on it, wincing as the pain washed over me. I staggered through the window of my room for what I hoped was the last time and hefted it over my shoulder, telling myself I was equal to it. Gently, I placed it on the roof next to the pots. Nonna was still determining the right moment for the ritual when I took another whiff of her creation.

"Have you ever heard of dogs-tooth? It's an herb from Greece."

"Yes. You probably don't remember this, since you would have been mortal at the time, but Zeus exterminated all of the herb, blasting the very roots from the Earth."

"Oh. Thessaly said her father Glaucos consumed it and became immortal. I was just thinking…"

"*Sì*, it would have solved many of our problems, mine and yours. But it is no more. Once its powers were discovered, it was destroyed."

Nonna always knew my mind, and she admonished me. "Stop feeling guilty. I know I was angry, and I lashed out. I'm sorry for that. Just because you get older and wiser doesn't mean you have to be perfect. We're still allowed to make mistakes." The naked old archon grabbed me by the waist and hugged me fiercely. I held on, feeling the pain of mortal emotions bubbling deep within as it replaced my immortal calm.

"I truly am at peace, Mamma. Now let's hurry this up

so I can do things to my mate that would make your hair curl."

"Oh god, Nonna. Seriously?"

She cackled just like old times and began chanting to the midday sun, butt naked. Her voice rose and fell, intoning, "Above and master, god of gods, O dark's disturber, thunder's bringer, whirlwind, Night-flasher, breather-forth of hot and cold, Shaker of rocks, wall-trembler, boiler of the waves, Disturber of the sea's great depth, I am SHE who searched with you the whole world and Found the great Osiris, whom I brought to you chained. I am SHE who joined you in war with the gods. I am SHE who closed the double gates and put to sleep the serpent, who stopped the seas, the streams, the river currents, and wherever you rule this realm. I have been conquered by the gods, I have been thrown face down because of empty wrath. Raise up your friend, I beg you, I implore. Grant me power."[1]

The winds whipped through the trees, and from this height, I saw the wine-dark waves rise up to meet Nonna's words. She bade me to take the scythe and dip it into the potion with her hands still in the air. I lurched over to it, the winds straining at the entire villa while thunder cracked in the blue sky and lightning zagged into the sea. The moment the scythe touched the liquid, everything stilled except for it. It took all of my new-found strength to hold onto the vibrating weapon, apparently because it was drinking a sliver of my soul. I watched in fascination as it absorbed the potion that not even the ancient gods knew. Only Thoth.

We had a fighting chance, I kept telling myself, as the scythe pulled power from me and the potion, adding to its own destructive energy.

Just as I was about to pass out, strong arms held me up

from behind. I looked and there was Aurick, bearing the weight with me. I could feel his chest go rigid as the power channeled through him, but he held onto me, never letting me down. We clung to the scythe, until the last vibrations faded away. It was finished.

Now, we lived or died by this weapon. Now, all I had to do was get close enough to rip out Thoth's rotten soul with holy water and then the scythe would take care of the rest.

"Ok, Tiberius," I said. "You know what to do."

His fur was glossy and his eyes fierce. He gave me a salute and a whisker kiss. "I will be back, my lady. Hopefully with reinforcements."

"You have my full confidence, Tiberius."

Aurick was already at the front door when I got down, holding it open for Nonna and avoiding any semblance of eye contact with everything except a rock outside. I suppressed a giggle.

"C'mon, Aurick," I said. "We need to warn the town."

"Good," he whispered. "I did not want to see what end-of-the world things Nonna and Culsans had planned."

The noises alone escaping from the kitchen were enough to drive us out for the night, but I could hardly begrudge her that. I wanted to do end-of-the-world things with my man, too.

Aurick must have had similar thoughts on his mind. His hand slipped around mine as we walked, our fingers interlaced. His strength helped me carry the scythe, which, I realized, would be my constant companion until Thoth arrived. Even this late in the season, I still got hints of cypress and moss in the salty tang of the wind.

"How are you feeling?" he asked.

"Everything. I'm feeling everything. The only good thing about the situation is that I'm no longer worried about losing Ava to the goddess."

"I wasn't," Aurick said, squeezing tightly. "Not for a moment."

"Well, I was. I was so worried I would lose Ava in the crush of memories. My time as Ava was a drop in the ocean of Tefnut's lifetimes."

"How do you separate them?" he asked.

"They're all there, but they're not actively escaping. I could peel back layers and look if I wanted, but even when I do that, they mostly horrify me," I admitted. "Ava ended up being so much stronger than even I expected. I should have never counted her out."

"I would have really missed Ava," Aurick said seriously. "You mean more than the world to me. Sometimes I look at you and wonder what you see in this old mummy. I have to admit, it's a little disconcerting being the younger man in this situation." He was trying to interject some levity, but I saw the insecurities for what they were. For the first time, probably in his whole existence, he felt inadequate.

I stopped walking and put the scythe down, slipping my other hand in his. For a moment, I let our gazes interlock like grooves in a moving gear. Butterflies danced in my stomach as we held the intimate moment. I hadn't felt butterflies as Tefnut. I'd felt the tug and pull of politics. Here, I felt the tug and pull of Aurick's own gravity, and I wanted to lose myself in it. The heat of his touch was enough to make me have to catch my breath. My body reacted whenever he was near and it had only grown more fierce. How could I make him believe that?

"Aurick, I stay with you because I want to. I don't need to. I can make my own way in life, have my own friends and my own source of income. My validation doesn't come from anyone else. So when I'm with you, it's because I want to be. There is no such thing as fate or destiny. I refuse to believe in soul mates. There is commitment.

There is compromise. There is respect. In that, you find the crux of true love."

"True love," Aurick said softly. "In all of my centuries, I never believed in it. I'd seen too much hate, death, and betrayal. No mortal made it an entire lifetime without experiencing some, if not all, of that. But when you put it so simply and couch it in terms of hard work, I believe in it. Just like I believe in you."

I smiled shyly, my nose wrinkling in pure joy. "I want to do the work with you."

"I can't wait to do the work with you, too," Aurick said. We were still paused at the edge of town, facing each other with our hands clasped in front of us.

"I've never felt so grounded before," he said softly. "Lately, I've spent my afterlife running from one job to the next, never giving myself time to settle in. Now, settling in is all I want to do. I want to experience all of it with you, but I know. I know we can't. I respect that, but I still want you."

Aurick leaned down to kiss my forehead, then the space between my eyes, the tip of my nose, and finally, pressed his lips to mine. I think he would have continued trailing down to kiss my chin before pulling respectfully away, but I held him there, moving closer to mold my body into his.

I had never felt this way with Thoth. With Aurick, I felt seen and accepted. Thoth had too many games to play, and Shu cared more about his status than love.

Neither of us were young or idealistic, but that didn't mean we were fatalistic, either. At this middle stage of our lives, we were realistic. True love was hard freaking work. But there would be beautiful moments that made it all worth it. I was consumed by his gravity. Nothing in this world or the next could make me move, caught like I was. The crazy thing was, I still felt safe, trapped in his orbit.

Aurick put this thumb on my lip and pulled it down to kiss just my bottom lip. Then my top. I threw my arms around his neck and went for broke. My hands slid down his back and over his torso as the taste of him developed on my palate, and, like any good appetizer, it left me hungry for so much more. So it was with complete hangry frustration that I almost howled when he pulled away, a wistful grin playing on his face.

"I know you're a big, strong goddess who could probably toss me like a discus to the mainland, but I want you to know I will guard you with my whole being. Everything I have is yours, Ava Falcetti."

"Thank you," I whispered. "I could toss you. But I wouldn't, just FYI."

He laughed that deep laugh that made me swoon, and too soon, we broke apart and gathered in Marco's Taverna, our unofficial official meeting place. The familiar scents enveloped me, although at Rosemary's yeasty hug, I had a pang of longing for early mornings with my friend, chatting, working dough, gearing up for a Spyro showdown. These were the little things I kept at the forefront of my mind, always. These were the things that mattered the most now. These were the things I would destroy Thoth to keep.

Marco was setting out pizza biancas with olive oil and Parmigiano-Reggiano while the fauns distributed enhanced oleander potions. Donatella started to hand me a glass bottle etched with curling rose vines in blush and gold but immediately jumped back.

"It's the scythe," I told her. "It radiates pain and grief."

"I'll leave the bottle where you can reach it then," she said, keeping her distance.

"Thank you," I accepted her gift and slipped the bottle

into my pocket, right next to the other one. I was becoming quite the walking apothecary.

She took my thanks elegantly. "I believe most have gone to retrieve old weapons we once wielded so we can dip them in oleander potion."

I sized up the faun in her flowery nightdress. She caught me staring and wagged a furry finger. "Our magic is all in a flick of the wrist," she said. Hilda made a circle with her hand and vines sprang up to encase me from head to toe. I barely had time to shred them with a flick of my own.

"Fair enough," I laughed, stepping out of the mulch. "I won't judge a faun by her clothing."

"We don't have long, do we?" Hilda asked.

Supernaturals are always good at reading moods and emotions. A little too good sometimes. "Unfortunately, we do not. That's why we came into town. Thoth sensed me in his Tablets. I'd be surprised if he isn't here sooner rather than later."

Coronis and Thessaly came up, a piece of pizza in both hands. Thessaly's teeth were sharpened points, but she looked at peace after reconciling with her mother and sending her back to Nibiru to begin scouting uninhabited areas where they'd like to live. "When will he come?" she asked.

"Soon."

Coronis set down her half-eaten pizza, her face a tableau of worry. "How long do you think we have? Honestly?"

I gave her the respect she deserved and locked her gaze on mine. "I don't know, but I would suspect a few days at most. I want Rosemary to start gathering the vulnerable townspeople in the basilica soon."

"And me?" Coronis gave me a wry smile. "What am I now?"

"Not exactly vulnerable, but—" I froze, the familiar sensation prickling up my neck.

"Ava?" Coronis asked. "What's wrong?"

I spun on my heel, shouting for Aurick. Coronis's eyes were large and frightened. I didn't want to, but I said, "Thoth is coming. Right now."

Chapter Twenty-Six

"OKAY. AVA'S LOST IT." Marco announced. "She's smiling."

"Thoth spent more time on Aradia than anyone, but it's not his home. It's ours. We know it's secrets, and we're protecting what is most dear to us," I said briskly, getting battle orders ready in my mind. "While this is a little sooner than I expected, it's better than having to attack him in Athens or somewhere in Egypt where he knows the land inside and out. Here, we have the advantage."

Coronis turned an ashen color as she tried to shift into a crow before remembering her wings were plucked. "No, don't worry about me. Worry about Thoth," she waved me off.

"I would feel better if you helped Rosemary," I told her.

Thessaly snarled. "Coronis is smart enough to know her limitations. Trust her as she trusts you."

I blinked. Twice. "You're right. Sorry, Coronis. Can you and Thessaly get everyone by the fountain who wants to fight? Tell everyone else to find a safe spot to ride out the battle. No one fights who doesn't want to, okay?"

Coronis gave me a hug, while Thessaly saluted me with her pizza before swallowing it in one slick bite and flipping into a doorway. Marco was busy arguing with Rosemary about going somewhere safe, but I could feel Thoth getting closer and closer.

I ran outside, scanning the sky. Aurick followed close behind. Together, we waited, feeling his presence gaining speed, spearing downward like a bird of prey with the cruel curve of his beak, a fatal tip aimed upon our land. There was no time left to hope this would come another day. It was here.

"You ready?" Aurick asked.

"As I'll ever be."

Within moments, Aradia lined up behind me, weapons in hand. They had oleanders wrapped around swords that were still coated in dust. Some had painted their faces in ancient displays of apotropaic images. They were snarling medusa faces, winged pegasi, and fanged griffins. All looked serious and prepared to defend their homeland.

The only sounds in the square were the bees droning around Mak and the creaking of bronze shields and swords as the supernaturals shifted. I wanted to pace and wring out this nervous energy, but instead I had to assure everyone else it would be fine. I even had to start to believe it. I lifted my chin and steadied my spine, pulling my shoulders back. Aradia needed me in this moment as much as I needed her. Time to prove my worth.

"Aradia, thank you for standing with me," I shouted, turning to face the crowd. Mae the maened had wild eyes and was brandishing a thyrsus. Mino had changed from his usual debonair attire into Spartan armor with arm greaves and a wicked looking bronze sword. Jo wore an evening dress with a slit up to her mid-thigh and a determined expression. Spyro stood next to her, aiming a steel-plated dildo like a spear, and I knew it would do its own weird amount of damage.

I steadied my voice. "You took me in when I didn't have a home. You became more than my friends. You became my family. I may look different and I may even look like an old, hated enemy, but I'm still Ava. I will protect this island with my entire body and soul, and I will not let it come to harm. You may think Thoth is scary and strong because he is a god, but he has nothing compared to what we have. We have Aradia."

"For Aradia!" everyone shouted.

Over and over, we banged our weapons and stomped on the ground. We embodied our old island and imbued it with our love. Nothing, not even a god, could stand against us.

For a moment, we waited, all of our hearts pounding in rhythm. Fingers clenched white around weapons as feet and claws and hoofs pawed at the ground.

And then?

He was there in the flesh. A god strode from the edge of town, fire and brimstone tornadoes forming all around him, their rotten-egg stench emanating across the square. I conjured a cloud of rain, dousing the flames only to reveal hordes of demons that had joined his cause. They snarled, spiked tails and razor-blade backs inching closer.

Thoth paused and held up a fist. They clanged to attention. Enyo, Daughter of Ares, stopped a few feet behind him out of respect, dressed in etched bronze armor made especially for her. Her upper lip curled as she stared at our ragtag army, probably thinking of all the destruction she would bring down upon them. Little did she know that Nonna's spells of victory were already soaking through our bodies or that death draughts dripped from our swords. We were outnumbered, but we had a chance.

Time moved differently in Nibiru. It also moved differently at the beginning of a battle. Seconds stretched to eternity as both sides merely stared. After all the running and illusions, there were no more tricks. No more near escapes.

For the first time in thousands of years, both of us stood before each other, wrapped in our full divinity. I hadn't been Tefnut since that day in the lemon-scented room when I dared to let him find me and dared to look unbidden inside his precious tablets. He hadn't been Thoth since that day on the battlefield. Every time he came to me since was nothing but an illusion.

Until now.

I could feel every pebble beneath my feet, and my skin tingled in the salted breeze of Aradia. None of my fear showed, although it simmered just below the surface. Thoth would sense it if I let my face twitch or licked my dried lips, and he would pounce on it like a cat with a plaything. Besides, any fear I felt wasn't for me. This could go on forever. No, my fear was for everyone assembled behind me.

So I made the first move as the square burned in his presence. His ancient names rolled off my tongue, both familiar and foreign at once. "Great Lord of Books, Reckoner of Time. Do you come in peace or strife? What is your aim?"

Thoth laughed, a deep rumbling sound that made all the animals on the island flee in leaps and bounds. His voice was silky and altogether too smooth. "That is your decision, my love."

Despite being in the shade of the cypress and walnut

trees, his face shone. His skin was like molded bronze, something not of this world. A beautiful evil.

Aurick bristled next to me. Thankfully, he wasn't some macho alpha male who had to sprint headfirst into battle at any perceived slight. He was much too smart for that. He was also confident in my ability to hold my own.

I raised my chin a millimeter, just enough that Thoth would notice. "Whether in strife or peace, everything you touch turns to ash. I guess it hardly matters which."

"You think so lowly of me?"

"I do."

"Your life will forever be entwined with mine. Our games will extend to eternity long after these beasts are gone."

His words bruised an already tender spot. Sometimes I wondered who I was without him. So much of my existence was tied to his. And if I succeeded in actually destroying him? What would I become?

Thoth swept his arm along the crowd of townspeople behind me, and I threw out a protective barrier. I guess I didn't freaking care what I would be when Thoth was gone. At least my people would be free of him. I couldn't fail them now.

The god laughed at my efforts. For once, I didn't let it get to me. "Our games will conclude today," I said softly.

He gave me mother magic when he cursed me with twins, and he didn't even realize it. That was his fatal mistake. Mother magic, as I had learned at Rosemary's Bakery, wasn't merely nurturing. It was also protective, like a mother lifting a car off of her child, or even destructive, like a mother striking down a would-be assailant and fiercely defending her babies. It grew strongest when she needed to protect her family.

I threw a stab of magic at Thoth, barely giving him

time to deflect it before shooting two, then three more. "You have no idea what you created. By turning me into a *lupa*, you gave me dual functions. By giving me children, you created a ferocious beast. By ignoring me, you created a monster. A monster specifically designed to hunt you, Thoth. I have learned throughout the centuries, and it has all led to this moment. I have learned what has worked and what hasn't. And now?" I paused, twirling the scythe like a baton and enjoying his discomfort at seeing such a dangerous weapon in my hands. "Now, I will destroy you."

Although he tried not to show it, for the first time, I saw fear dot his eyes. Not the illusion of fear that he had used to trick me before, but true fear. It distorted his handsome features, making him seem vulnerable for a tiny second.

"I have control of my god magic. I have control of my mother magic. I have friends who help me willingly. I am more formidable than you ever imagined, Thoth."

"Bravado gets you nowhere, my love."

"For once, I agree with you." All around us, creatures from myth threatened our land with their fear and hatred. Thoth had brought sons of the soil, water serpents, and all manners of demons. He'd recruited sphinxes that had been locked away under the Arch and other creatures that believed they would be better served with Thoth in charge. Cold rains poured from my fingers, and then I unleashed a flood.

Thoth's magic flared around him, but I wasn't aiming for him. A large swath of his army instantly disappeared, washed to the ocean in a river of cries and screams.

"Seems your army just got smaller," I said. "You never were good at thinking about others." I intended to keep him off-centered, out of control, mistaken. I remembered how Thoth had been wounded and nearly been taken prisoner and banished in the last battle of the Archon Wars. It wasn't impossible. The impossible was getting close enough to strip his soul and slash it with an angry scythe. And this time, I wouldn't save him.

Thoth forced a smile. "They were always dispensable, my love."

I rolled my eyes in a very Ava way. "Yeah, I'm sure your troops love hearing that."

Electricity crepitated from Thoth's fingers, and I threw up another bubble of protection. His spell sizzled out.

"Everyone here is under my protection. You will not harm them."

"My intentions are good. I wouldn't dream of doing harm."

I almost barked a laugh at that. "No wonder you brought an army of monsters with you, then."

"Merely protection, in case I was poorly received."

"And what would you consider a good reception?"

Thoth smiled. His true intentions about to come through. "You, by my side."

"You have always asked for the impossible."

"Yet, I still always get what I want."

"Not this time." Once again, water droplets formed at my fingers, but Thoth didn't wait for me to decimate his army a second time. Despite his blustering, he needed them to do his dirty work.

The air exploded with chaos, the magic he stole from me. It winged through the air like a terrifying flock of birds descending on Aradia. I met it with my own dampening magic, and it arrived as a flock of butterflies. Effective, but it was merely a distraction. Already, Thoth's army was on top of us.

All around, the sounds of battle rang out. I saw Aurick flinging grave goods and stabbing demons with dual daggers. Mak stood on top of the fountain in the middle of the square. Diseases gushed from his hands, sickly green and sinking to the ground in curls like dry ice. A harbinger of death, he let loose dark green clouds that raced outward, enveloping our attackers and stopping demons in their tracks as they dropped to their knees in agony, boils and pus oozing from sores that erupted on their skin. Mak's face was grim. Clearly, it took a lot of courage to use the side of him that wasn't healing but destroying. The cost was written all over his body language.

A horde of baby sphinxes galloped from the east, forming the cutest attack flank I'd ever seen. They batted at each other like it was a game and they were playing rough and tumble.

"He did not," I cried, angry at the Council for keeping them locked up and at Thoth for using them. "Rosemary," I shouted. "Can you guide the babies to safety somewhere?"

Rosemary's face dropped at the sight. "Oh, how could he?" she cried. "Yes, I'll herd them to the basilica and lock them up there. They should be safe until..." she cut off.

"It will be over and we will win," I said, finishing her sentence. "Get them to safety and protect them."

She gulped. "I know it. I believe it. *Buona fortuna*, Ava." She whirled in the air on her wings, beckoning and luring the playing babies away from the battle.

With both Rosemary and the baby sphinxes taken care of, I turned my attention to Tiberius. He was back from his mission, riding on the helmet of the Knight as the Italian housewife spat curses at demons. The Knight's chest was puffed with pride as he led a contingent of ghosts from Nibiru into battle, just as he had in his crusading glory days. With his sights set on sons of the soil, he lifted his sword and yelled, "You cannot hide, you liver-bellied infidels! For glory! For Ava! For Aradia!"

The ghosts spread across the town like a white sheet, and my heart swelled to see my girl gang fighting alongside them. Queen Dido looked particularly sublime as she rode on the back of a decaying elephant in rotten armor and—

My breath hitched.

"Mestjet."

The ghost of Mestjet changed course, speeding toward me, and bowed. "My lady."

"What are you doing here?" I asked.

"I didn't want to move on without seeing you one more time. Then, this blustering Knight came and said we could fight the gods and that you were leading the charge."

"I'm sorry I murdered you."

Mestjet blinked her owlish eyes. "You made me who I am. Why would you not have the power to take it away?"

"Because gods shouldn't have that power."

"And so you are fighting it now. Goodbye, my lady. I do not think we shall meet again."

"You will drink the waters of Lethe?"

"You gave me more time than I could have ever imagined. I am ready." Mestjet drifted into a clump of manticore demons and sank her fingers into their scales. Scarab beetles emerged, crawling and disintegrating each beast, one by one. It was gruesome to watch. No wonder I had chosen her to protect my story.

When I looked back up, Thoth had disappeared. The scythe screamed hatred in my hands, but I couldn't let it fall. Nor could I use it, it seemed. All I needed was a moment in his presence. A quick spell and a good swipe. That's all it would take, but now I realized my folly. My magic was more powerful, but Kronos had something I didn't have. The element of surprise.

More and more demons marched into Aradia, spurred on by false promises from Thoth. Chimeras shrieked, spitting flames that caught Jo's evening dress on fire. I quickly put it out, leaving a smoking hole where lace had once been. Jo gave me a nod of thanks and spread her arms over a clump of lion-snake monsters. They immediately began licking their privates while Spyro laughed delightedly.

I saw Mino charge into a group of sons of the soil and lift one up by his waist. He roared, bouncing it over his head before using him as a bowling ball. The rest of the demons fell like pins. As they went down, they cracked and shattered, howling, but it was completely drowned out by Mino's victory roar. He looked a tad manic, like something you'd see in a dark labyrinth seconds before you realized you were lost and not going to make it out alive. I merely gave him a thumbs up and watched approvingly as he pulled apart another demon like cheesy bread, throwing his body parts at scorpion shifters.

Everywhere I turned, the ebbs and flows of the battle raged. I watched from the fountain, using my goddess senses to intervene wherever I saw someone in need, blasting a demon here, sending some protective magic there. It kept my friends safe and the tide turned in our favor, but it wasn't a long term solution. I needed to find Thoth, but he was cloaking himself, letting others do the fighting for him. If I wanted to end this thing, I needed to find the heart. I needed to destroy him.

The sky darkened with his armies as winged creatures descended on our shores. As they came, they clanged swords and cutlasses on their shields. I unleashed a storm. It raged around us like a hurricane, spinning and turning and sweeping the demon armies from the sky. They disappeared in the fog and rain, swallowed by the raging ocean below.

I strained with the effort, and still, more came. Each battalion that I destroyed was instantly replaced. There were a lot more than I'd ever dreamed would side with Thoth. Pretty soon, they were going to tighten the noose around our town and pop off our heads. We were too outnumbered, out-demoned, out-sworded.

Mak took out a good portion of their ranks with disease in truly gruesome fashion, the boils exploding from their scaled faces in bursts of pus, but the rest of the townspeople were barely making a dent in Thoth's forces. Most had to fight them one-by-one, and that would never succeed with such a large horde.

Then, my heart dropped. In the distance, I saw a fleet of ships that stretched from one horizon to the other. Their bows cut the waves, and their red sails strained in the wind, painted with images of… seals?

Coronis appeared around the corner, a huge grin on her face, which didn't exactly feel appropriate for our situation.

"I always told you the selkies know how to throw a party, Ava!" she laughed, delighted.

"What are they doing here?" I asked, stabbing the blunt end of the scythe into a manticore's orbital region. It howled and fell backwards.

"They're here to stop Thoth. He's a threat to every supernatural being. Always count on a selkie to bring a crowd."

I stared at Coronis.

"You should probably kill the storm now and let them enter Aradia."

"Oh, right." I released the energy flowing from my chest,

and instantly, the air around us calmed. More and more ships were sailing into the harbor where my own ferry from the mainland had failed to dock months ago. It felt like years ago. "I can't believe you got the call out to other supernaturals."

Coronis nodded. "Of course. Thoth doesn't have the monopoly on gathering the troops. Remember? Trust your friends. Now, your circle of friends just got a whole lot larger."

I looked closer with my enhanced eyesight. Some of the ships were full of djinn with sails of fanged black snakes, while others held what I could have sworn were leprechauns. My breath hitched and my heart swelled when I realized that one of the boats was full of neon-haired sirens, hissing and holding bone shards they'd sharpened into weapons. They'd decided to help after all.

My heart felt fierce, beating a drum of gratitude and faith. I even recognized the stone statues flying over the ships. The gargoyles and grotesques had joined the fray! They landed on the island before the others, and my old friend from Washington University held up her clawed, stone fist from afar as her mouth opened wide and she did truly unholy things to a manticore.

"Coronis, I could kiss you. Have Thessaly meet the ships at the cliffs. She and the rest of the sirens can slip past the hordes of demons with their liminal tricks. Then, we'll crunch the attackers between our two forces like a rotten nut."

She saluted me. "Go. Find Thoth. Kick his sad ass to oblivion."

"I intend to, but Coronis? If the tides begin to turn, don't let the townspeople play hero. There's always another day, another strategy. The Archon Wars were centuries long. We can draw it out if we need to."

"We won't need to," she said confidently and ran to tell Thessaly the good news.

I would have felt better about our plan if it wasn't for the fact that I still couldn't find Thoth. That made me uneasy. Striding around, swinging a soul-stealing scythe wasn't exactly helping matters. Even if Thoth didn't know about Nonna's potion pulsing secretly on the blade, he was at least aware of its history. He kept out of sight and hid like the coward he was.

Anger blistered through me like a burn. He was content to let his army and that demigoddess fight his battles, saving his strength.

For the next hour, we played a cat and mouse game, racing and fleeing along cobblestoned roads between village houses and down the dirt lane to Nonna's villa and back. Evening turned to night, and not once did I get within striking distance. Not even close.

Thoth twisted in and out of streets, sometimes emerging to taunt me with bursts of chaos that destroyed whole sections of Aradia. Each time, he beckoned with a grin, only to wisp away again, nothing but a scent of something wrong in the places where he used to be. He let me glimpse him occasionally, only to make me angry so I would misstep.

I could bring a flood that would destroy cities. I could surround the helpless with protections worthy of motherhood. I could give really bad bunions. Yet, I couldn't defeat Thoth.

Somehow, he always won.

Constant attacks lit up the sky with bursts of spells and pearly ghosts rampaging the demons. I knew this could continue for days, if not weeks.

If not centuries.

I couldn't let that happen. Eventually, Aradia would be

damaged beyond repair, a graveyard of the second great war with the gods, and eventually, my friends would die. I couldn't protect them forever. I knew what I had to do. It was the only way to stop the carnage, to keep things from getting out of control.

Slowly, I took the two vials out of my pocket and placed a drop of the separation spell into the concentrated oleander. Then I put the Faun's bottle back in my pocket and returned to the square, sweeping aside demons along the way. When I got to the fountain, I dropped my hands to my side and lifted my chin to the sky.

"I've missed our game, my love," I called clearly and loudly, my voice echoing throughout the island.

Chapter Twenty-Seven

I HATED the way the townspeople turned and looked at me in horror, as if I were betraying them. But there was only one way I could get Thoth alone and on my own terms. I had to make my gambit.

This wild seed in my chest would not fail. Despite every setback and failure, I would not let it die. I went from suffocating in a small pot in St. Louis—the endless office meetings where I was practically invisible to my own husband—to suddenly getting replanted in exotic, loamy soil. Over the last few months, these people had nurtured my soul. Now, I must cling to them. Thoth would not uproot me. Not when I finally found my home.

I hoped they believed in me, too.

Thoth appeared at the edge of the square, his soldiers parting to let him pass. He kept a respectable distance between us. I had done enough to make him wary of me in a way he'd never experienced before. Maybe that was my mistake, because now I needed him to trust me.

"I think we've had enough of this," I called as the angry din of battle slowly dissipated.

"Have we? I know how much you like to run."

"I see that you are mad," I acknowledged. "Does that make us even? You did, after all, curse me for thousands of years."

"Which is what in the lifespan of an immortal?" he grinned.

I met his smile with my mouth closed so he couldn't see my gritted teeth. "What indeed?"

"What do you propose, Tefnut?"

"I want to parlay."

"Drop the scythe, then. We can't do that with you holding that monstrosity."

Instantly, I let it fall from my fingers. It clanged to the paver stones, and everyone stared. I looked at no one, not Thoth or even Aurick.

No one, but Luca.

He nodded once, although his face was pained. Without a backward glance, I walked down the familiar road to Villa Venus. The night air was crisp, the sea breeze salted and comforting. If I closed my eyes, I could nearly pretend I was walking back from apertivo hour.

Thoth rippled into view, and we walked side-by-side, testing nothing except the silence. It wasn't until we reached the villa that we paused.

"It's a bit rundown for your style," Thoth said, breaking the silence as he stared at the rusted iron railings and peeling paint.

"I've changed. Evolved."

Thoth's laugh was mirthless. "The gods are unchanging. That is what makes us great. Mortals count on our unwavering personalities. It is the only constant in an unstable world."

"Funny. I don't see it that way."

"How else could you? When mortals die, they are

happy to know some things are immune to death. In a world of constant flux, it is comforting to know some things never change," Thoth said lightly.

"To stay in place is death. For the gods, it's a living death, but it's still death."

"And running is the answer? I think you were just running so you didn't have to face your problems."

I paused. "You think I ran to escape? You know what I think? I think this slow death is why you love your games. My grandchildren's lives were pieces on a board to move and play, because what else was there? And still, you watch death coolly, as if counting on your abacus. One. Two. Three. One thousand. Two thousand. Three thousand. Lives are mere beads to move back and forth. They mean nothing to you."

Thoth kept his voice neutral, but I could sense resentment bristling off of him. "You were once that way. I think you'll find you still are, deep down."

"As I said. I've changed. You should try it sometime."

"I have adverse reactions to change."

"So why do you still want me if you hate who I've become?" I asked.

Thoth held the villa's door open for me. I stepped inside first and led him to the kitchen table, that sacred place where so much of my new life had transpired. Thoth stopped me from sitting down, taking my wrist and engulfing it completely. He swirled me into him, our bodies touching at every point, and lifted my chin. He smelled like the desert sands I knew and loved as Tefnut. He smelled like a homecoming. But it was all sour to me now, nothing more than spoiled milk.

"Call it personal growth. Weren't you always begging me to grow? Well, I love you despite who you've become."

"You made me this way," I reminded him. "I would

have never become Ava without you." I felt Thoth's growing desire between us, but I still had to wait. He so enjoyed our banter.

"What are you planning, Tefnut?" he asked, his gaze boring into mine.

Aurick's bone dagger was heavy on my conscience. I called it forward and stabbed Thoth in his lower belly.

"Tefnut, come now. You must be more sneaky than that," Thoth admonished, turning the dagger into a lotus blossom with a flick of his wrist before it gutted him. "And here you are, pretending to have grown and changed. I can't say that I'm terribly disappointed. I liked the old Tefnut." He caught the flower by its stem and tucked it behind my ear, its sweet fragrance perfuming the air between us.

"It was worth a try. Would you expect any less?" I let him kiss the line of my jaw, his delight at our renewed game evident in the predatory way he held both my wrists together with only one of his hands. This was the Tefnut he knew. This was the Tefnut he trusted.

He pushed me against the table, taking my neck in his other palm as he continued to kiss me and whisper in my ear. Games like this were catnip to a god who craved power.

"Was this moment not worth all of those years of pain?" he asked, putting his weight against me.

"If I said yes?" I gasped as he bit my earlobe. "What then? Would our life go back to the way it was before?"

"Is that so horrible? We would rule this realm together."

I repulsed him with a protective bubble of mother magic and watched Thoth stagger back a step. I hadn't hit him hard, just enough to make him think I hadn't given up too easily. I straightened my blouse and fluffed my hair as

Thoth watched, a hungry look on his face. We were paused in this dance, a dance so new no one knew the steps.

I faced away from him. "All this fighting has made me thirsty. I'm going to make some tea."

Thoth came to watch, his body overshadowing me at every turn. He was silent as I pulled out the Faun's vial and emptied it into a sauce pan. It was amusing in some way. I may have laughed at the town hall meeting, but here I was, inviting Thoth to a tea time.

"Why oleander?" he asked as I set two cups in blue and white porcelain saucers.

"I've grown a taste for it since my return. Isn't it more delicious knowing that no other beings could possibly drink this and survive but us?" I gestured to the chair. "Sit down. Have some tea. There's honey in the cabinet and milk in the glass jar."

"Please," he gestured. "Make ours both."

I bent my head and reached for the honey, taking the wooden honeycomb dipper and drizzling Mak's sweet concoction into our cups. Next, I poured just a drop of milk and watched the white cloud swirl. "I don't think it's a proper tea, but I like milk and honey."

Thoth was silent. He couldn't figure out this new game, but he was curious enough to let me continue. Gods of wisdom are easy in that way. They always hunger for knowledge.

I held my warm cup to my lips and blew curls of steam off of it. Thoth scooted his toward me, and I gave a small laugh. "I see. Here, I'll take a drink from both if that makes you feel better."

Thoth sat back, his arms crossed against his chest. "Just a precaution, you know."

"Of course." I drank the tea, an explosion of apricots and vanilla bursting on my tongue while I waited a beat, my heart hammering into my chest. "I think this is where I pretend to gag and foam at the mouth in hysterics and then say, 'Gotcha!'"

"Is it?"

"Yes, and then we laugh and make love and go back to our games. Come now, you don't look amused."

Thoth took my cup, leaving his for me, and sniffed it, detecting only the sweetness of the oleander. "I must admit I'm curious why you're so intent on this tea."

I went back for seconds, drinking tiny sips and waiting. "I enjoy a cup of tea with my conversations now. Did you think it would take so many lifetimes before I came back to you?" I asked, genuinely curious.

Thoth raised his glass in salute and took a tentative sip, enjoying himself now. He wanted to believe me, craved it as the truth so much that he let himself believe, if only for a mouthful. And all I needed for my plan to work was a taste.

"I could never read you very well. It's what drew me to you. The way you changed your mind like a desert storm, mercurial on the drafts of a cloud."

"Yes, I always was hard for you to read. Even now."

"What do you mean?" he asked, a smile at his lips.

"See, Thoth, I used all those overt attacks so you wouldn't suspect the real one. I know how much you appreciate subtlety."

"Are you suggesting this tea will somehow harm me?"

"I am."

"Come now. You said yourself that oleander could not kill us."

"And it wouldn't. By itself."

Thoth scoffed. "There is nothing you could put in this tea that could harm a god."

I laughed at his confidence, galling him further.

Thoth restrained from slamming his fist or shouting or anything of the kind. It wasn't like him. Instead, he used his words. "There is only one master magician in this world, one god powerful enough to destroy another god, and I am here before you. Enjoying my tea."

"Correct, my once-love. But you practically brewed this tea yourself."

The cup froze inches from Thoth's lips. "You found the spell? But that's impossible."

No Thoth, I found both.

"Not alone, of course. Your protections were too strong. But that's something you never understood: even gods are stronger with help. You never did like to rely on others."

"This tea will kill you, too," Thoth strangled out. Naked shock shone on his face as the poison worked its way down his body, and we began to convulse. His fingers curled in agony around the cup, shattering it instantly before he dropped to his knees, his shoulders hunched and shaking. I could barely answer at this point with the poison working its way down my own body.

His mouth gaped open, and although his cheek was pressed to the floor and his eyes rolled in the back of his head in his death throes, Thoth began chanting the spell I knew he would, the one to throw our bodies back into stasis to fight this out another day, another century, another lifetime, before the oleander completed its deadly duty. Chaos curled around his fingers, inky black and dangerous.

But this time, I was ready.

Chapter Twenty-Eight

ONE DID NOT SUCCEED in besting a god. Not easily. And not without paying a heavy price.

At his moment of triumph, I had eluded him, and now Thoth resembled an ibis snapping at a fish in the Nile only to land in the mouth of a hippo. In his surprise, his face transformed with rage and true fear as he grappled for life.

Despite my own weakened state, I let mother magic wrap around his body in a protective bubble, this time not worried about my inability to summon chaos magic or even Tefnut's water magic. That's one of the reasons I failed before on the field of battle. I wasn't relying on what truly made me powerful: being a mother and trusting in my friends to help me.

My mother magic acted like a shield around him, warding off any attempts to practice magic on his own body, and right now, he needed it. Nonna's potion had stripped our souls, ripping it from our bodies, leaving them weakened and exposed. The enhanced oleander tea did the rest, killing our bodies so we could never return. It was agony. I was raw, exposed to the world for what I truly was.

It felt as if my very skin was being flayed in long strips from my body.

As we lay dying, I locked eyes with Thoth. "Take courage," I told him as we convulsed on the familiar, terracotta floor of this beloved kitchen, and his fingers reached for mine in his moment of death. "No one is immortal."

In the pain, I saw his face unguarded, as bare and raw as my own, and there, I found the Thoth I had once loved. It was startling to see traces of that love reflected back. It had been overshadowed so many times by my anger.

"The game is not over. It will never be over," he choked out. But my vision was turning to stars and a black void, as vast as the universe, waiting to fold me into its arms.

As my eyesight grew dim, I saw Luca standing over my convulsing body, holding a moss-covered jar. And then I saw nothing.

When I woke, my left hip ached and I had under-boob sweat. Even my teeth hurt from the migraine pulsing at my brain. If there was any doubt, I was definitely in my old body. I was Ava. Ava Falcetti. Except now, I was complete. All of my memories were here, my entire being inside of this immortal soul. Tefnut's body was killed forever, along with Thoth's. But he was right about one thing; this wasn't over.

Shakily, I got to my elbows as strong arms swooped down to lift me.

"Ava?"

I blinked at the hovering figure, bringing it into focus. It was Luca, his face twisted in worry. "I could kill you," he said.

"Too late." I whispered, my voice rough after my time

in stasis. "Nonna, Mak, and the faun sisters already took care of that."

He frowned. Okay. So, it was too soon for murder jokes.

"You promised me this was only a back-up," he said, accusation and relief suffusing his voice in equal measure.

I swallowed a few times. "I had complete faith in your necromancing abilities. How did you catch it?"

Luca was still staring at me in wonder, the moss jar broken in two on the ground by the bed. "I lured it here with powerful bait. Something I knew you'd love." He pointed to the remnants of a biscotti and a small glass of espresso sprawled near the glass shards.

"You caught my goddess soul in your weird glass jar with caffeine and sweets? What if that didn't work?"

Luca smiled, quite proud of himself. "There's a little pasta in there, too. Nonna prepared it herself."

"Of course."

Who was I kidding. He could have used dirt from Aradia and it would have worked. This island was in my bones.

Luca shook his head, wonder in his voice. "Isn't it funny? I never would have been able to strip your soul the first time I tried because it wasn't fully there."

"We've had one hell of a ride together, huh?" I was struggling to remember. There was something else I still had to do. A promise I had to keep.

Luca pointed to the scythe in the corner. "Aurick brought it. He said you needed it, and he made me promise to give it to you the moment you woke up."

"Thank you. I do need it still," I said, gratitude pouring through my body for my mummy, a man capable of carrying a god's burden. "Is he gone?"

"Yes, he—Hey, what are you doing? You shouldn't be out of bed."

"Luca," I said desperately, taking him by the shoulders and shoving him toward the front door. "You have to go now, too. Leave the house and don't come back."

"What?"

I grabbed the scythe. It weighed about a thousand pounds in my mortal hands, but I didn't have a choice. While our godly bodies may have been destroyed by that cursed tea, our immortal souls hadn't been touched. Mine lived in Ava, but Thoth's was still out there. Hopefully, still disoriented and trapped in the protective bubble I had thrown around him. Hopefully, it would buy me enough time.

Luca helped me remove the rest of the mummy linens around my legs, and I shakily ran to the kitchen, hanging onto the scythe with every ounce of my mortal strength. "Luca, I'm serious. You have to get out of here. This thing isn't done. Not yet."

"I won't leave you."

"You've done your part. Let me finish this."

We entered the kitchen together and found Thoth's soul exactly where I left it, next to the kitchen table. It banged against the walls of my protective barrier, which was weakening fast against the onslaught. All around us, braids of garlic and dried peperoncini and bottles of limoncello shook from the force of his soul's desperation. I calculated seconds before it broke free.

Luca's face paled as he finally understood the gravity of the situation.

"Luca, stop being noble and run," I shouted.

A crack formed, and Thoth's soul slithered through it like a great snake emerging from its den. It was charcoal and cobalt, pulsing in its reckless desire to find something to inhabit. I charged, swiping the blade at the swirling cloud, but Thoth's soul was quicker than my human reflexes. It was also quicker than Luca.

"No!" I screamed.

Before Luca could get to the door, the roiling orb sunk into his chest. He staggered, his eyes blinking milky white, then cosmic black, before becoming Thoth's shade of brown. He reached for me, but Luca must have fought back because the next blink was his, and my friend stared miserably at me.

"I'm sorry, Ava. I wasn't quick enough."

"Luca, no," I choked, my hand going to my mouth as a sob escaped. This wasn't part of the plan. This was the opposite of the plan. "No, it was me. I wasn't quick enough."

But Luca was already looking beyond me. "Do it quickly before he takes complete control," he managed to get out, his movements already becoming jerky.

"If I use the scythe on you, it will disseminate your soul, too. You won't go to the afterlife. You won't go anywhere. You will be nothing."

Luca's face blanched as he realized what that meant, but he gritted his teeth, a tear rolling down his face. "Ava, do it before he gets away. Do it now!"

"No! I refuse."

Looking frantically around, I jumped to the table where my cup of lukewarm tea was still half-drank and shoved it at Luca. "You have to drink the tea to expel both of your souls. It will kill your body, but your soul will survive."

Luca looked like he was about to protest, but his face was going through a series of emotions and not all of them were his. He was fighting Thoth, but for how much longer?

I massaged open his jaw and poured the tea down his

throat. Luca fought me, gagging the whole time, but I also saw him swallow.

It didn't take long for him to die, his body only convulsing once before his eyes rolled in the back of his head and he collapsed. His face took on a bucolic quality. "Gianna?" he called as he died with a smile and his wife's name on his lips.

A glittering orb escaped from Luca's open mouth. It was small and fragile looking. I let it pass, waiting for my prey. Sweat made my grip on the scythe precarious, but I clung to it, ignoring every ache and pain and bit of grief threatening to weigh me down.

Then, Thoth's soul exploded out, black and threatening. He didn't wait around, instead winging toward the open window.

I didn't think. I ran.

I had no more tea, no more potions. I had only the scythe. I couldn't let Thoth inhabit anyone else. I had to destroy him forever.

I was good at running.

The scythe dragged on the ground behind me, slithering Stygian rivers of decay where it touched. But I refused to believe my muscles would stop working. They didn't have a choice. There, at the edge of town, just like I asked him, Aurick waited. His face was a mask of worry until he saw me. I watched as it lit up with the same beautiful moment of relief that Luca had upon seeing his wife, my name on his lips, asking if I was okay.

"Get away from him!" I screamed at Thoth's soul, terror making me preternaturally fast.

I surged a bubble of magic to throw Aurick to the side and slashed the massive golden weapon with the strength and quickness of a goddess. And this time, I hit the mark.

·

Thoth's soul made a retching, screeching noise as it detonated into glittering nothingness. A crackle began in the center of my chest, radiating to my fingers and toes. It coated me in a warmth that equaled Ra's rays. In rapid fire moments, I saw all of the women I had ever been and their fated twins. I saw my twins now as they staggered on the sidewalk near their dorm room, strong magic wrapping them in a cocoon for just a moment, just the quickest of moments, so that they couldn't be sure it had actually happened. And I gasped.

The curse was broken.

The world was a pregnant silence, a loud buzzing in my ears as the dust settled. I let the scythe fall from my fingertips.

Already, Aurick was bounding back to his feet to get to me.

"Luca," I gasped.

Aurick's face dropped in understanding, and together, we sprinted back to the villa. My fingers trembled as I opened the door and saw the bodies. Thoth, Tefnut, and Luca. The orb that was Luca's soul was gone. Ignoring the others, I sank to Luca's body. His eyes had a glassy, glazed look, yet I still reached to shut them.

Aurick went to the ground with me, rocking me in his arms as I cried. He didn't try to tell me it was okay or make anything better. He just held me and smoothed back my hair and let me cry. His body was real and solid against mine.

"I wasn't quick enough," I kept repeating. "I just wasn't quick enough."

"I know, Ava. My beautiful Ava, I know," Aurick murmured into my hair.

I blew my nose and kept sobbing, a tsunami of emotions rolling over me like waves, one relentlessly after another. Much like Thoth, in my own moment of triumph, I had ultimately failed.

And then I saw it. The orb had returned, and it was growing into a familiar shape. Luca was a ghost. I jumped to my feet in awe. "Luca?"

He stared at his body, unblinking. I let him process, but after a few moments, he looked over at me. "Thank you, Ava."

"I'm so sorry, Luca," I cried, fat tears rolling down my cheeks, "I wanted to save you."

"I didn't need saving."

"Everyone needs saving sometimes, Luca. Even you, even me."

"Yes, but in this case, I am glad to give my life in true service. I want you to know that."

And then, another orb appeared, colliding into Luca like two atoms. The only thing to ease the burn of Luca's loss was to watch his face as the second orb took its form. It was Gianna, somehow feeling his death. She spun wildly into his arms, before turning to me. "Ava, you're alive! I'm glad, but don't you have an island to save?"

Chapter Twenty-Nine

WE DRAGGED Thoth's body to the town square, his head flopping grotesquely on the ground as we tugged. All around us, the battle still raged, and I had to bellow to be heard. Many ignored me still, perhaps not realizing it was actually me without Tefnut's commanding presence.

"Give me your bone dagger," I said suddenly.

"You have it."

I remembered Thoth turning it into a flower. It must still be in Tefnut's hair. "Uh, right. We should talk about that later. In the meantime, do you have anything else sharp?"

He pulled out a misericorde and handed it to me. I swallowed at its thinness. This wasn't going to be pretty. I tugged at it.

Aurick wouldn't let go. His eyes met mine over the weapon. "You can't be serious."

I tugged again, harder. "How come you always know exactly what I'm thinking?" I complained. "Do you read minds?"

"Of course not—hey!"

"Oh, don't be so dramatic. It was just a little shock," I said, getting ready to hack away at Thoth's neck with the misericorde, which was now in my hand. While beheading him might not have mattered, what with his soul disseminated forever, it felt poetic. Also, it was effective as hell for grabbing people's attention.

"Enough!" I cried, holding Thoth's head like an ancient trophy. It was totally gross, but as Tefnut, I'd done worse.

Those around stopped fighting and stared at me. "Thoth is dead. Whatever orders he gave you died with him."

Soon, the news was yelled from every rooftop as weapons dropped to the ground and supernaturals came to peer at the once great god. Even in death, they kept their distance.

A few demons, however, still hadn't stopped, spurred on by Enyo. She stood at the head of her battalion giving orders. "What will it be, Daughter of Ares?" I shouted. "Peace or strife?"

She turned to me and advanced, ready to test my strength as Ava. Big mistake. She made it three steps before I turned the ground around her into mud with Tefnut's water magic, and then forced the dormant seeds to sprout with my mother magic. Instantly, she was entangled in vines of wisteria and bundles of flowers. Where she once stood was now a beautiful garden. I bound her so tightly, she had trouble dropping her spear in surrender, so I went closer and plucked it away for her. With a great *snap*, I broke it over my knee and threw the pieces to the ground. In short order, the rest of Thoth's army followed suit.

Now that everyone was on the same page, I gestured to Thoth's body. "The gods are defeated once again. Whatever Thoth promised you will not be delivered, but I can promise you that everyone who abides by the original accords will be treated with decency and respect. There will be no more warring."

Everyone was too stunned to move, shocked by the sudden end to the battle, so I clapped my hands together. "C'mon people. Gather your weapons and tend to your wounded. If you came here with Thoth, you have until sunrise to leave Aradia and never return, or I will turn you all into our latest garden sculptures. You'll be our living displays."

That did the trick. All around me demons and supernaturals worked together in teams, clearing the field, making a makeshift field hospital by the basilica. I shielded my eyes from the early morning light and searched for two ghosts. I found them giggling by the cliff where Luca used to sit when he thought about his wife. Except this time, she was there next to him.

Gianna gave me a little wave before turning her complete attention back to Luca. He lifted her up, twirling her around as they knitted themselves together in a kiss. I raised my hand back as they disappeared, arm in arm.

Luca was gone. But he had found Gianna.

Aurick came up behind me, wrapping his arms around my shoulders and bending his head down to mine. "Are you okay?"

I nodded. "I will be. I'm glad they're together. Maybe she'll show him the ropes for a while before drinking from the River Lethe." While Luca's death wasn't the outcome I wanted, he was at peace and I had to accept that.

"Look at what else you did. I've never seen supernaturals work together so well."

"Maybe we should threaten them with flower power more often."

He smiled. "Can you believe you killed a god?"

"Don't shortchange me now," I poked him, although it barely made a dent in his chest. "I also killed Tefnut. That's two for the bingo card."

Aurick raised both eyebrows. "So she's separate from you?"

I thought for a moment. "No, she's in me, but she's no longer the dominant one. Thoth thought that after centuries without divine power, as nothing more than a weak mortal woman, I would beg to be reinstated as Tefnut. He didn't realize how much I'd enjoy it."

"He underestimated you in every life, Ava."

"You don't."

He pushed back a tendril of my sweaty, snotty hair. "I try not to, at least." Aurick lifted me up the rest of the way, holding me tightly. "But I still do."

I turned to him, staring deeply into his gold speckled eyes. "What do you mean?"

"I've always believed in you. How could I not? You're incredible, and yet every time I think we've reached your limits and you can't possibly go further, you always find a way forward."

I leaned back into his arms with a chuckle and elbowed him in the ribs. "Yeah, I've never been good at respecting my limits, as Ava or as a goddess."

Aurick snuggled my ear. "Ava will always be a goddess in my eyes."

Epilogue

ACANTHA LIFTED her nose and wrinkled it, but she held her tongue. I considered it growth. The water world I had created in Nibiru for the sirens was nowhere near as grand as their old masterpiece, but it was leagues better than before. Sunning rocks dotted the watery depths, and fish crested the surface to catch bugs. Their scales shimmered rainbow colors in the artificial light that Mak had helped create. He much preferred using Apollo's beneficial powers over his plague powers, but I couldn't blame him. I probably would have tried to forget those existed, too.

We'd also gotten the faun sisters to create kelp forests and reedy beaches, and Mino graciously donated pottery to replace their skull bowls.

The sirens had a real community now, including a few supernaturals who decided to join them—once there were assurances the sirens didn't have their power of deadly song. Old fears died hard. Mae the maenad even decided to move there permanently in order to play her frenzied music and start a dance club.

Grandmother made her way to my side, holding a beautifully painted kylix drinking cup with dolphins frolicking on the lip. She raised the glass and drank to my health.

"What will you do now, goddess?"

"Ava will do," I reminded her for the tenth time. "Am I truly a goddess without the body or the pantheon?"

"Aye, of course. You will always have a woman's innate sense of the goddess divine. Whether you are a real one or not."

I raised my own glass to her. "In that case, I'm going to live. I won't have to look over my shoulder, worry about my sons, or even think about Thoth. I'm going to enjoy the hell out of my early retirement."

"Sounds almost sinful to be so happy."

"Doesn't it?" I let out a contented sigh. "Moving to Aradia feels borderline illegal."

"Thessaly seems to enjoy that island, too. Although she'll have to come back regularly to Nibiru."

"To visit her family?"

Grandmother laughed. "To negate the curse. You weakened the rock's pull, but it wasn't your curse to undo. She must return here regularly to stay strong, to resist it. Although in time, perhaps she will be excited to see her family as well."

"That's the only solution?" I asked, watching Thessaly scowl at being splashed. Vigorously, she rubbed her arms like she'd been dunked in ice. "It seems unfair we truly can't break Poseidon's curse. I felt mine break the moment I disseminated Thoth's soul."

Grandmother stooped to pick up a clear, turquoise stone and turned it over in her palm. "It's good penance for her. And, it will give her a chance to reconnect with Acantha every week."

I turned to Grandmother with a narrow-eyed look. "Every week, eh?"

She skipped the stone across the water three, four, five, six times. A small shrug lifted her shoulders once. "Thereabouts."

I examined my own stone. It was a brilliant pink in the palm of my hand, and I held it up to let Mak's fabricated sunlight radiate through. "You know if Thessaly finds out she doesn't have to come back that often to keep the curse at bay, she'll probably find a way to curse you."

"She'll have to get up a lot earlier in the morning to figure out how to best me, my dear Ava."

I laughed. "Of that, I have no doubt."

For a moment, we watched a scene that hadn't been possible for centuries. Sirens laughed as they did full body strokes and squirted each other with water like kids in a pool. Most kept their distance from Thessaly, but I had a feeling she was fine with that. She didn't need their acknowledgement to know she'd done a good job. The more she visited, the more used to her they'd get. I also had no doubt that Grandmother knew exactly what she was doing by telling her granddaughter to come home so often. Thessaly was plain lucky to have her. She was also lucky to have Coronis, who had already pledged to go with her whenever she needed the extra support.

A single tear escaped Grandmother's eye as she saw Acantha pat her daughter's shoulder. She caught the tear on her wrinkled fingertip and stared at it in wonder as it shimmered in the sunlight.

"Did you know you could do that?" I asked.

She shook her head, and her voice was soft when she spoke. "Thank you, Ava. Thank you."

I smiled. "You come whenever you want to Aradia. If you need anything, I will be there." We embraced, and I watched Grandmother hobble to where Acantha was, holding her tear high for all to see.

It was lovely, but I couldn't linger on the scene. I had some important business to attend to. Aurick had been in St. Louis for the last round of voting for a new head of the Council of Beings, and I was looking forward to seeing him again. As the only surviving high-level employee that had battled Thoth, he had made it through each round with ease. As proud as I was, I selfishly did not want Aurick to take the position and live in St. Louis. I loved the guy, but that was asking a bit much. I mean, I'd do it. Probably.

Either way, I was antsy to hear the news.

Thessaly helped me ascend from Nibiru, and I quickly made my way from her old rock to Villa Venus. Aurick was waiting, his hand slung casually in his jean pockets. He wore a fitted button-down tucked in, and his golden-reddish locks were brushed back from his forehead. He had a half-smile, wry and full of promises.

My breath caught at the sight of my mummy. After all we'd been through together, he still made my heart flutter. Although, it more flopped from one side of my ribcage to the other in a rather ungraceful somersault.

With a grin, I ran and surged into his arms, my hips only aching a little as I wrapped my legs around his waist and nuzzled against his neck.

"That's quite the hello," he joked as I finally hopped down.

"I think that's the appropriate greeting when one sees the brand new head of the Council of Beings," I replied.

"If that's what this is about, you'll be disappointed."

I gave him a funny look. "What happened? You were a shoo-in. It was almost obscene how easy that vote was going to be."

He shrugged, a smile at the corner of his mouth.

"Aurick! Tell me what happened." I yelled, a tiny rain cloud forming over his head.

"Okay, okay, woman. Enough with the threats. You know how I convinced a few people from Aradia to participate for variety?"

I nodded, waiting.

"I threw Mak's name in the ring. At first, it was to annoy him, but I made such a convincing argument, the only supernatural that didn't want Mak to be head of the Council was Mak. Well, and I guess Spyro, too. He thought bribing the voters with sex toys really would work."

"So, Mak is the new head?"

He winked. "Of course. His dismay was drowned out by everyone's cheers. They even managed to drown out Spyro's objections. He'd brought 'Free the Willy' bumper stickers."

"He has what it takes," I said confidently. "Mak, that is. Plague magic to protect us, healing magic, and a general desire not to be in power. All good things to have in a leader."

"My thoughts exactly. I think he's just sad to leave Aradia full-time."

"I don't blame him." Without an archon powering the bone daggers under the Arch, we'd quickly realized astral travel was about to become a thing of the past. "I've lived in both places, and while St. Louis has its charms, nothing beats an Italian apertivo hour."

Aurick smiled. "Well, fortunately he doesn't have to choose."

"Nonna figured it out?"

Aurick beckoned me to the villa. "She cooked up a

strega spell mixed with archon blood. As long as he doesn't misplace his dagger or let you borrow it, Mak can come back for his morning espresso whenever he wants."

"That was hardly my fault," I objected while Aurick grinned. We settled into an easy stride together, and I sighed. "Well, I'm glad for him. Espresso really isn't the same anywhere outside of Italy."

The sun was setting over Aradia as the spring began to take hold of our island. Without Thoth under the basilica or Nonna feeding it her archon blood, Aradia had gone from a feral creature to a gorgeous island. Ghosts still roamed, and Marco still roared, but there were no sudden sinkholes or rumbling earthquakes. Supernaturals weren't called to her shores. Nonna figured even MILF tourists and ferries could potentially start to make a comeback. If the townspeople wanted it, of course. By the way Jo and Spyro's eyes lit up, I had a feeling we'd have to call a few more town hall meetings to set ground rules before that happened.

For now, I was enjoying the scent of almond blossoms and orange blossoms, the riot of bright red poppies poking their heads up, and the carpet of clover that covered Nonna's yard. Blue flax and yellow mustard blanketed the grove of walnut trees, too, although I couldn't call it Nonna's anymore. Nonna was about to leave for her last great adventure, and soon it would be all mine.

Aurick slipped his arm over my shoulders, and I inhaled his woodsmoke and desert scent. It sent shivers coursing down my belly that ended as a tingle in my toes. His power eddied and swirled around him, pressing and surging in its rawness against me. His gaze almost made me buckle under its intensity, but I would gladly fall if only to let him catch me.

I ran my hands down his chest, feeling how decadent it was to finally let myself indulge in the thundering of my heart and the flutter of butterflies in my stomach. Finally, I didn't have to worry about curses or rogue gods or anything else.

Aurick bent his lips to mine, hovering just an inch apart, enjoying the anticipation. Then he swooped down and tugged at my bottom lip with his teeth. It was a teaser, a taste of more to come. And then, swift and demanding, he stole my breath and my kisses.

Surprised by his sudden passion, as quick as a summer thunderstorm, I opened my mouth and let him in, moaning only the tiniest bit as the butterflies became outright beasts, slamming against my body in constant spits of heat.

Aurick led me back to the empty villa, his eyes dark and stormy. I barely noticed as we entered or as I tripped over a piece of firewood by the oven. Aurick caught me, and he refused to put me down, so I let him carry me, his fingers and hard abdomen burning desire into every place we touched. We were near my bedroom, but I couldn't tell much else. I only had eyes for what I wanted to do to him.

Feverishly, I yanked at his buttons, popping them off, one-by-one. They pinged to the ground as our eyes stayed locked on each other. My skin scorched to the touch, but Aurick's hands worked their relentless rhythm, sliding my shirt over my head and pulling me onto his lap. I leaned into him, wrapping my arms and legs around his torso. With shallow breaths, I strained to keep myself from rocking against him as he unclasped my bra.

"Remember Venice?" I whispered, begging myself for at least a good showing of self-control. Five minutes, at least.

Aurick dragged a finger in a winding trail from the hollow of my neck to my belly button. He met my heated gaze. "I remember how beautiful the moonlight complimented your pearls and how bright your eyes were when you realized what we were really doing. But mostly, I remember the way you gasped when I did this." He lifted a breast with his palm and ran his tongue in a circle. My stomach knotted and excitement roared through me as he nipped and kissed and moved to my other breast. A few dew drops accidentally erupted over us and they steamed where they touched my overheated skin. Aurick blinked as they curled away. With a growl, he suddenly stood, bringing me with him.

In one fluid twist, he threw me on the mattress and straddled me, only allowing my hands to pull down his jeans before locking them to the bed with his own. "I've been dreaming of doing this to you since the moment you tried to use your magic on me in the lemon grove. It was so..."

"Reckless?" I suggested, although my voice was hoarse and wanton. *Keep it together, woman!*

"Feisty. Brave. Fearless." For each word, he kissed a different part of me, lingering below and inhaling my scent deeply. His tongue dipped and explored, ferocious as the wild creature he was. I moaned and scrabbled at the bed, but he gave no mercy. "I want all of you, all of the time," he said when he could speak again.

I wriggled my wrists, but Aurick held me firm. "Do you trust me?"

I could only nod, my back writhing as his hands moved across my skin. His first thrust made my eyes squeeze shut and my hands tremble. I folded them together across his back as he thrust again.

We moved in concert, the heat spreading between us. I

felt full but never sated as my chest rose and fell against his. There were moments when the brightness and intensity of what he was doing blinded me, and I could only hold on tighter.

As he pulled out and thrust at a new angle, I couldn't help but crash the houseplant that was on my dresser and use its vines to hold him in place. His look of shock was quickly replaced with delight, as this time, I held Aurick down to wring out every last drop of pleasure from our bodies. The entire villa shook and I vaguely heard something else break when we reached the top.

And then, slowly, we came down together. Aurick held me tightly, kissing my scalp with lingering passion and a little bit of teeth as I could feel him wanting me again. "I think we broke a picture frame," he murmured.

"Worth it."

"No, Ava. You're worth it. I love every single bit of you. I adore what you've helped me become."

"Someone who stays?"

"Right next to you," he promised. "Here I will want for nothing."

"How are you like this? I've lived a thousand lives and still don't know the right things to say. You've never pushed me in any way. You never told me what I should do or look at me in disapproval when I did things my way. Even when I was terrified of becoming Tefnut or hurting others, you were there with nothing more than your constant belief in me. I just…"

Aurick scooped me under his arm, his body hard against mine. "I would feed you Imo's from my own hand if it made you happy, Ava. I might even take a bite myself."

"You promise?" I laughed, trailing a finger down his chest to spool over his stomach.

"On my death, I promise."

He worshipped me again, and I fell asleep in his arms with a smile. When we woke up, tangled together, the comforting promise of Sunday dinner wrapped us in a warm hug. I indulged in a yawn and stretched to get out all of the kinks.

"Hello," I said, my voice still husky.

"Hello," he replied with a kiss. "Did you sleep well?"

"Like an uncursed baby. Did you watch me the whole time?"

"Basically. I should have known you'd snore."

"I do not!"

"Don't worry. They were these cute little exhalations. It took me a few minutes to figure out what it was even." He kissed the tip of my nose and the little cupid's bow above my lip before sweeping me into a more passionate embrace so that I had no time to protest or even gasp for air before he took me under again. It was delicious to do nothing but spend the morning and afternoon in bed, and I couldn't help reaching up to cup my hand around his jaw every so often and stare into his laughing, quick eyes, just to remind myself this was real. This was now.

Eventually, we heard the banging of pots and pans in the kitchen. "Guess we should get up," Aurick said wistfully, his eyes burning again as I slid out of bed to put on… something. My mind was mush. He stopped my fumbling and kissed the hollow at the base of my neck. "But I can't wait to sneak away later tonight and taste you again," he promised.

I shivered at his touch, grinning like a fool.

When we finally made it out of the bedroom, Nonna was giving Culsans a taste of something at the stove. His tongue licked the spoon as his tail slid around her waist and drew her close. I knew where this was headed. I cleared my throat jet-level loud, but just the sight of them made it difficult, and tears pricked at my eyes.

Nonna turned around, her hair in place and her makeup on point. She wore a smile to stun the sun, but I still continued to well up. They'd be leaving today.

Forever.

Nonna saw my face and tsked. "Come now, Mamma. You can't feel guilty for the rest of your life. It's entirely too long for that, now that you've got your immortal soul. Imagine the emotional baggage. You'd never be allowed on a plane again."

"Want to bet?" I blubbered.

"What good does guilt do?" she chided. "Anyway, this isn't a true death. As archons, we will wander the realms of the dead and explore until we pass on. Culsans always was trying to talk me into it, but I preferred Earth to Nibiru." She gave me a small kiss on either cheek. "My centuries alone have disabused me of that notion. I don't want to spend any more time here if it's without him. I'd much rather go to the next great unknown. Does that take some of the sting away?"

"Sting? Your death isn't a sting. It's the whole damn hornet's nest."

Nonna laughed. "Don't forget, time moves differently in Nibiru. I've still got life left in these old bones, and I intend to use it. Hold on a second, Mamma. I've got something for you." She plucked the wooden spoon from the pot of sauce and, bowing gravely, handed her favorite utensil to me, still dripping bolognese. "I bequeath my Sunday sauce spoon to you. *Vivi bene, ama molto, ridi spesso.* Live well, love much, laugh often, my beautiful Mamma."

I clutched it with all of my strength, which, admittedly, wasn't as much as Tefnut had, but it was more than enough for this life. "Thank you, Nonna. For everything."

The archons bowed together, but the solemn moment was broken by Culsans tickling Nonna with the fuzzy end of his tail and causing her to sneeze and swear like a siren.

"Let's get this food outside," I suggested, grabbing a blue-checkered tablecloth and matching linens. Aurick took the candlesticks and white porcelain plates, and we headed outside.

In no time, Marco and Rosemary arrived, carrying loaves of roasted garlic ciabatta and caramelized eggplant focaccia. There was pillowy gnocchi drowning in homemade tomato sauce and broiled in the open hearth with fresh mozzarella and fragrant basil. Culsans carried out the bubbling pot of bolognese with bucatini pasta and tons of flaked Parmigiano-Reggiano arranged in a teepee on top. There were salads, and long cutting boards filled with prosciutto and melon, candied walnuts, cured meats, dollops of whipped 'nduja ricotta, and oozing balls of burrata.

I loved eating in the open air, smelling the perfume of the spring flowers and the salt of the sea. I had to practically pinch myself to remind me that this was real. Aradia was my forever home.

I FaceTimed the twins before the rest of the guests arrived. Josh answered and I could see Jacob waving behind him. Already, they looked better. They wore big smiles, and there wasn't an undercurrent of tension like the last time I'd seen them. Thoth's curse had been broken for good.

"Hey, Mom. Oh, is that focaccia? Did Nonna make it?" Josh asked, trying to look around me at the laden table.

Jacob licked his lips. "I love her cooking. Do you think she'd mail us a care package?"

"I can cook and mail, too, you know."

"Right, but there's just something special about a real-life nonna making real-life Italian food."

I bit back a laugh at their earnest faces and smiled. "I think she could be persuaded. But Nonna's going to be taking a long trip with her boyfriend, so don't get too used to it. How's classes? Do you need any money re-loaded on your dining room cards?"

"Nope," Jacob said. "We're all good. Hey, did you hear that Marla broke up with Dad? In Italy!"

I blinked. "I might have heard something about that."

Jacob was still hooting. "Italy! Can you believe it?"

"It feels like some sort of divine justice," Josh added while I worked to school my face to neutral. Boy, did it.

"I'm sure she had her reasons," I said.

"Yeah. He's a jerk."

"Boys," I said half-heartedly. "He's still your father, and you still deserve a relationship with him. Just have one on your terms."

They rolled their eyes and sighed in rhythm. "Fine, Mom. You're probably right."

I loved to see it.

"When can we come visit you in Italy again?" they asked.

"How about you come stay at the villa for part of your summer break? You'll be starting jobs soon enough, so we'll have to make a lifetime of memories during this one summer in Italy. I'll book your flights."

"We can't wait."

I blew them kisses and hung up. My heart was light for the most part. In fact, I hadn't felt this good in centuries.

"How were the twins?" Aurick asked.

"Great. Really, truly great. I can't wait for them to come this summer."

"It will be nice to get to know them better," Aurick agreed, giving me a decadent kiss.

Soon, the ghosts arrived, including Piero and his lute, the Knight, and the sixteenth century housewife. The faun sisters brought beautiful bouquets of jasmine, violets, and even a few oleander flowers in honor of the battle. Jo had taken over Mae's wine and cheese shop, and she had Mino carrying a crate of Tuscan red and white wine. Rosemary put a huge tray of Tiramisu in the kitchen for later.

"With Mae gone, we can have chocolate in the bakery again," she said when she came outside. "You will be coming back to work, won't you, Ava?"

"Don't worry. I'll be at the bakery bright and early. I haven't eaten a sugary *bomboloni* in at least two weeks. That's a criminal offense in my book."

"*Perfecto*. Oh, I can't wait to dive into some of my chocolate books. Did you know Jacques Torres once ate a bonbon right out of my hand?" She sighed with a faraway look in her eyes and fluffed up her crazy frizz. "This hand right here."

"Wow, I can't wait to try this famous bonbon."

"Pretty soon, I'll have the whole town eating out of the palm of my hand!" she joked as she slid into her chair between Marco and Coronis. Thessaly was on Coronis's other side while I took my place between her and Aurick. Coronis was showing off her new, glossy black feathers that were growing back where Thoth had plucked them.

As soon as everyone had their wine glasses filled, Tiberius started squeaking, "Speech, speech!"

Everyone took up the chant.

"Fine, fine," I said. I picked up my wine glass and stood, and for a second, I merely took in the scene. All of my friends were gathered, the food smelled delicious, the air was perfect, and the wine was delectable. I wanted for nothing. Aurick squeezed my hand and shot me a little wink.

With a deep breath, I clinked my wine glass with the side of my fork. "Thank you for coming tonight. It's an honor to be around good friends and eat good food. First, I want to have a moment of silence for those we've lost."

We bowed our hands and waited. After a few moments, we all poured out a bit of wine for Luca and then Manu.

I cleared my throat and gave people a minute to gather themselves. "I also want to have a moment for those we will lose. Nonna and Culsans, will you please stand so we can adore you one last time?"

Laughing good-naturedly, they rose next. Nonna took a few deep bows while Culsans shook his head with a smile. We toasted and wished them a long vacation through Nibiru.

"Can you get messages to us through Tiberius?" I asked hopefully.

Tiberius wiggled his whiskers. "Yes, absolutely. They just can't risk coming back. The journey would age them terribly."

"Don't worry, Mamma. You're not quite rid of my impeccable advice yet."

I merely held up my glass to her again. "This is where I'm supposed to say something profound," I choked out, barely able to speak from the well of emotions. "Yet all that comes to my heart is thank you. Thank you for taking me in and thank you for being there for me through everything."

Aurick smoothly put his hand over mine while I sat. "I think it's time to eat," he said.

Piero broke into song, and Nonna threatened to hunt him down in Nibiru if he continued, so he carefully put away his lute. It was a wise decision. I doubted she was joking.

After that, the waves breaking on the cliff became our soundtrack as we talked and ate. We indulged in all of the best possible ways, and throughout, I caught myself watching the love and knowing in the marrow of my bones how lucky I was.

Too soon, the sun set and we only had the light of the moon over the ocean and the flickering candles to light our way. Too soon, Nonna came over to say goodbye.

As I embraced her, she whispered in my ear, "*Chi si volta, e chi si gira, sempre a casa va finire.* On Aradia, no matter where you go, you will always end up at home."

Culsans came up behind her, bowing low. "Goodbye, Ava. I am so glad I got to meet this version of you."

After that, they only had eyes for each other, but I called softly, "Take care of one other," and wiped away tears as they disappeared into the walnut grove under a beam of moonlight, hands clasped.

Aurick gently wrapped his arms around me, pulling me into that perfect spot where I fit without effort. "It's going to be weird not having Nonna around." he said.

I agreed. "But I'm excited for her. I've never seen her so happy."

"What about you?" Aurick asked, kissing the tender spot below my ear.

For his answer, I gave him a sly smile, a kiss, and a naughty little finger crook as I beckoned him back to the villa.

And you know what? Forget centuries. I hadn't felt this good, ever.

La Fine.

What a ride! Thank you for punching your ticket to Aradia one last time. It's been an emotional year as I conceived, wrote, and birthed this series. As I neared the end, it became even more so. My writing buddy of over fourteen years, my cat Loki (yes, before Marvel was cool), suddenly became sick. One day, he was jumping on counters, snuggling all afternoon on my lap, and sneaking food from the kids. And the next? He collapsed from the cancer eating his stomach that we didn't even know he had.

While I wrote significant death scenes in this book, I was also facing the death of one of the most constant presences in my life. Loki was a unique cat, and our bond was beyond weird. He hated all humanity, except for me and my two kids, and happily chased away any friends or family who ever had the courage to visit. But he was also needy and spent a solid chunk of his day on me or following me. It's odd to have this void of loneliness without him wrapped in my lap or curled over my shoulders like a fashionable fur stole. Yes, he was literally so needy, he'd taken to riding around my shoulders just to be close. (It started when I began breastfeeding and didn't have space for the baby and him in my lap.)

So you see, mourning him is complex. Mourning the end of this series is also complex. While I'm happy to see it take flight, I'll certainly miss our Siren Squad. Thank you for joining the Squad with me. Rest in peace, my little Loki.

Please consider leaving a review if you also enjoyed your last trip. It truly helps me so that I can continue writing new and fun books. And let's be honest; writing is cathartic. It's been helpful to focus my attention.

If you're looking for more, try my take on Hades and Persephone next. The grudges are as old as the gods… Flip for a sneak peek of my new book, *Of Thorns and Bones*, and don't forget to check out my afterword!

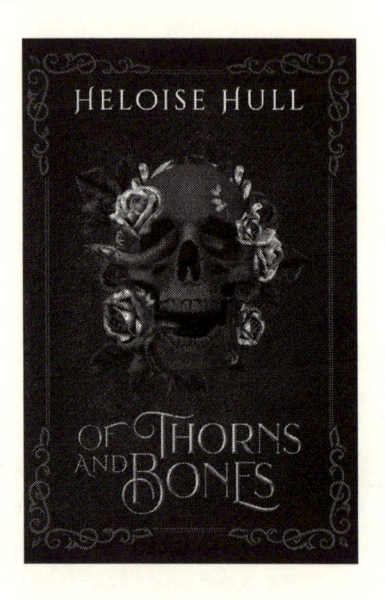

Chapter One

PERSEPHONE

VARNA, Bulgaria
   Summer, 2001 CE.

The god of death was watching me. I could feel him.

The manticore dressed in a stolen Adidas tracksuit accessorized with fake gold chains and a white baseball hat was also watching me, but I probably looked like an easy target to him.

Music pulsed from the row of nightclubs in the resort district, reverberating through my skull and making my chest thump as I pick my way over the cobblestones. The Eastern Bloc really came alive in the summer. Stilettos clacked loudly as young women tittered and laughed on the arms of the wealthy oil tycoons and contractors vacationing on the Black Sea, but I was merely slugging home in my sensible tennis shoes and blue jeans after work.

I glanced at the darkened alley I'd swerved into on purpose and took stock. Two rats throbbed with life energy, and another teetered on the brink of life and death. There was a mortal five meters away at the edge of the chain link fence, but walking fast the opposite way.

As for the manticore? Well, he just radiated death.

The demon rimmed his lips with a blood red tongue and smiled with two, bright gold teeth that I knew were fake, because I sold them to him last week. A tiny wave of apprehension skated over my skin, leaving goosebumps to pimple my arms. This was what I'd been waiting for. A chance.

I'd been waiting for something to come, but perhaps not exactly him. Manticores would easily rip mortal limbs off to suck the marrow from their bones' sticky center. Add forbidden magic to the mix? I was downright irresistible. A mystery. Something to be savored and then devoured all at once.

My advice? Always let them underestimate you.

My pulse thrummed at my throat as the warm summer breeze off the bay kissed the back of my knees. The manticore moved closer.

"I knew something smelled off about you," the manticore said, stumbling a little. He didn't notice his misstep, though. Instead, he stood watching me, his eyes dilating in his excitement. The gold chains around his neck jangled together like a delightful sea shanty. "The moment I stepped foot into that pawn shop, I said to myself, I said, 'there's something off about that one.' And I'm never wrong."

Resisting the urge to roll my eyes, I put my hands together in a prayer. "Oh please, good sir." Here I winced. That might be laying it on thick. When was the last time 'good sir' was in vogue? I couldn't keep track. "Oh please, sir. Why don't you swing by the shop tomorrow? I'll give you a real good price. Whatever you want. Jewelry, watches, more teeth. All yours."

·

"Cute. But you know what I want." His red tongue skimmed his lips again. "I'd rather not run and have you scream. Others might hear and then I'd have to share you. Trust me. You do not want to be shared, girl."

Girl. That word, abhorrent to me in the old tongue. It was equally detestable in any language and the very reason I refused to ever look younger than thirty in any incarnation. Believe me, I did not look like a girl. I looked like woman in her mid-thirties who was tired of putting up with handsy tourists and had the crows' feet from frowning to prove it.

My patience for playing the gullible part splintered into threads.

While it was true I was practically neutered in this realm, and my stockpile of hoarded magic dwindled by the week, I was, still, a goddess. I let my cloak of immortality diffuse in rose petal pink and enjoyed the way my prey's eyes feasted on it.

He wanted me. Badly.

"What's a girl like you doing with magic like that in this realm?" he asked.

Hm. So perhaps not as thick as I thought. Honestly, he didn't look like he had two brain cells to rub together and keep himself warm. And there it was, again. That abhorrent word.

"Black market," I tried, stretching my toes in preparation to lunge.

"Nah. I know everyone that comes through. You? Never heard, seen, nor sensed you before."

I lifted an eyebrow. "Oh do you?"

The manticore picked his lion fangs with a sharpened point of bone. "Yeah. I do." He tossed it over his shoulder to thud against the cobblestones and cracked his neck in both directions. He shook out his mane as he transformed from mafia to manticore. His hands widened into paws the size of my head and a serpent's tail flicked back and forth. I had the distinct feeling he wanted to whip me with it first.

Good luck, buddy.

The goddess inside of me wanted to obliterate him with carefully curated death magic, but the been-too-long-on Earth goddess settled on jabbing my fingers into his windpipe and flipping his body over my shoulder as he gagged and coughed.

He squealed in surprise as his track suit tore along the rough stones before jumping to his feet, menacing closer. He had no caution whatsoever, which suited me fine. I lifted my chin in a quick, jerking movement, egging him on.

He cracked his neck left, then right. "That wasn't very ladylike," he commented.

"Oh good. I thought for a second I was being too delicate."

The manticore narrowed his eyes, but I tossed a lentil seed at him, willing it to sprout before he could flick his deadly tail again. My seed somersaulted through the air, spreading its arms like some grotesque but adorable alien. They netted around the manticore's head and clung tight as he stomped through the alley, roaring and demolishing dumpsters as he struggled to remove the network of shoots. I smiled grimly when they finally managed to gag him.

The shoots continued to grow, wrapping their arms around his back and trussing him like a pig ready for slaughter, forcing him to his knees. I couldn't see his face anymore, but every line of his body twisted in anger.

For a moment, my body glowed oil-black with my true form. Glittering stars cascaded down my hair and power churned through me. I felt fanged and dangerous, hungry for more—and I liked it. It was sweeter than the ripest strawberry on my tongue and I savored the power burst.

"What are you?" he gasped. "I deserve… to know… what slayed me."

I bent down to whisper my name in his ear. As his body shuddered one last time, I added. "And I want him to know it was me."

Too soon, the power coursing through me dissipated as his essence splintered like dried spaghetti and he left this world for the next.

I don't want your kiss. I don't want your crown. I want to burn your kingdom to the ground.

Of Thorns and Bones will be in *stores Halloween 2021. Pre-order pricing at $3.99!*

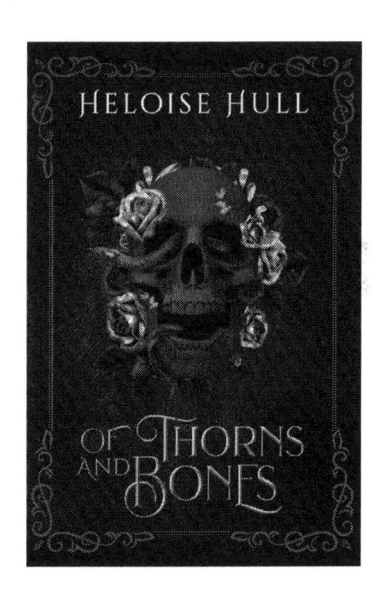

Afterword

Culsans is the name of an Etruscan god of doors, which felt appropriate given the archons' roles in my story. He is the precursor to Janus, Roman god of two ways. Culsans

Nonna's real name, Culśu, is the female equivalent in Etruria and means the gateway between worlds. I had the great fortune to visit Pamukkale, Turkey as an undergraduate and see the magnificent salt beds there. Beautiful terrain! It served as my inspiration for the cursed siren village.

Do you want to read the original Little Mermaid by Hans Christian Anderson? Of course you do! There's a link for that: The Little Mermaid

Please do go check out the image of the amethyst bracelet Tefnut wears to meet Thoth. It's real and was found in King Tut's tomb!

These spells really were written down for Egyptian magicians in the ancient world, and by the Roman period, Egypt was well known for their magicians. Here's a link to some of the spells and texts found from that period, including all the spells for the ones I mentioned in the

Tablets, such as the donkey faces and insomnia. And yes, the spell to separate spouses did invoke Tefnut's name! This source is from the University of Chicago Press, an impeccable research university near my home in Hyde Park. The Greek Magical Papyri in Translation Including the Demotic Spells

I promise, even the lettuce and epically weird battle between Set and Horus is from history. The story was first written down on papyrus during the Twentieth Dynasty coinciding with the reign of Ramesses V. All quotes from Set and Horus are, sadly, true from the text. I actually took a little liberty and had the semen come out of his ear instead of his temples as the myth does, because there's only so much nonsense I could take… Lettuce and Kings: The Power Struggle Between Horus and Set

And for the love of flowers, don't make oleander tea or even use the stick of one to roast a marshmallow. Here's the link to an article about a woman who died drinking oleander tea. Case report Oleander tea: Herbal draught of death

Notes

Chapter 25

1. An incantation and ritual from the Demotic Spells for Nephotes to the immortal king Psammetichos. See: the Greek Magical Papyri in Translation from the University of Chicago Press. I took the liberty of changing HE to SHE. Please forgive the intrusion.

About the Author

Unlike her namesake of medieval infamy, Heloise doesn't intend to have her midlife crisis in a nunnery. She'd much rather drink espresso martinis and chant in fairy rings while wearing socially questionable clothing.

In her other pen names, Heloise writes romance, nonfiction, and epic fantasy with tinges of the ancient world all thanks to dual degrees in archaeology and Classics. She splits her time between St. Louis and Chicago with her husband, two kids, and ~~two~~ one cat, and is too heartbroken to plot how to bring in a puppy for the moment. Hug your real babies and your fur babies.

Manufactured by Amazon.ca
Bolton, ON